Everyone has secrets... but some are fatal.

1932, London. Late one December night Simon Sampson stumbles across the body of a woman in an alleyway. Her death is linked to a plot by right-wing extremists to assassinate the King on Christmas Day. Simon resolves to do his patriotic duty and unmask the traitors.

But Simon Sampson lives a double life. Not only is he a highly respected BBC radio announcer, but he's also a man who loves men, and as such must live a secret life. His investigation risks revealing his other life and with that imprisonment under Britain's draconian homophobic laws of the time. He faces a stark choice: his loyalty to the King or his freedom.

This is the first in a new series from award-winning author David C. Dawson. A richly atmospheric novel set in the shadowy world of 1930s London, where secrets are commonplace, and no one is quite who they seem.

1

London, December 1932

The body was buried under a pile of rubbish in the unlit alleyway. Simon would have failed to see it, if it were not for the cat.

That December evening London was shrouded in a thick yellow smog from power stations and the smoke of thousands of coal fires. It was impossible to see more than a few feet in any direction. Simon was late as he hurried down the lower end of Oxford Street. When he came upon the alleyway, he hesitated for only a moment before choosing to take the shortcut.

He had discovered the route during the summer when he had begun working at the BBC's new wireless studios in Portland Place. It cut several minutes from his semi-regular sojourn to the Fitzroy Tavern on Charlotte Street. On summer evenings it had been a pleasant stroll through the back streets, away from the noise and smell of traffic, and crowds on the main thoroughfare.

But now, in mid-December, the alleyway was dark and forbidding, a much less inviting place to be. The fog deadened the sound of London's traffic to a low rumble, and the visibility was even worse than in Oxford Street. Simon trod carefully and extended his gloved hands in front of him. It was harder than walking in the dark, because the acrid taste of the fog got into his nose and mouth, and made him cough loudly.

Up ahead he heard muffled voices followed by a *thud*. The noise was indistinct but threatening. He stopped, and considered turning to go back to Oxford Street. If there was villainy ahead, he wanted no part of it.

Pull yourself together man, he thought. *This is Bloomsbury, not Whitechapel.*

He resumed his slow trudge along the alleyway, his eyes fixed on the comforting glow of a distant street lamp. Once more he extended his arms to forewarn him of any obstacle ahead.

It was after no more than a few dozen yards that the cat startled him. It emerged from a gap in the wall to his left and hissed. Simon recoiled, his foot slipped on the uneven cobblestones, and he fell backwards onto the ground.

Which was when he saw the hand.

It was a woman's hand. The long fingers caked in dirt, the red polished nails were chipped. The arm and the rest of the body to which it was attached were covered by several grubby hessian sacks. Simon scrambled to his feet. He brushed down his mohair coat, and leaned against the wall to catch his breath.

From this viewpoint, the protruding hand was not visible beneath the pile of sacks. But Simon knew it was there. He could recall the scratches on the fingers, the cracks in the nail polish. He took a deep breath to prepare himself for what he might find, and crouched down to inspect it more closely. As he did so he gathered the hem of his coat to avoid it coming into contact with the muddy cobblestones. He reached out to the nearest of the sacks and lifted the fabric, taking care to avoid touching whatever might lie beneath.

The hand was indeed attached to an arm. There was a delicate gold bracelet around the wrist, just below the cuff of a fur-trimmed coat. Simon grew bolder and gave the sack a firm flick to remove it.

The woman was beautiful. She was in her early twenties and her pale skin had a smooth sheen like a china doll. She had high cheek bones and her features reminded Simon of a woman he had once seen perform at a Berlin nightclub. In addition to the fur-trimmed coat, the unconscious woman wore a fur hat. The outfit added to her foreign appearance. Her body lay contorted on the ground, one leg twisted at a hideous angle. On the cobblestones close to her head was a smear of fresh blood.

Her eyes were closed. There was a coarse black scarf knotted tightly around her neck and a rag stuffed into her mouth. Simon removed the rag and her mouth dropped open. He fumbled with the scarf until he succeeded in loosening it and could remove the ligature. She made no movement.

He leaned forward to examine her. As he inhaled, the scent of her perfume filled his nostrils. It was delightful, a hint of rose petals and apple blossom.

Despite the gloom of the alleyway, he could see contusions on her neck. When he ran his fingers over her skin it still felt warm. He found the carotid pulse in the groove of her neck. It was faint, but she was still alive.

Simon raised his head and called out into the murkiness of the fog. "Help! Police! I need help here."

The woman stirred and a rasping groan emerged from deep inside her. Her lips moved, and Simon lowered his head close to her. "I'm going to get help," he said into her ear. "There's a police box on the corner. I can telephone for help from there."

Her breathing was laboured and curious gurgling noises came from her throat. Her lips parted as if she was trying to speak.

"Don't move," Simon said. "I have to leave you to get help. I'm not medically trained. If I try to move you, I might injure you more."

The woman coughed and her eyes flickered open.

"Curling," she seemed to say. She raised her hand to her face and winced.

"What's your name?" Simon asked.

When the words came, they were little more than a hoarse whisper. "Curling."

Simon frowned as he tried to understand.

"Curling in cover," she said.

Her hand fell limp against the side of Simon's head, and her fingernails grazed his cheek. He took the hand in his and found a small, hard object nestled in its palm. He took the object, lowered her arm back down to her side, and inspected what he had found. It appeared to be an ornate, metal button. Perhaps she had torn it from her assailant's coat. Simon slipped it into his coat pocket. It might prove to be useful evidence in tracking down her attacker.

The woman's eyes had closed again. Once more Simon felt the side of her neck for a pulse. She was still alive, but the pulse was very faint. He used the discarded hessian sack to create a makeshift pillow for her head, stood, and headed for the nearest police box.

"Are you sure this was the spot where you found the lady, sir?"

The evening had taken a confusing turn. When Simon had telephoned for help from the police box on the corner of Oxford Street and Tottenham Court Road, he had had little more than ten minutes to wait before a constable arrived. He had quickly explained the reason for his call and led the policeman through the fog and back to the alleyway. When they arrived at the spot where Simon had first seen the young woman's hand, her body had disappeared.

"Absolutely, officer." Simon bent down and picked up a hessian sack. "Her body was covered with these."

The constable took the sack from Simon's outstretched hand, held it to his nose, and sniffed. He shook his head and handed it back to Simon.

"I thought I might get a hint of perfume," the constable said, by way of explanation. "If it was used to conceal a woman's body."

He took a large white handkerchief from his pocket and blew his nose explosively. "All I can smell is horse manure." He wiped his nose with the handkerchief and thrust it back into his trousers. "Now, sir." The constable took a notepad and pencil from his top pocket. "As you telephoned us, I am obliged to write a report. Let me start with your name."

"But she must be here somewhere." Simon bent down again and examined the cobblestones around the pile of sacks.

The constable sighed. "Your name, sir?"

"Simon Sampson."

The policeman's pencil paused, suspended above the notepad. "Are you the same Simon Sampson as what writes the *Sleuth* column in *The Chronicle*?"

Simon shook his head. "Not any more. I work for the BBC

now. I'm a news announcer."

"Pity." The policeman resumed writing. "Address?"

"Flat 21, Bellman Buildings, Dorset Square, Marylebone." Simon noticed a dark patch on the cobblestones glinting in the light. "Look here, officer." He beckoned the constable over. "There's a blood stain over here." He dabbed at the mark. "It's not dry. Still fresh. I think the young lady's assailant came back and removed her while I was telephoning you."

The police officer sighed again. He hitched up his trousers and squatted down beside Simon.

"Rats."

"Rats?" asked Simon.

"Rats, sir." The constable hauled himself back to an upright position. "They're everywhere. Either that or foxes. You see, sir," he resumed writing on the notepad. "They scavenge. Lots of rubbish from the restaurant kitchens thrown in this alleyway. It'll be blood from some animal, no doubt."

Simon stood. "Are you saying I'm making this up?"

The policeman leaned towards Simon and sniffed. "Been drinking, sir? It is nearly Christmas after all. I wouldn't blame you if you have."

Simon was furious. "No, I have not. How dare you insinuate that I'm drunk."

The officer raised his hand. "Please calm down, sir. I was merely attempting to find an explanation for the absence of the body of a young lady you claim was here not fifteen minutes ago. Either she got better and decided to go home, or she wasn't here in the first place."

"Or there's the third explanation I've just mentioned." Simon was not to be deterred. "That her body was removed by her assailant while I went to telephone for help. He might have been nearby when I was examining the poor unfortunate woman." He shivered. "I was lucky he didn't decide to attack me as well."

"*Habeas corpus*," replied the constable.

"I beg your pardon?"

"*Habeas corpus*," the policeman said again. "It means—"

"I know full well what it means," Simon interrupted. "I read law at Oxford. *Habeas Corpus*, otherwise known as The Great Writ of Liberty, protects a person from wrongful arrest or imprisonment. It was an ancient prerogative, strengthened in the Habeas Corpus Act of 1679 under Charles II. Although, these days—"

"Really, sir?" The constable looked surprised. "And I simply thought it meant 'have the body'. Which was why I used the phrase in this instance." He gestured around the fog-smothered alley. "We clearly don't have one, do we, sir?"

He continued to write on his notepad. "Could you give me a description of the woman you claim you saw? I'd better take it for completeness sake."

Simon gave as much information as he could remember.

"Shoes?"

Simon shook his head. "I'm sorry, constable, but I don't recall."

"But she was wearing some?"

Simon tried to retrieve an image of the woman to his mind. But he had been so concerned with the scarf knotted around her neck he had failed to retain a complete impression of what she had been wearing. He slipped his hand into his pocket and withdrew the brass button he had discovered in the woman's palm.

"Look. She was holding this. It must have come off the coat her attacker was wearing. It's an important clue."

The policeman took the button from Simon's

outstretched hand and held it up to the light.

"Lots of people wear coats with buttons on, sir. It's hardly much of a clue."

He handed the button back to Simon and put his notepad and pencil away. "I don't think there's any need for me to detain you longer, sir. I'll finish writing up my report in the early hours of tomorrow morning. When you're probably safely tucked up in bed, sir."

"Is that it?"

"I have everything here, sir." The constable patted his top pocket. "If we get a report of a missing person, the station might be in touch with you again."

"What's your name, officer?" Simon asked.

"Constable Smith, sir. Eric Smith." He turned away and headed back down the alleyway. "I'm at Bow Street if you ever need me," Constable Smith called over his shoulder, and disappeared into the fog.

Simon rubbed his face and counted to ten. He was both confused and furious in equal measure. How could the body of a beautiful, injured woman disappear in less than fifteen minutes? And why was there no clue to her disappearance?

He squatted down, picked up the discarded hessian sack, and sniffed it cautiously, as Constable Smith had done so a few moments before. The police officer was right. There was a strong smell of horse manure, but no hint of rose petals or apple blossom. He put the sack to one side and lifted more of them out of the way, intent on finding some evidence of the woman's former presence in the alleyway.

As he picked up the last sack, he noticed something glistening inside an old orange crate next to them. He reached in and found a small clutch bag, made from fine leather, strung on a gold chain and secured with a gold clasp.

Bingo, Simon thought.

2

"You're late tonight. What 'appened? Did the BBC keep you behind for bein' a bad boy?"

The barman at the Fitzroy Tavern winked at Simon when he got to the pub. Jonny Manning was a round man. He had a large round head with big round eyes surrounded by deep crinkles of laugh lines. A big fat neck joined his round head to an enormous round body, which he heaved around the bar of the Fitzroy Tavern with increasing difficulty. His round, pudgy fingers tapped the beer pump in front of him.

"Your usual pint of mild, Mr Sampson?"

Simon shook his head. "I need something stronger this evening, Jonny. Get me a double whisky, will you?"

The barman reached behind him for a glass. He uncorked a bottle and poured a generous measure.

"I thought you weren't lookin' too good when I saw you come in, Mr Sampson. What's the matter? Comin' down with the influenza what's goin' 'round, are you?" He put the glass on the counter in front of Simon. "Here. Try that. One of my customers brought it in for me last week. Twenty-year-old single malt from the Highlands."

Simon raised the glass to his lips and took a sip. He held the liquid in his mouth and rolled it around with his tongue to absorb the rich palette of flavours. When he swallowed, he felt the warmth of the whisky stroke the back of his throat.

"Thank you, Jonny. A taste of heaven. And a far greater medicine than any they might offer in Harley Street."

Simon leaned on the bar and looked around him. The smoky interior of the Fitzroy Tavern was not as full as usual, possibly the thick fog and the plunging temperatures had kept some of the regular patrons away. Those who were there were all men, dressed in their office suits and ties, with overcoats either slung over their arms or hung on a line of coat hooks close to the bar. The majority sat in pairs at small round tables, chatting and smoking. A few drinkers were on their own, standing at the bar or seated on stools at a long counter against the side wall.

Simon took off his heavy overcoat and placed it onto the barstool next to him. He smiled at two men who had turned to stare at his dinner jacket and black tie. He wore it because the BBC required all their announcers to wear full evening dress when performing at the microphone. Simon was much the best-dressed gentleman in the Fitzroy Tavern that evening.

He took another sip of his whisky. "I'm not sickening, Jonny old chap. But I've had the most sickening fright." He leaned across the bar and lowered his voice when he spoke. "Tonight, I discovered the barely conscious body of a woman. The victim of a vicious attack. I went to summon help, and when I returned with a constable"—He paused to create a moment of anticipation— "the victim had disappeared." He sat back and awaited his intended reaction.

Jonny's large round eyes opened even wider. "Lord, Mr Sampson. No wonder you look like you've seen a ghost." He laughed and shook his head. "It's because you 'ave done. Are you sure this fallen woman was actually there in the first place?"

"She most certainly was." Simon was aggrieved by Jonny's scepticism. He nodded in the general direction of the outside world. "She was in that alleyway at the end of Charlotte Street. About a hundred yards up from the corner."

"And what were you doing there at this time of night, darling?" There was a woman's voice from behind him. "On the prowl for a man to have a good time with?"

Simon lowered the glass from his lips and turned to face her.

"Don't be vulgar, Florence," Simon said. "This is a matter of great importance. I was telling Jonny how I stumbled across the victim of an attempted murder tonight." He hoped his voice contained the right amount of drama, without spilling into melodrama.

"Don't call me Florence when we're in here." The woman wore a dark three-piece suit, well-tailored with a narrow pinstripe. She clenched a cigarette holder between her teeth and peered at Simon over the top of her half-moon spectacles. "You know perfectly well I'm only Florence Miles during the day. When we're out gadding you must refer to me as Bill." She tapped her glass. "You can stand me another gin for that. Make it a double."

"You expect me to pay again?" Simon was certain he had been bludgeoned into paying for Bill's drinks the last time they had met in the Fitzroy. That had only been four days ago. And she had drunk a great deal that night.

"Oh, but darling." Bill ran her fingers over the shoulder of Simon's dinner jacket and picked a piece of lint from it. "It's you who's the voice of the BBC at six o'clock. You must be absolutely loaded by now. I'm just a menial backroom person in the great Corporation."

"Don't be ridiculous, Bill." Simon was sure she was on a higher grade than he was. "You know as well as I do the BBC pays atrociously. They expect us to work simply for the honour of serving them."

"No matter." Bill shoved her hands into her trouser pockets and leaned against the bar. Simon admired the exquisite cut of her suit. He made a mental note to ask who her tailor was.

"Tell me about your gruesome find," she said. "And spare me no details."

Simon recounted the events of the past two hours, ending with his frustrating and ultimately fruitless attempt to persuade Constable Smith to pursue an investigation. Bill roared with laughter. The sound cut through the buzz of conversation in the crowded saloon, and the patrons in the bar turned to look for the source of merriment. She waved a hand in gracious acknowledgment of their sudden attention.

"Bill." Simon was exasperated with his companion. "Please take this seriously. Why you always try so hard to make yourself the centre of attention is beyond me."

"Oh, darling." Bill took out a large crimson handkerchief and blew her nose loudly. "You're perfectly well aware that I spend my working days hiding in the shadows. At least allow me the liberty of taking centre stage when they let me out."

"This is the Fitzroy Tavern." Simon sniffed dismissively. "Not the Palladium."

"No difference, my dear. All the world's a stage."

She gave Simon a sideways glance. "What I don't understand is why you went down that alleyway in search of one of your tall, dark men. I'd have thought it was a very dangerous and exotic location to explore. Especially on these dark wintry nights."

"I wasn't in search of 'a tall dark man', as you so tastelessly put it. It's a useful shortcut to get here."

Bill ignored his protest and gestured towards the men in the bar. "Once again I'm the only woman here tonight. And yet I feel completely safe. Surely this is a better place to pursue your need for illicit male companionship. It's not been raided since—" She turned back to Jonny. "When did you last receive a visit from His Majesty's brave police service?"

Jonny shook his head. "Don't you worry about that, Miss Miles." He leaned in close to Simon and Bill, and dropped his voice to a whisper. "I'll say no more than that I made them a very generous offer last year, and they've chosen to look elsewhere ever since."

"Bribery?" Bill's voice was louder and shriller than Simon expected.

"Please, Miss Miles." Jonny looked around, as though concerned that a plain-clothes policeman would emerge and arrest them. "There's no need to use language like that." He tapped the side of his nose. "Let's just say, there's a gentleman of high rank in the Metropolitan Police who is also of our persuasion. He and his friends are regular and discreet patrons of this establishment. They wouldn't like to be exposed to the unpleasantness of a raid by members of their junior ranks."

Simon stared at the faces of the men in the bar. Jonny's statement was a surprise to him. The Fitzroy Tavern was well-known to be more popular with artists and Bohemians than civil service types. It was why he and Bill had chosen it as their regular, in preference to other central London establishments sympathetic to *"people of their persuasion"*, as

Jonny had phrased it. As far as Simon was concerned, the members of the artistic community who patronised the Fitzroy were far more interesting to talk to. Maybe the *"gentleman of high rank in the Metropolitan Police"* and his friends Jonny referred to felt the same.

Jonny shook his head. "No, Mr Sampson. They're not in tonight. And I certainly won't be pointing them out to you. But rest assured, you'll be undisturbed by the boys in blue for the foreseeable future."

"I don't think darling Simon's afraid of our boys in blue." Bill raised her gin glass to Simon. "Cheers, m'dear. After all, you recently spent time in the company of—who was it you said?—Constable Smith?"

Simon snorted. "Much good that it did me. If only the police were to spend more time investigating real crimes instead of hounding people like us, the streets would be far safer."

"Real crime?" Bill asked. "I must say I feel a certain sympathy for poor old Smith. He's called out on a freezing foggy night to a bleak alleyway frequented by prostitutes and scoundrels—"

"That's somewhat of an exaggeration," Simon protested.

"You said yourself you feared for your life."

"Well, it was dark." Simon felt he was losing control of his dramatic story. "And there were strange noises muffled by the fog. I'm sure you'd have been just as nervous if you'd been there."

"You've been reading too many ghost stories recently." Bill banged her glass down on the counter top, and signalled to Jonny for a refill. "Your imagination got the better of you."

Simon reached into his coat and retrieved the small clutch bag he had found. He placed it on the bar in front of Bill with a flourish.

"Very nice." Bill looked from the black leather bag to Simon. "It goes with your eyes, darling. But if you want to avoid another run-in with the police, I wouldn't walk around in public with it."

Jonny returned with their drinks. He moved the gold chain of the clutch bag and put the glasses on either side of it. "Is this to be the new fashion for men in 1933?" he asked. "Only if it is, I'll 'urry down to 'arrods tomorrow and order mine."

Simon retrieved the bag from the counter and waved it in front of Bill's face. "I found this close to where the body lay." He fumbled with its clasp. "I'm certain it was the lady's, and that her attackers left it behind in their haste to remove her body while I went in search of the constable."

The clasp clicked. Simon tugged the bag open and inspected its interior.

"Well?" Bill asked. "What have you found?"

Simon shook his head. "Nothing. It's empty." He let go of the bag and watched it collapse shut again. He felt deflated. "I suppose her attackers removed everything from it before they discarded it."

Bill picked it up and ran her palm over its surface. "It's very good quality leather." She peered at it to examine the gold chain. "I'm not really an expert, but I could well believe this to be real gold. How on earth did it end up in that Godforsaken alleyway?"

"There's an easy answer to that, Miss Miles," said the barman.

"Jonny, darling." Bill put the bag on the counter top in front of him. "Please stop using that name. I prefer Bill."

"Beg yer pardon, Bill." Jonny reached forward to pat her on the shoulder. He saw the look on her face and hastily withdrew his hand. He winked at Simon, picked up the bag, and turned it over in his hands. "It's my bet that some rogue nicked this from a woman in Belgravia or someplace posh, took what 'e wanted, and got rid of it." He held the gold chain in his fingers and examined it. "If this is gold like Bill 'ere says, 'e might 'ave 'idden it there with the aim of comin' back another time to retrieve it."

Simon shook his head. "You're forgetting about the woman. I know you don't believe me. You two are as bad as that constable. But she *was* there. And I'm certain this belonged to her."

Jonny put the bag back on the counter. "Well, if the police won't do anything, I'd say you're the next best man to investigate this curious incident. A former crime reporter for *The Chronicle*, and now a journalist at the BBC."

Simon wrinkled his nose. "I'm afraid that's a misrepresentation. I'm an announcer, not a journalist. All they let me do is read the news written by others who work in the department. And for the most part, they're limited to rewriting government statements. It's not like my days on *The Chronicle* at all."

"So why on earth did you take the job?" Bill asked. "Especially if you think they pay us so poorly."

"Because, my dear Bill," Simon replied. "You suggested they take me on. And it was the BBC asking me. Of course I took the job. I was very flattered. Don't forget I'm their only announcer with a background in journalism. And the youngest."

Bill roared with laughter, and once again the hubbub in the bar dipped in volume.

"And that's of some great significance?" she asked. "Thirty is no longer young, but neither can it be considered old. It's the no man's land of age." She grasped her lapels dramatically. "If you want to play with dates, don't forget that

I'm the youngest head of department at the BBC. At the tender age of thirty-five."

"I hadn't realised you was so elevated Miss Miles, er, Bill," Jonny said. "I thought you only did office work."

Simon held his breath and waited for Bill's response to this slight. She turned to the barman, straightened her back, and appeared to grow one or two inches taller. "Mr Manning. I have a staff of seventy-five reporting to me. Without them, the BBC would collapse."

This time it was Simon's turn to roar with laughter. "Darling Bill, you run the libraries, not the engineering department."

Bill gave Simon a withering look. "And where would you and your chums with their typewriters in the News Department be without our ready index of fact-checked information? You'd have nothing to announce and your voice would be silenced."

"She's got you there, Mr Sampson." Jonny picked up a cloth and wiped the counter top.

"Wait a moment," Simon fumbled in the pockets of his coat. "I completely forgot. There was something else. It fell from the lady's hand. I've got it here somewhere."

He retrieved the small brass button he had shown to the constable earlier. He held it close to the lamp at the end of the bar to examine it. The button was shaped like a shield, with a sword extending down its length, and an odd, wheel-shaped symbol on the handle of the sword.

"May I see?" Bill took it from Simon's hand, closed one eye, and squinted at it.

"I hope you find it interesting," Simon said. "Sadly, Constable Smith gave it hardly a moment's thought. He didn't seem to care two hoots about the evidence I found. That button. The blood on the cobblestones. The police are simply not—"

"--this is fascinating." Bill's voice had raised in pitch. She stared at Simon. "And it's very sinister. If I'm not mistaken, this is from—"

"Bill! I thought I'd lost ye." The warm Scottish voice came from behind them. Simon turned to see a handsome young man with a beaming smile. His face was a mass of ginger freckles and he wore a tailored black coat.

The man's arrival had a surprising effect on Bill. She smoothed down her hair, which was cut in the short Eton Crop style, and pulled back her shoulders.

"Ah, young man," Bill said in a much deeper voice. "There you are."

"Had ye forgotten about me?" The man glanced from Bill to Simon. "Who's your charming friend? Ye must introduce him."

Simon was amused by Bill's sudden basso profundo voice. It was an occurrence he had become used to when they were *"out gadding"*, as she called it.

"My name's Simon Sampson," he said. "And you are?"

"Cameron McCreadie," replied the young man. He took Simon's hand and pumped it up and down with enthusiasm. "Bill and I were exchangin' indiscretions about guardsmen over in that corner. I popped out for a Jimmy Riddle, and when I returned, he'd buggered off."

Cameron leaned in towards Simon and his eyes widened. "Did ye say Simon Sampson? Ye'll not be, by any chance that *Sleuth* reporter in the newspaper, will ye?"

Simon shook his head. "Not any more. I left earlier this year. I've started working on the wireless. For the BBC. What do you do?"

Cameron passed a hand across his forehead as if wiping

sweat from his brow. “Och, there’s a blessing. I’m not supposed to mix wi’ the lowlife of Fleet Street.” His broad smile at Simon’s frown was beguiling. “Don’t worry. I’m only teasing. I work for the king. Buy me a wee drink, and I might be indiscreet.”

3

Cameron accepted the whisky from Simon and raised his glass.

"To new acquaintances," the Scotsman toasted. "May we never stray from this path of ultimate damnation that people such as us are embarked upon."

He smiled his broad, beatific smile at Simon once more. "I didn't know Bill was wi' another gentleman. It wasnae my intention to steal him away from ye. I was merely looking for conversation and companionship in a venue hitherto unknown to me."

"Not at all." Simon smiled. He enjoyed listening to the lilt of Cameron's brogue. And Bill had clearly succeeded in convincing him that she too was a man. It was a game she relished. "Bill and I were meeting this evening, but I got delayed on my way here. I'm only glad that he found an agreeable chap like yourself to while away the time with."

Cameron nodded towards Bill. "Are you and he—?"

Simon waited for Cameron to complete his sentence, but the man seemed unable to do so. "Are we what?" Simon asked finally.

Bill looped her arm through Simon's. "Don't embarrass the boy, darling." She winked at Cameron. "Simon's a great friend. We've known each other for nearly over years. And we're both—just so."

"But do ye live together?" Cameron asked.

"Good God, no." Bill snorted and raised her glass to her lips. She paused, and lowered it again. "Exactly how old are you, young man?"

"Twenty-two next birthday." The beatific smile had disappeared. "Is that of any consequence?"

"My God, he's a child," Bill whispered to Simon. She unhooked her arm and continued her inquisition. "No consequence, Cameron dear. We'll try to remember to buy you a gift. How long have you been in this great cesspool called London, as Sherlock Holmes once described it?"

"It was John Watson in *A Study in Scarlet*, not Holmes," Simon said quietly. He enjoyed correcting Bill on the few occasions she was wrong. "You say you work for His Majesty the King. Are you at the Palace?"

Cameron nodded. "St James's Palace that is, not Buckingham. I'm in York House."

"And from the sound of your accent," Simon said. "I imagine you previously worked at Balmoral. Am I right?"

"All my life." Cameron smiled and it was like the sun breaking through the clouds on a winter's day. "I mean, not at Balmoral. But I was born in Crathie, a wee village not far from the castle. My da' worked on the estate and he used to take me wi' him from when I was a bairn. Have you ever been to Scotland yourself?"

Simon nodded. "Once. My father borrowed a cottage from a friend one summer. It was near Loch Lomond. We stayed there when I was eleven. Is that how you came to work at Balmoral? Through your father?"

"Aye, it is," Cameron replied. "They were a couple of men short when His Majesty stayed four summers ago and hosted a grand banquet. They got me in because I happened to be workin' in the grounds at the time." He straightened and pulled his shoulders back. "I was the right height."

"The right height for what?" Simon asked.

"Holding the haggis salver when they piped it in." Cameron held his hands out, palm up alongside his shoulder, and mimed holding a heavy dish aloft. "There were four of us, one at each corner."

Bill chuckled.

Cameron glowered at her. "It was a great honour," he continued. "And Queen Mary apparently asked who the new man was bringin' in the haggis, and commented how fine I looked. So, I got the job."

Simon pictured Cameron in black breeches and stockings, with a crisp white shirt and red tailcoat. He must have looked very fine indeed.

"What brings you to the Fitzroy Tavern?" Simon asked. "And on a night like this? It's a fair distance from St James's. Or Buckingham Palace, for that matter. I would have thought the Running Horse was more likely to be your local haunt."

"Aye, it is," Cameron wrinkled his nose. "But it's a wee bit too close for comfort, if ye know wha' I mean."

Bill laughed. "Full of the queens from the Palace, I suppose. I've heard it said that the vast majority of the male staff who work there are—just so. I find it deliciously ironic that Queen Victoria, who allowed her government to pass the Act which imprisoned dear Oscar Wilde, was herself surrounded by men who were no different to Oscar."

"I'm not sure Her Majesty could ha' done much to stop the law," Cameron said defensively. "And anyway, there's a lot o' married men wi' families who work for the king. Ye cannae say it's the majority who are looking for"—he paused as if in search of the right phrase—"homogenic love."

Simon was delighted to hear the young man stand up to Bill's sweeping generalisations. She was far too eager to dominate a conversation. In the presence of this tall, young Scotsman, he felt a sense of *schadenfreude* as she struggled to assert herself.

"Ah, homogenic love," Bill said. "Or *the love that dare not speak its name* as Oscar described it so aptly. And what do you know of that?"

Cameron's demeanour changed completely. A laugh erupted from deep in his chest, and he gave Bill a playful slap on the arm. His face betrayed the cheeky appearance of a schoolboy who had much to hide.

"Only a little, I'm afeared to say." Cameron said. "But I'm learning. My accidental encounter with a guardsman in Hyde Park in late May made me curious, and taught me a few wee things. But none of my subsequent encounters can be remotely described as love. Not of any kind."

Bill sighed. "Alas, my dear. It's the way for so many of us. Nature is against us. Dear Noël told me not to run after love. He thinks we should leave love waiting off-stage until we're good and ready for it."

"Noël? Cameron was star-struck. "Do you mean Noël Coward?"

"Of course, sweet boy," Bill replied.

Simon sighed and leaned against the bar. He knew this was the opening Bill had been waiting for. An opportunity to flaunt her connections.

"I was his factotum," she continued. "While he staged *Cavalcade* at the Drury Lane Theatre."

"One of two assistants," Simon interjected.

"Dear Noël was very fond of me." Bill turned her back to

Simon. "Sadly, he keeps leaving us. Infatuated with New York, that other cesspool across the Atlantic."

"So, Cameron," Simon interjected. "If you're at York House, can you throw any light on these rumours about Noël and Prince George?"

"Simon, darling." Bill's voice was chiding. "Always the gutter reporter. Why do you have to pry into other people's private affairs?"

"Because they're fascinating," Simon replied. "And, given that you've always been so tight-lipped about it, I thought this young man might tell all." He nodded to the glass in Cameron's hand. "After all, he did promise to be indiscreet if I bought him 'a wee drink'."

"It's true the prince lives at York House," Cameron replied. "His brother, the Prince of Wales, is there at the moment too. But as to his personal affairs, I really cannae say. My responsibilities are to the housekeeper. I have nae personal contact wi' their Royal Highnesses."

Simon grudgingly admired the man for his loyalty. But he tried one further attempt to encourage Cameron to say more.

"Surely there's a network amongst you chaps? Isn't there chatter about what their Royal Highnesses get up to? They're in the gossip columns all the time."

"Buy me another drink or two." Cameron winked at Simon. "I'll see what I can remember then."

Bill looked at her watch.

"Dammit," she said. "I've got a late supper appointment. I'm going to have to dash."

Simon glanced at the clock behind the bar. It was nearly nine. "Supper? At this time? Who are you meeting all of a sudden?"

Bill leaned over to Simon and whispered in his ear. "I'm

not going to play gooseberry with you and young Rabbie Burns here all evening."

Simon opened his mouth to protest but Bill continued. "And don't deny it. Your eyes are practically out on stalks. I'll see you tomorrow, no doubt."

She turned to Cameron and held out her hand. "Delighted to meet you, young man. You must come by this way again. Or we could have a spot of lunch at The Lily Pond."

Cameron furrowed his brow in confusion.

"Bill means Lyons' Corner House on the Strand," Simon explained.

"Oh, I didnae realise." Cameron took Bill's outstretched hand and shook it. "I'm afraid lunch's a wee bit tricky for me. Although I do get occasional Wednesdays off."

Bill reached into her pocket and handed Cameron a card.

"Here's my number if you get a free Wednesday." She turned to Simon. "Goodbye, my tardy friend. Do let me know if your murder victim turns up. I'm intrigued."

And she was gone.

"What did he mean, 'murder victim'?" Cameron asked.

Simon turned and waved to Jonny, who had moved to the other end of the bar.

"I'll tell you in a moment," he replied. "Let's get some more drinks first."

Cameron showed none of the scepticism expressed by both Bill and Jonny as Simon retold the story of his encounter earlier that evening. When Simon produced the clutch bag, Cameron took it and turned it over in his hands. He undid the clasp, and examined the interior, feeling the delicacy of the lining with his fingers.

"It's a fine wee bag." He peered at the metal frame to

which the clasp was attached. "Very fine. There's something stamped on the metal. Here. But the writing's tiny."

He said the word *tiny* towards the back of his throat, with the Scottish emphasis that seemed to fill it with extra vowels. There was a musical rhythm to Cameron's voice. At the BBC, Simon and his announcer colleagues were all expected to speak in the same standard way. It was known as Received Pronunciation. Announcers were not permitted to have regional accents on the wireless. Simon thought the ruling was narrow-minded of the Corporation. Given that the Director-General, Lord Reith, possessed an accent very similar to Cameron's, Simon also thought it was hypocritical.

"I think there's a name inscribed here." He held the bag out to Simon. "On the inside edge. D'ye see?"

Simon peered at a spot in front of Cameron's finger.

"The engraving's extremely fine." Simon screwed up his eyes to focus on the delicate sweep of the letters. "That might be an S at the start of the first letter. And perhaps a C at the start of the second. But it's impossible to say with certainty." He closed the bag and put it back into his coat pocket. "I have a glass at home and electric light. I'll examine it later."

"What are ye goin' tae do now?" Cameron asked.

"Well, I thought I was going for supper with Bill. That was before he announced he had a prior engagement. So, I might just stroll home and have some left-over kedgeree from the pantry instead."

Cameron smiled. "I meant about the missing body. Are ye simply goin' tae forget about it?"

Of course he meant the missing body, Simon thought. What a presumption on his part to believe the man was interested in his social arrangements.

"I'm not sure what I can do," Simon replied. "I reported it to the police. They've taken my name and address, although I must say I don't hold out much hope they'll take it any further. It's simply a mystery."

Cameron shook his head. "I hae to say, ye disappoint me, Mr Sampson. First ye tell me ye were the great *Sleuth* reporter from *The Chronicle*. Now ye say it's a mystery and ye willna do anythin' about it. Has all that sleuthin' left ye, now ye sit behind a microphone in a dinner jacket, 'announcin' the news for them that listens?"

Simon would have felt stung by Cameron's comments, if it were not for the man's cheeky smile. And there was a grain of truth in his accusation. It had not taken long for Simon to become a cog in the mighty institution of the BBC. Nothing more than a man who read scripts penned by others.

"Are ye not in the least bit curious to find out more?" Cameron persisted.

"Well of course I am." Simon felt obliged to defend himself. "And I suppose that, when I went back with the policeman, I did find fresh blood on the cobblestones. Although Constable Smith dismissed it as rats."

"'Rats' indeed." Cameron laughed. "And d'ye think it wa' rats?"

"No, I suppose I don't."

Simon shoved his hand into his pocket. His fingers grazed the small metal button that had fallen from the woman's hand. He felt a sense of the old excitement returning to him from the time he had worked on *The Chronicle*.

"And here's another thing." Simon retrieved the button and held it in front of Cameron's face. "The woman had this button in her hand when I found her."

Cameron took it from Simon and examined it.

"I think it's an important piece of evidence," Simon said. "She could have ripped it from her assailant's coat in the struggle."

"It's unusual," Cameron said. "And I think I might hae seen something like this before." He handed it back to Simon. "But I cannae recall where."

"Would you excuse me." Simon picked up his glass and finished his drink. "And thank you. You've prompted me to go back to the alleyway and take another look. Maybe I'll find something else to give a clue to the missing woman."

"I'll come with ye, if I may." Cameron's broad smile lit up his face. "It could be a dangerous place. It certainly wa' for that young lady."

Simon was grateful for the offer. He would feel safer in the company of the tall Scotsman. And perhaps he might be persuaded to come back to Simon's for a kedgeree supper afterwards.

4

Cameron was more than an agreeable drinking companion. When he and Simon returned to the alleyway fifteen minutes later, he proved to be resourceful as well. From the pocket of his tailored black coat he produced an electric torch.

"A perk o' the job at the Palace," he said by way of explanation. "They gi' it tae me in case I wa' required tae be called oot late at night. Fortunately, it's an occurrence I've managed tae avoid so far."

The torch's beam was of limited usefulness in the fog, reflecting off the swirling yellow mist instead of penetrating it. But it proved more valuable when they reached the alleyway, and Simon crouched down to inspect the cobblestones and the detritus covering them.

"Are ye sure this is where ye found the lassie?" Cameron asked. He squatted alongside Simon and waved the torch into the gloom ahead.

"Yes. Look. Shine the torch here." Simon indicated a spot in front of them. The beam reflected off the still-drying blood smeared on the cobblestones he had discovered earlier.

Cameron flashed the beam to an area a few yards away.

"There's more over there." It was a much larger pool of blood. It seemed to Simon that the woman had been subjected to a more serious injury. Perhaps the person who had attacked her initially had not only come back to take her away, but also to make sure she was dead.

Simon stepped forward to the pool of blood and motioned Cameron to join him with the torch. Its beam lit up a box of Swan Vesta matches a short distance away.

"Do you smoke?" Simon asked Cameron.

Cameron nodded.

"I think it's a filthy habit," Simon replied. "Whatever my doctor tells me about the health benefits." He pointed to the match box. "I presume that's not yours?"

Cameron shook his head.

Simon took a handkerchief from his pocket and carefully picked up the box by its ends.

"Then this might have belonged to the woman. But I doubt it. She looked more the type to either use a cigarette lighter or have someone light her cigarettes for her." He turned the box over in the beam of the flashlight. "It could have been discarded by anyone walking through here. Except the owner had blood on their hands when they last handled it." He pointed to two bloody fingerprints on either side of the box. "Which makes me think this belonged to her attacker."

"It's mighty cold tonight," Cameron said. "Surely he would ha' been wearin' gloves?"

"Have you ever tried lighting a match with thick winter gloves on?" Simon asked. "I might be wrong. But I think this attacker got careless." He wrapped the box in the handkerchief and put it into his pocket. "It could be useful evidence. If the police won't do their job, then it's up to us to leave no stone unturned."

The old orange crate in which Simon had discovered the

woman's clutch bag was shoved against the wall at the side of the alleyway. He returned to it and peered inside.

"This is where I found that bag," he said to Cameron. "Shine your torch inside it, there's a good chap. Although I'm pretty sure it's empty now."

The beam of electric light illuminated an empty crate, save for a few scraps of old newspaper. Cameron looked up and flashed the beam along the brick wall. There was a circular metal sign fixed about six feet from the ground warning that dire legal consequences would result if pedestrians loitered in the alleyway.

"I'm surprised ye didnae get arrested by the constable for breakin' the bye-laws," Cameron remarked with a chuckle. "You cannae go anywhere in London wi'oot a sign like this mindin' yer business for ye."

As the light from Cameron's torch moved away from the sign, something caught Simon's eye on its lower edge.

"I say, throw a light on it again will you, old chap?"

Simon peered at the gap between the rough metal edge of the sign and the wall. He could see the corner of a piece of brown paper jutting out. He reached for his pocket penknife and flicked open the nail file.

"What is it?" Cameron asked. He moved the torch closer to the sign as Simon hooked the end of the nail file into a fold of the piece of paper and tugged. More of the paper emerged until Simon could see it was a sealed brown envelope.

"Voila!" Simon said. "Evidence upon evidence. This alleyway is a veritable treasure trove of clues. We should have this mystery solved by sunrise at this rate."

Somewhere ahead of them a bottle clattered on the cobblestones. Simon slipped the envelope into his coat pocket, turned to Cameron and raised a finger to his lips. Cameron switched off the electric torch and they headed back to Oxford Street, away from the disturbance. They turned right at the end of the alley and carried on up the street until they reached a department store doorway.

"I think it wa' wise we made our exit at tha' moment," Cameron said. "It might hae simply been that same cat that disturbed you before. But after what we've just seen, I'd rather not remain to find oot."

"Exactly," Simon replied. "And I for one am frantic to discover the contents of this envelope. Let's retire to somewhere a little warmer. Would you like some kedgeree?"

Simon's one-bedroom apartment was on the fourth floor of a mansion block adjacent to Marylebone Station. The entrance to Bellman Buildings gave a clear indication of the faded grandeur that lay within. The wooden doors were scuffed and battered from years of careless use by the fifty or so residents who lived there. A broken glass pane in the left-hand door had stayed boarded up for over a year. An electric lamp set into the awning above the entrance flickered on and off. More off than on.

"Comfortably shabby," announced Simon as he held open a door for Cameron. "But it's home."

Cameron stopped at the threshold. He appeared hesitant about entering the building.

"What's the matter?" asked Simon. "Have you suddenly remembered a more pressing engagement?"

"No, no," Cameron nodded towards the lobby and half whispered to Simon. "It's just that I see ye hae a porter on duty. Is it nae a problem for me tae be seen visiting ye at this hour?"

Simon smiled. "You're wise to be cautious, my friend. I've

heard of some porters who take great delight in reporting late night gentleman callers to the local constabulary. But Mr Pethers is a kindly old buffer. As long as you depart before midnight and give him a wave as you go, it won't give him cause to be suspicious about me having a gentleman caller stay late."

There was a mischievous look in Cameron's eyes as he responded: "And wha' if you chose to have a gentleman caller stay late?"

Simon considered carefully before he replied. "A word of advice to a young man in this 'cesspool called London', as Bill misquoted earlier. Take care not to flirt so easily with every man you meet."

Cameron's expression took on that of a child whose balloon had been taken from him and burst before his eyes.

"We men of the shadows live in a dangerous world," Simon continued. "As you've correctly observed, I am indeed a gentleman and therefore honourable. Not everyone you meet will be. Nor will they necessarily be of our persuasion. The police have been known to set traps using their prettier constables. I'd advise you to beware." He smiled. "However, for future reference, I've had occasion to use the rear stairs to the building. But there won't be a need to do so on this particular evening. Not on a first acquaintance, if you get my drift."

Cameron smiled. "I do kindly, sir. It wa' clear to me on first meetin' ye this evenin' that ye wa' a man o' fine principles."

Simon was relieved the young man had listened to his solemn sermon without offence. In truth, he would have liked nothing better than for Cameron to stay over. But Mrs Nowell would be arriving on the dot of eight tomorrow morning to do her twice-weekly clean-and-tidy. She was much less understanding about his occasional visitors. Not for reasons of prudery. Simon doubted she could even contemplate the realities of his associations with other men. But her concern was that they had *"no consideration for the extra trouble their intrusion causes a hardworking housekeeper like myself."* Good housekeepers were hard to find in London. Simon had no intention of upsetting Mrs Nowell for the sake of a brief dalliance.

He gestured towards the lobby, and Cameron entered the drab hallway of Bellman Buildings. Simon followed, and pulled hard to close the entrance door, which had a tendency to stick in the winter weather.

Benjamin Pethers sat in his usual spot on a tattered armchair adjacent to his porter's desk. His head nodded forward. An open book was on the point of falling from his hand. When the front door slammed shut, Pethers jolted awake, the book fell, and Simon hurried forward to retrieve it from the floor.

"I'm terribly sorry to have disturbed you, Mr Pethers." Simon handed the book to the elderly porter who was struggling to stand. "No need to get up, my dear chap. Mr McCreadie here is joining me for a late supper before he returns to his duties at the Palace later."

The porter brushed down the front of his shabby tunic. He retrieved his cap from the reception desk and replaced it at an odd angle on his head.

"The Palace, eh?" he said, and sniffed. Simon's attempt to place-drop failed to impress Pethers. "Buckingham Palace or Crystal Palace?"

Cameron laughed. "I'd nae be venturing south of the river a' this time o' night to the Crystal Palace. Mr Pethers, is it?" He held out his hand. "Cameron McCreadie, sir. Very pleased tae meet ye."

Pethers regarded the outstretched hand for a moment before grasping it and shaking it. "And you too, young sir. Good manners are always welcome in Bellman Buildings."

Simon led the way to the main staircase. "There's a lift but it's got an unfortunate habit of getting stuck between floors. I'm on the fourth floor so it's a bit of a trek. Hope you don't mind." He began to climb without waiting for Cameron's response.

"Hang your coat up on one of those hooks." Simon closed the front door of his apartment and indicated a row of coat hooks in the hallway. "Come in and make yourself comfortable." He walked through to the sitting room, and switched on the electric wall lights.

"Fortunately, this building benefits from a very efficient centralised boiler, so we're as warm as toast in the winter." He crossed to the windows and drew the curtains. "But I can fix you another whisky if you want to shrug off the chill from our walk."

Cameron stood in the doorway and looked around the sitting room. "It's a grand place ye have here. Ver' cosy." He pronounced the adjective with a charmingly short Scottish 'o'. "I'll gladly take another wee dram. But don't ye wanna open yon envelope first? I'm fascinated tae know what's inside."

Simon reached into his pocket and took out the brown envelope they had found in the alleyway. He placed it on a small wooden bureau set against the wall adjacent to the window. "Of course. I'm as eager as you are to discover its contents. And while I'm investigating..." He reached back into his pocket and withdrew the metal button he had found in the woman's hand. "...I'd like you to take another look at this object I showed you earlier. You said you'd seen something like it before. I'd like you to wrack your brains for me and try to remember."

Simon handed the button to Cameron and walked back into the hallway to hang up his coat.

"I said I might hae seen it before," Cameron called after him. "I cannae be certain. And what about that bag with the engraving on it?"

Simon returned to the sitting room with the woman's leather bag in his hand and placed it on the bureau. "All in good time." He picked up the envelope and prodded it cautiously. "I'm presuming it's too small to contain a bomb. And I can't feel anything metallic. There don't seem to be any wires inside." He turned it over. "Nothing written on the outside. I can only presume it's a document of some kind."

He opened the drawer of his bureau, took out a letter opener, and gently slid it into the narrow gap at the top of the sealed flap. He sliced through the closed end, set down the letter opener, and pulled out a thin manila folder. Inside were five foolscap-size pages. Simon spread them out on the gate-leg dining table next to the bureau. Four of the five pages were thick, almost like cardboard. They were covered in diagrams and what appeared to be engineering drawings. The fifth page was much thinner and covered in text.

"Intriguing." Simon picked up one of the diagrams. "This one looks like a wireless tower. But the others are a complete mystery to me." He picked up the fifth page. "This is German. But it doesn't make any sense at all."

Cameron laughed. "I'm nae surprised." He looked at the paper in Simon's hand. "How do ye know?"

"I spent a little time in Berlin a couple of years ago." Simon peered closely at the heavy black Fraktur typeface.

"They're German words. But they're not proper sentences. Just a random collection of nonsense." He shook his head. "It's no good. I'll show it to Bill tomorrow. She, I mean he, might have an idea."

"Can he read German?"

Simon shook his head. "Not at all. But he knows all sorts of people. He might be able to come up with someone who can help." He turned to Cameron. "Now, my dear chap. I promised you kedgeree. Are you hungry?"

Cameron winked at him. "I could eat anything right now."

5

Weak, wintry sunlight illuminated the soot-stained buildings of Portland Place when Simon strode towards the BBC's new headquarters in Langham Place the next morning. Today, as on most days, he stopped outside the main entrance to look up and admire the curved façade of the Art Deco style building, adorned with sculptures of Ariel and Prospero. It stood like a stately ocean liner at the head of Upper Regent Street.

Simon pushed open the heavy brass doors and entered the high-ceilinged lobby. It was over six months since he had left his job at *The Chronicle* and he still felt a frisson of excitement whenever he walked into the building. One never knew who one might meet there. From writers and poets, to performers in the theatre, to big-wigs from Whitehall or band leaders like Henry Hall, Broadcasting House was like the giant stage-door of a theatre. And it had now become a world theatre. The BBC's new Empire Service had started the day before, bringing the voice of the BBC to many countries in Europe and in Britain's empire. The king himself was rumoured to be referring to it in his first ever Christmas Day broadcast.

The thrill of working for the BBC did not completely offset his growing frustration with the role he had been given in the News Department. When he had joined, he had been promised he would work as both a reporter and a news announcer. But the government had pressured the BBC not to compete with the nation's newspapers. The Corporation lobbied to expand its news operation, but had so far been unsuccessful. Simon was impatient and missed the satisfaction he got from working on an investigation.

He took the lift to the sixth floor and followed the carpeted corridor around to room 612. The building's similarity to an ocean liner continued on the interior. The many studios were placed in the bowels of the building, like a huge broadcasting engine room, while the offices were distributed around the perimeter, like cabins on a ship. The white-painted walls of the corridor reflected sunlight that streamed through tall metal-framed windows placed every few yards.

Until now Simon had never visited Bill's office. They had either met in a charming little restaurant in Great Titchfield Street or at the Fitzroy Tavern. But today he had a sense of urgency. Under his arm, he held a leather attaché case containing the manila envelope of documents he and Cameron had puzzled over the night before. He knew Bill would be frightfully busy, or at least, give the impression of being frightfully busy. But he hoped she might at least spare him a few minutes of her time.

Halfway along the corridor he encountered Daphne Goodmayes and her tea trolley. It was Daphne's duty to provide tea to senior management three times a day. There was a delivery first thing in the morning, then at eleven o'clock, and her last round of duty was at three in the afternoon. If the Director-General was feeling generous then she would have digestive biscuits to offer as well.

"Good morning, Mrs Goodmayes," Simon said brightly. "Have you been to Miss Miles yet?"

Daphne was on her hands and knees, clearing up some spilt sugar from the floor. "Morning, sir." She peered suspiciously at Simon through the thick lenses of her spectacles. "I've not seen you on this floor before."

Simon stooped to help her back on her feet. "No, I'm not as grand as the chaps here. I'm Simon Sampson. The news announcer."

The tea lady eyed him up and down. "Where's yer dinner jacket then?"

"Well, I only wear it when I'm at the microphone, Mrs Goodmayes." Simon had hoped for a more admiring reaction. "Actually, it's being pressed this morning. I'm collecting it this afternoon before I read the six o'clock news." He looked down at the mass of cups on the trolley. "If you haven't got to her yet, can I take Miss Miles's tea? I'm heading that way."

Daphne Goodmayes sniffed. "It's 'ighly irregular, sir. It's me what's supposed to take them their tea. Not some gentleman claiming to be an announcer. How do I know who you are?"

"It's perfectly all right, Mrs Goodmayes." Bill's voice echoed down the corridor. She strode towards them, a lighted cigarette hanging from her lips. "Simon's not a Bolshevik spy come to poison me." She stopped at the trolley and took two cups from it. "Let me take ours back with us to save you the trouble."

"But 'e's not from this floor, Miss." Daphne glowered at Simon. "I've already said it's 'ighly irregular."

"Please don't concern yourself, my dear." Bill handed the two cups to the tea lady. "Mr Sampson's my visitor. I'm permitted tea for my visitors. And a digestive as well."

Daphne Goodmayes sniffed. "If you say so, Miss." She took the cups and filled them with tea from a giant brown teapot. "It's not for the likes of me to say what's right and what's wrong." She handed the cups to Simon. "'Ere. You be the gen'leman. Milk and sugar's there if you wants it." She turned to Bill. "I don't have no digestives this morning. They're only allowed on afternoons."

"Thank you, dear lady," Bill said. There was a sickly-sweet smile on her face. "Come along Mr Sampson. I can give you ten minutes."

"Bloody woman." Bill slammed shut her office door and stalked over to the desk. "Give these people a trolley and they think they're in charge of Boadicea's bloody chariot."

Simon was just as irritated with Mrs Goodmayes. She had been quick to put him in his place and highlight the difference in seniority between him and Bill. It rankled.

Bill slumped into a large leather swivel-chair, swung her legs up onto the desk, and waved her cigarette imperiously. "Put the tea there and sit down. How did you get on with your Scottish youth? Another Sampson conquest?"

Simon was shocked. "We'd only just met, my dear Bill. You know how particular I am. And I certainly wasn't going to risk raising Mr Pethers' suspicions last night."

"Pethers? Your doorman?" Bill chuckled, and then coughed on a lungful of smoke. "You crafty blighter, Simon. You took the poor boy back to yours last night, didn't you? Intent on having your wicked way with him, were you?"

"Nothing was further from my mind." Simon reached for one of the cups on the desk. "I had some leftover kedgeree in the larder and it seemed appropriate for me to feed a strapping Scotsman like him. And seeing as you chose to cancel our supper appointment—"

"Oh, nonsense." Bill swung her legs off the desk and leaned forward to take the other cup. She tipped some tea into its saucer and slurped noisily.

"Do you have to indulge that disgusting habit?" Simon asked.

Bill finished the contents of the saucer and refilled it from her cup. "It's practical, Simon dear. It cools the tea and lets me drink it more quickly. I told you, I can only spare you ten minutes. I'm very busy. What do you want?"

"I could start by asking you to pay for your drinks in the Fitzroy occasionally." Bill's office was larger than he had expected, with a double window looking out on Portland Place. He pointed to the painting of a female nude on the wall. "Especially when I see how well the Corporation is treating you." He opened his attaché case and removed the manila folder.

Bill sniffed and held out her hand. "What's that?"

"I really don't know." Simon handed her the folder. "We found it hidden behind a metal sign in the alleyway last night."

"'We'?" Bill picked up her glasses from the desk, perched them on the end of her nose, and removed the pages from the folder. "Did you force that young man to go gadding with you in that disreputable alleyway after I left?"

"I didn't force him, Bill. He offered to help. He's very accommodating."

"Yes." Bill peered at him over her glasses. "I don't doubt he is." She pushed aside a pile of the morning papers and laid out the five sheets of paper from the envelope on her desk.

"I suppose you saw?" Simon said, indicating the newspapers.

"Saw what?" Bill's head was bowed as she studied the sheets of paper.

Simon picked up a copy of *The Chronicle* from the top of the pile. "Nothing in the paper about last night."

Bill looked up. "What do you expect? Since you left, they've lost their star reporter. You said yourself the police wanted nothing to do with it." She gestured to the five sheets of paper on the desk. "Is this all there is?"

After three years of knowing her, Simon still found it difficult to reconcile Bill's imperious abruptness with their friendship. Her tongue was sharp, like the cut of her clothes.

"Why do you ask?"

Bill tapped one of the sheets of paper. "Because there are page numbers on four of them, my simple friend. They start at seven and finish at twenty-five. These are but a selection from a larger document."

Simon was annoyed with himself for missing this simple detail. Last night he had been so engrossed in the content of the pages he had failed to notice. Bill took a silver cigarette case from her jacket pocket and opened it.

"Damn."

She rummaged in one of the drawers of her desk, found a packet of Senior Service, and refilled the cigarette case. She lit a cigarette and inhaled deeply.

"I'd say these are copies." Bill exhaled smoke over the four thicker pages. "I think they've been photographically reproduced. What's this last one? German, isn't it?"

"That's right," Simon replied. "But it makes no sense."

"I'd have thought with all your trips to the fleshpots of

Berlin you'd be able to translate it." Bill looked over her glasses at him. "Didn't you get arrested with Dietrich?"

"Who told you that?"

"You did." Bill drew on her cigarette and blew the smoke in Simon's direction. "On a particularly boozy night in your flat on the occasion of your thirtieth birthday." She laughed. "You were so maudlin that evening, bemoaning the end of your *"roaring twenties"* as you so delightfully put it. I think you confessed everything to me."

"Well don't go blabbing it to all and sundry," Simon replied. "When the judge released us on a caution the next day, there was a charge officer who was very smitten with Marlene. He very sweetly erased all note of the arrest. Frightfully daring of him. It meant the dear lady was able to travel to America to launch her Hollywood career without fear of being stopped. If it ever got out that she had a police record they might deport her back to Germany."

"Her secret is safe with me. I would never betray a sister." Bill picked up one of the photographic copies. "This looks like a radio tower."

Yes, that's what I thought." Simon pointed to another of the pages. "And this one's some kind of wiring diagram. But no idea what. If we could make sense of the German, we might get a clue as to what it's all about."

Bill stubbed out her cigarette, leaned back in the chair, and rested her legs on the desk once more. "Do you mean a native speaker?" She waved a hand in the direction of the door. "The place is swarming with foreigners. They're all running around like ballyhoo with this new Empire Service."

Simon wrinkled his nose. "I'm really not keen to share this with all and sundry. What if it's some top-secret document that's gone missing? If someone shoots their mouth off about it, they could get me into all sorts of hot water."

"Then take it to the police. Or at least the Head of News. Don't you have a duty as an employee of the Corporation to do that?"

Simon shook his head. "That's not what I do. I never did at *The Chronicle* and I'm not going to start now. Hang the BBC rules. The police couldn't be bothered to do anything when I called them. This is *my* investigation."

Bill roared with laughter. "I understand. You're becoming frustrated now that you're confined to the wireless studio and can't get out solving crimes like some character in a Dashiel Hammett novel."

It was true. Well, maybe not about wanting to be a character in a Dashiel Hammett novel. But in his five years at *The Chronicle* Simon had been fortunate to investigate several very juicy crimes, including the Stage Door Killer. It was while he had been working on that case that he had met Bill, who had often accompanied Noël Coward to His Majesty's Theatre in Haymarket during the run of *Bitter Sweet.*

"Any ideas, Bill? Someone you can ask discreetly? You're in a better position than me to pull a favour. The only person I can think of to ask is Binkie Bradbury from *The Times*. And he's out in Berlin right now, reporting on all the shenanigans with Herr Hitler."

Bill gathered the five pages together and put them back into the manila envelope. "There's a rather sweet Polish girl along the corridor here. Very charming and she speaks fluent German. We both buy our cigarettes in the same shop in Great Portland Street. She's working her socks off on the Empire Service but she might have time. And I'm sure I can prevail upon her to be discreet."

"Is she sapphic-leaning?" Simon asked.

"What's that got to do with it?"

"I see," Simon replied. "You've got designs on her, haven't you?"

"That's none of your business." Bill sniffed and looked away. "You know, you can be most awfully rude sometimes."

There was a knock at the door.

"Come in," Bill shouted.

The door opened and a youth in a dark blue uniform stood on the threshold. "Beggin' yer pardon, Miss Miles. A telegram's arrived for you. From America."

Bill waved him in. "Bring it here." She took another cigarette from the silver box and lit it. The youth crossed to the desk and handed her an envelope. She tore it open and withdrew a sheet of paper.

"Good Lord."

"What is it, Bill?" Simon asked.

She looked up, the cigarette hanging from her lips. "What are you doing for Christmas?"

"Trying to avoid visiting the parents in darkest Wiltshire. Why?"

Bill waved the telegram at him.

"I've got your perfect excuse. It's Noël. He's staying in New York over the holidays, performing in *Designs for Living*. He's offered me Goldenhurst, his little farmhouse in Kent. Come on, Simon. Let's go gadding in the countryside for Christmas."

6

The lunchtime editions of the newspapers still contained no reports about a woman being attacked. In fact, they had very little news to report at all. Parliament had a few days left before it rose for Christmas, but in truth, the government was doing very little business. Many MPs had already departed for their homes in the country, as had their civil servants.

In the early afternoon Simon sat in a corner of the large office occupied by the News Department and flicked through the pages of *The Chronicle*. It was dispiriting to see acres of newsprint devoted to suggestions for last-minute presents, or Christmas recipe ideas for harassed housewives.

There were a few items of serious news. The paper had printed the minutiae of the new Trade Unions Bill. It also reported that a tram had crashed into an omnibus in Greenwich with several people injured, and that the Prince of Wales was recovering from a chill at York House. There was little else of interest. Simon knew that the two journalists working on the six o'clock news report were struggling to find items to fill it.

He wondered if there might be a repeat of the fateful day two years ago, when listeners had tuned in to the evening news to hear the announcer say "There is no news tonight." Instead, the BBC broadcast fifteen minutes of piano music and then switched to a performance of *Parsifal* at the Queens Hall. It was before Simon had joined the Corporation, and was one of the reasons he had had for accepting the invitation, tempting him away from *The Chronicle*. But the management's original promise of using his crime reporting experience to improve the BBC's news output was yet to materialise.

So far his suggestions for additional news items had been rejected as being "*too common*" for the high standards demanded by the Director General. Simon could see little future for himself in the News Department, neither could he face asking the bulldog-like editor of *The Chronicle* to give him his old job back.

At least there was the imminent prospect of a week-long holiday to savour. Simon's head of department had already released him from his news announcing duties over the Christmas period, because he himself wanted to do that job. It was probably no coincidence that the man had cancelled all news announcements for Christmas Day, saying that it was "*to give the listeners a respite from the troubled world*".

Simon was looking forward to "*gadding*" with Bill down in Kent. It was kind of her to invite him, and it gave him the perfect excuse to avoid a repeat of his Christmas last year. As usual, he had travelled to the family home in Wiltshire to join his parents and his two older sisters with their husbands and young families. Cook had been given a day off, and so it had fallen to Simon's mother to prepare the lunch, with limited help from his two sisters. Simon had offered his services in the kitchen, and had fallen into a row with his father over the role of a man in the modern household. His mother had been reduced to tears, his father had stormed out of the house in a fearsome temper, and the lunch was burnt.

Surely, this Christmas had to be much more fun.

"Sampson."

Reggie Worthing, one of the journalists, waved a telephone receiver at him from across the office.

"Some fellow called Bill asking for you."

It was unusual for Bill to use her after-work name during working hours. Even more so on the internal telephone system. Simon walked over to Reggie and took the receiver.

"I hope that's not a personal call." The voice came from the doorway of a small office at the end of the room. Simon had failed to notice his head of department was back from lunch.

"No, sir," Simon replied. "Bill works in the Libraries Department."

"Really?" The head of the department looked puzzled. "Don't remember a chap called Bill there. Must be new." He turned, went back into his office, and slammed the door behind him. Simon put the receiver to his ear.

"Am I your personal assistant all of a sudden?" Bill's voice was loud, even on the crackly telephone line. Simon pressed the receiver closer to his ear to make sure no sound escaped from it, in case Bill made an indiscreet comment.

"What do you mean?" he asked.

"I've just received a call from that young Scotsman working at York House, asking if you might be free later this evening."

Simon smiled. The day had got markedly better. "Well, you did give Cameron your card last night."

"And you didn't give him yours?"

"I don't have one," Simon replied. "Announcers must remain strictly anonymous at the BBC."

"Oh, poppycock." The consonants exploded in Simon's ear and he lifted the receiver away, only to clamp it to the side of his head again as Bill continued. "This is the last time I act as a go-between in your amorous trysts. Mr McCreadie says he's got some news from the Palace you might want to hear."

"From the Palace? Did he say what it was?"

Bill coughed on her cigarette. "Of course he didn't. He asked me if I could suggest somewhere discreet for you two to meet."

"And what did you say?"

Bill snorted with laughter. "I suggested the first-floor restaurant at the Lily Pond."

"Oh really." In his exasperation, Simon had nearly slipped up and said darling. He corrected himself just in time. "It's hardly discreet."

"Nonsense, darling," Bill replied. "I'd say the waitresses at the Lily Pond are the most discreet in the whole of England. You know perfectly well that all the rich and famous take their boys there before they go off for a bit of nookie. Yet not a word of scandal has ever broken from a waitress's lips."

"I suppose you're right. What time did you say?"

"You know, this is most depressing." Bill sighed. "Here I am, BBC senior management. And yet I'm forced to pimp your next assignation for you."

"It's not my fault he called you instead of me."

"And this is the last time." Bill sighed heavily again. "Piccadilly Circus. Eight o'clock under Eros."

"Piccadilly Circus?" Simon chuckled. "He'll be lucky if he's not been picked up and robbed by the time I get there."

Reggie twitched his head and there was a disapproving look on his face. It was probably unwise of Simon to discuss his social arrangements within Reggie's earshot. The man was a stickler for observing the head of department's rule of no personal calls in the office. But Simon had little time for deference to BBC hierarchy. And Reggie was a very mediocre journalist.

Bill chuckled. "I thought it was time the boy was introduced to London life. He's got a far too sheltered existence over at St James's. Are you still all right for Goldenhurst at Christmas?"

"I certainly am," Simon replied. "Looking forward to it."

"Patsy Prendergast says we can borrow her motor for Christmas," Bill continued. "She's staying in London and doesn't need it. What day do you finish?"

"The twenty-third. This Friday," Simon replied. "How splendid. We can motor down in the evening. Where in Kent is it?"

"You won't know it," Bill replied. "It's in the tiniest of villages. A place called Aldington, almost at the sea. If you kept going, you'd end up in Folkestone."

"Sounds idyllic," Simon replied. "We can go for a bracing walk on the sands. You're such a brick, Bill."

"I know."

Reggie poked a pencil in his side to get his attention, and pointed towards the head of department's office door. It was open.

"Look, Bill. I have to go—"

"Before you do, there's something else. I had a spot of lunch with Anna today."

Simon was puzzled by the conversation's new turn. "Who's Anna?"

"I told you this morning," Bill replied, sounding exasperated. "She's the sweet Polish girl I told you about. Working on the Empire Service. I asked her if she might take a look at that document you showed me and she said yes."

"Sampson."

The head of department stood in front of Simon.

"Look, Bill. I really must go."

"How rude. I do you a favour and you cut me off."

"It's not that Bill. But—"

"No matter. I've given her the page of German text and I'll hang onto the other ones. I've got an idea about them. Toodle--oo."

Simon handed the receiver back to Reggie and smiled at his head of department.

"I've told you before Sampson about using BBC telephones for personal calls."

"It wasn't a personal call, sir," Simon replied. "If you must know—"

"'Must know'?" interrupted the head of department. "In my position as Head of News I have a responsibility to know everything my staff are doing. What was the purpose of your call?"

Pompous old fool, Simon thought. The man had no idea about news and would have lasted no more than five minutes in Fleet Street. He had been promoted beyond his ability and strutted around like Simon's old headmaster. He had already dismissed his request to investigate the discovery in the alleyway the night before.

"As I said earlier, sir," Simon continued. "I was enlisting the help of the Head of Libraries in a small investigation."

"Not that ridiculous story you told me this morning?" The Head of News grunted his disapproval. "I told you then and I'll tell you now. The police tell us if there's an investigation to report. It's they who enforce the law in this country, not us."

Simon said nothing. One of the few pieces of sage advice

his father had given him was *"battles not lost are not fought, merely battles not worth fighting for."* He decided against putting up any further argument.

The Head of News picked up a newspaper from the desk and waved it at Simon.

"We're the BBC. Not some common rag down in the gutter. Now get on with some useful work and don't go wasting BBC resources again."

He threw down the newspaper and retreated to his office.

Simon waited until his boss left for a drinks party with the Director General and a few other members of senior management. There was little happening on the news front, and Simon's two colleagues seemed content with the running order they had decided upon earlier in the day. They sat smoking and discussing the *"shocking waste of money"* the BBC was spending on its television experiments. Simon was not needed until half an hour before the news broadcast at six o'clock. He collected his hat and coat and headed outside.

The day was getting colder, and Simon shoved his hands into his pockets as he headed down Upper Regent Street. His fingers came into contact with the metal button that had dropped from the woman's hand the night before. He remembered showing it to Bill at the Fitzroy and her reaction to it. She had called it sinister and was about to say more when Cameron had arrived. He thought about turning back and paying a call on her, but he decided it could wait. There were about three hours left before he was due back in the office. Plenty of time to do some investigating. He took a left on Margaret Street and headed for the alleyway.

Five minutes later he found his plan for the afternoon thwarted. The entrance to the alleyway was roped off and a police officer was guarding it. The officer was not the same one Simon had encountered the night before. He smiled and hoped the policeman would be more helpful than Constable Smith.

"Can't I get through, officer?" Simon asked. "Only I need to look for something in that alleyway. I think I left it there last night, when I was coming back from the Fitzroy Tavern. I won't be a moment."

"I'm afraid not, sir," the policeman replied.

"Why has it been blocked off?"

The officer shook his head. "I'm not at liberty to say anything, sir. Official business going on here."

"What kind of official business?" Simon asked.

"I can't tell you, sir."

Simon took out his now expired identity card from *The Chronicle.*

"I'm from the press."

"Then you certainly can't enter," the police officer replied. "All inquiries must be made to Scotland Yard."

A man wearing an overcoat and smoking a pipe emerged from the shadows of the alleyway behind the constable. He carried what appeared to be a heavy sack, tied at the neck. Simon stepped around the policemen and approached the rope barrier.

"Excuse me," Simon called. "I'm from *The Chronicle.* Is this about the woman who was assaulted here last night? I may be able to help you. I was a witness."

"Constable." Pipe man ignored Simon. "Don't let this gentleman through. I thought you were supposed to be guarding the entrance?"

Simon felt the officer's hand on his shoulder. "Now look

here, sir. I've told you already. Official business going on here—"

"Let go of me." Simon turned and thrust his identity card in the officer's face. "I have a right to be here. I'm with the press."

The constable took the card from Simon's hand. "It's out of date. Six months out of date." He handed it back to Simon. "Move along please, or I'll be forced to arrest you."

Pipe man put down the sack and fumbled with the rope barrier. Simon tried again. "Look. I was here last night, so I know what happened. Are you from Scotland Yard?"

"Yes, that's right." The man untied the rope barrier, stepped past it, and bent to retie it. Simon took out his notebook and pencil.

"What's your name, please?"

Pipe man finished tying the rope, reached into his pocket, and took out a packet of cigarettes. "All inquiries have to be referred to Scotland Yard. I can't speak to you." He lit his cigarette.

"But at least tell me your name and rank," Simon insisted. "You're from Scotland Yard, you say? Then you must know Detective Inspector Robbie Mountcraft. He's a good friend of mine."

Pipe man nodded warily. "Yes, I know him."

"You work with him, right?"

Again, the man nodded. He bent down and picked up the sack. "I told you before. Speak to Scotland Yard. Maybe your friend Mountcraft can tell you more." He walked away with the sack to a large black van parked nearby.

"But why won't you talk to me?" Simon called after him. "I'm a witness. A woman was assaulted. Surely you need to interview me." Simon went to follow, but again he felt the constable's hand on his shoulder.

"Now, now," the constable said. "This is your last warning. Let him get on with his official business. There's no need for any more witnesses here."

Simon opened his notebook to write down the number of the black van. It was then he noticed it had no number plate.

7

"Relax, my dear, and have another gin."

"I can't relax," Simon replied. "I'm certain he was an imposter. He said he was from Scotland Yard and knew Robbie. But if he did, he'd know his last name's Mountjoy, not Mountcraft."

Bill took Simon's glass and carried it over to the drinks cabinet in the corner of her office. "Easy mistake to make, especially if he doesn't know him that well. Or maybe there is a Robbie Mountcraft at Scotland Yard that you don't know about."

"I don't think that's likely." Simon shook his head. "No. There was something not right about what was going on there. I'm beginning to wonder if that was even a real policeman guarding the entrance."

"Impersonating a police officer?" Bill turned, a bottle of gin in her hand. "That's taking a hell of a risk in the centre of London, isn't it?" She waved the bottle at him. "Single or double?"

"I mustn't," Simon protested. "I'm at the microphone in

half an hour. It's bad enough that I've had one already. I certainly shouldn't have another."

"Phooey," Bill replied briskly. She poured a liberal splash of gin into his glass and topped it up with tonic. "From what I've heard of your broadcasts, it'll improve your diction." She handed back the glass. "Come on, darling. Take a little medicine to relax your throat muscles."

Simon gave in to her persuasion. After all, it was almost Christmas. "I thought you'd be at that drinks party the Director General was throwing this afternoon," he said. "My head of department skedaddled off to it soon after he gave me a dressing down."

"Pah!" Bill slumped into her chair, leaned back, and swung her legs onto the desk. Papers and files tumbled to the floor. She glanced at the mess she had created and dismissed it with a wave of her hand. "They didn't want *me* there." She inhaled on her cigarette and blew an enormous smoke ring that hovered in the air between them.

"You mean you weren't invited?"

"No."

"But I thought you were senior management like them?"

"Senior management, yes." Bill swung her legs off the desk, lurched forward, and searched through the papers that remained on it, scattering them to left and right as she did so. Simon was certain she had already started drinking before he arrived.

"Here. Read this." Bill tossed a single sheet of BBC headed paper across the desk. It was a memorandum from the Director General, addressed to all senior staff. The heading was *Christmas social arrangements*.

Simon was confused by what he read. "But this *is* an invitation," he said. "So you were invited."

Bill gave him a withering look. "I thought as a journalist

you were supposed to be able to read." She snatched the memo from his hand and read the first paragraph:

"The Director General, Sir John Reith, requires all gentlemen of senior management to join him in his office for a brief celebration to mark the BBC's first Christmas in the new Broadcasting House. Soft drinks will be served."

"You didn't go because he wasn't serving alcohol?"

"Don't be so obtuse." Bill crumpled the memo into a ball and threw it at Simon. "Didn't you hear? It's addressed to *all gentlemen*. Damn Reith. Impertinent little man. I might wear trousers, but I'm still a woman."

"I admit it's rather clumsy of him. But you're the only woman on senior management. It was probably an oversight."

"How dare you take that vile man's side." Bill stood with such violence that her chair crashed over behind her. "Don't you know what an egotistical little prig he is? He despises people. Makes it very clear. And I'm certain he reviles people like us. Men and women. Damn him."

"That's not what I've heard."

"Of course he does," Bill replied, a note of impatience in her voice. "He despises people who are—just so. I've seen him cut dear little Joe Ackerley dead many times. And Joe's a man who makes no secret of his preferences."

"Well." Simon took a drink from his glass. "All I know is what I was told by an old regiment chum of Reith's in the Fitzroy one night last year. Apparently after the Great War, it was widely known Reith had at least one passionate affair with a chap."

Bill's hand froze, carrying her cigarette to her lips. "Really?" She inhaled on the cigarette. "I must remember that." She blew out another smoke ring. "Whatever. From the day he got his hands on the place he's never allowed theatrical types near the microphone if he can help it. He's been opposed to all forms of light entertainment on the BBC. It's only because of Radio Luxembourg's test transmissions and the threat of their popular programming that the government's leaning on him to give way. He's going to have to give in before long. But he'll still resent people like us. And if what you tell me is true, that makes him a hypocrite to boot."

Simon was shocked by the vehemence of Bill's tirade. She had often complained about what she saw as irritating obstructions the Corporation's bureaucracy threw in her way. But only now did he realise how personal her frustration was. Simon had met the Director General twice, and each time for no more than a few minutes. He was an imposing man, well over six feet tall, with an abrupt way of speaking. Like a general addressing his troops. In her senior position, Bill must have met him on many more occasions and for longer. Simon put his glass on the table and stood.

"I'm sorry, Bill. It's clearly not a good moment. I'll come back another time."

"Oh, darling, sit down and stop being so bloody sensitive." She picked up his half empty glass and walked back to the drinks cabinet. "I'll top this up. Then we can plot your next move in the case of the missing lady."

Simon decided it was pointless protesting about the drink and sat down again. He wished he had eaten something at lunchtime. He was going to feel very lightheaded by six o'clock.

"I'll go and talk to Robbie at Scotland Yard," he replied. "And if he won't talk to me, I'll go over his head and insist on speaking to the Commissioner."

"Trenchard's the new man at the top of the Metropolitan Police, isn't he?" Bill poured another generous shot of gin into

Simon's glass. "Ex air force. You'll be lucky getting to see him. I'm told he surrounds himself with flunkies to avoid any contact with the public. Or 'the great unwashed' as he sees them. Haven't you got anything else to go on?"

Simon reached for his coat and rummaged in the pocket. "Actually, I have." He found the metal button and retrieved it. "Last night I was showing you this shortly before Cameron bowled up. I'd found it in the young lady's hand. You said you thought you'd seen something like it before."

He took the full glass Bill offered him and handed her the button in return.

"Ah, yes," she said. "Der Sturmabteilung."

"I beg your pardon?"

Bill held the button at arm's length in front of her and saluted smartly with her other arm. "That's what I was trying to tell you before Cameron interrupted. It's military. Rather fringe German military, I'm afraid."

"How do you know?"

"I'm the BBC's head of libraries," she said, and gave him a withering glance. "I'm expected to know everything." She lowered her saluting arm and held the button for Simon to see. "That jagged A-shaped symbol? It's the emblem of Der Sturmabteilung. Also known as the Storm Detachment, or brownshirts. Very nasty group of people. Fascist. They go about smashing places up. Particularly Jewish places."

"Of course," Simon said. "They're the ones behind that fellow Hitler who keeps popping up on news agency reports from Berlin. He's getting awfully popular."

Bill nodded.

"Yes. He's got this funny little man with glasses running them. Ernst Röhm. Another nasty piece of work. Although the rumours are he's of our persuasion." She looked closely at the button once more and handed it back to Simon.

"If you say it was in her hand when you found the poor woman," Bill continued. "Then my guess is it came off her attacker's coat during the struggle. I wonder how someone in London got hold of a coat with *Sturmabteilung* buttons on it."

Simon shoved the button back in his coat pocket, took a drink from his glass, and choked. "Good Lord, Bill. This is pretty well neat gin."

Bill shrugged. "I must have forgotten the tonic. Never mind. It'll put hairs on your chest. Is there anything else you can remember from last night?"

Simon took out his notepad. "She said something odd. I wrote it down. It was when I was telling her I was getting the police." He flicked over a couple of pages on the notepad. "Here we are. It sounded like 'curling'. And then when I asked her to repeat it, she said something like 'curling in cover'."

"'Curling in cover'?" Bill sat down in her chair and reached across for Simon's glass. "Look, darling. If you're not going to drink that, can I have it? Waste not, want not and all that." She took the glass before Simon had a chance to reply, and drank from it. "'Curling in cover'?" she repeated. "Something to do with a book, do you think? You found that folder of documents hidden under the sign in the alleyway. Perhaps there's something hidden in the cover of a book. But what book?"

"If I'd managed to get back into the alleyway. I might have been able to find it."

Simon looked at the clock on the wall of Bill's office. He stood, and swayed slightly as the room floated in and out of focus. "Good God. Is that the time? I'm supposed to be in the studio by now. I've got to run."

He crossed to the door, opened it, and turned to stare bleary-eyed at Bill. "If I manage to read the news script tonight without stumbling it'll be a bloody miracle. Please don't ever let me drink before a broadcast again."

Simon arrived at Piccadilly Circus at ten minutes to eight that evening and waited to cross the road to the statue of Eros on its traffic island. This part of London always gave Simon a thrill of excitement. It buzzed with activity, like a giant beehive. There were swarms of people hurrying from work, or strolling towards a restaurant, theatre or pub. The beehive metaphor was apt, because within fifty yards of where Simon stood there were so many queens.

Across the road was The Trocadero. Its Long Bar was always guaranteed to provide a gay evening for gentlemen in search of pleasure. A little farther on was the Empire Theatre in Leicester Square. Its Upper Gallery was popular with painted boys and men dressed in smart suits who spent an evening either exchanging acid-tongued witticisms or seeking a friend for the night.

Even at that time of the evening the traffic on the roads leading to Piccadilly Circus was almost stationary. Simon stepped off the pavement and wove his way between taxis and omnibuses queuing to drive up Shaftesbury Avenue or down the Haymarket. Cameron was waiting for him, and Simon was pleased to see he was once again soberly dressed in his immaculate black coat. This time with a grey scarf and black leather gloves. Young men of a similar age to Cameron were also standing on the steps of Eros, and they wore far more flamboyant clothing. Simon preferred to be inconspicuous when out with a gentleman friend. There was less chance that they might draw the attention of the police, or *busys* as his friends in the Fitzroy Tavern would call them.

"I do hope you've not been waiting long." Simon took Cameron's outstretched hand and squeezed it firmly. "It's getting awfully cold. I think it might snow this Christmas."

Cameron reached out his other hand and rested it on Simon's hip. Simon pushed it away. "Best not here, old chap," he whispered. "Awfully public you know."

He released Cameron's hand and pointed across the road. "We need to head towards Leicester Square. The Lily Pond is two roads up. And we can walk past the Trocadero on the way and see who's out gadding tonight."

"I'm glad I'm wi' ye," Cameron replied. "I'm still finding ma bearin's in London. I've nae come down to this part of town since I moved to York House."

"Oh, you should." Simon led the way through the still stationary traffic to Coventry Street. "It's frightfully exciting. And you can always be sure of meeting someone interesting." He pointed to the corner of Glasshouse Street. "That's the Regent Palace Hotel. Awfully good bar. Perfect place to meet gentlemen from overseas, and they can hire a room for you by the hour if that interests you." He grabbed Cameron's arm and pulled him to safety as a motor car attempted to circumvent the traffic jam and drove up onto the pavement.

"Try not to get yourself killed, my dear."

The first-floor restaurant of Lyons' Corner House was very busy, and Simon was grateful to Bill for having telephoned in advance and reserved them a table. Cameron looked around at the all-male clientele with a broad smile on his face. He leaned in to whisper to Simon.

"Are all these gentlemen, you know—"

Simon caught the eye of a waitress, and she scurried over to their table.

"Excuse me," Simon began. "My friend is asking why there are no ladies dining here this evening. I was about to tell him how well you and the other waitresses keep us protected from those who are not *'like us'*."

The waitress covered her mouth with her hand and giggled. Despite her obvious nervousness she held her shoulders back with a natural poise. Like all Lyons' Corner House waitresses or nippies as they were known, she wore a simple black and white uniform, which highlighted her slim waist.

"Oi don't know wha' you mean sir." She spoke with an accent that was not from London and it accentuated her shyness. The letter *i* sounded more like *oy* and she rolled the letter *r* around her mouth. Simon guessed she was from a more rural part of England, such as Oxfordshire or Kent. "All oi've been told is you gentlemen prefers each other's company to that of ladies. And we don't want no trouble." She took a notepad and pencil from her apron pocket. "Are you ready to order? Only kitchen's very busy tonight."

"Thank you, my dear," Simon replied. "We'll have the braised beef and onions if you still have any left." He grinned at Cameron. "It's always reliable here." He turned back to the waitress. "And a bottle of bordeaux. It should go with the beef very nicely."

The waitress took a note of their order and left. The atmosphere in the restaurant was lively. The wooden floors intensified the buzz of conversation, the clatter of plates and the occasional explosion of raucous laughter.

"You told Bill you had some news from the Palace that might interest me," Simon said.

Cameron looked around and leaned in towards Simon. "Are you sure we can't be overheard in here?"

Simon nodded.

"I'm pretty certain that international coups and major bank robberies have been plotted in here before now and no one's been any the wiser." He nodded in the direction of two men at the next table. Their fingers were intertwined and their heads almost touched as they gazed lovingly at each other.

"Everyone's far too concerned with themselves," Simon said in a low voice to Cameron. "They don't care what's going on around them. Is what you have to tell me so top secret?"

Cameron shook his head. "Not really. But I'm not supposed to speak about what goes on at the Palace in front of strangers."

Simon took his hand, lifted it to his lips, and kissed it. "There. These people can't hear you. And we're no longer strangers. You can confide in me."

8

The waitress returned with their wine, and Cameron hastily tugged his hand away from Simon's. She filled two glasses and placed the bottle on the table.

"Aren't you supposed to taste it first?" Cameron asked Simon.

Simon smiled at the waitress. "It's my friend's first time here. He doesn't yet know that you serve only the finest wine and there's never any need to taste it."

She looked awkwardly from Cameron to Simon. "Didn' I do it roight? Oi've not been 'ere long. Oi'm still gettin' the 'ang of it."

"You were faultless, my dear," Simon said. "Why don't you go and check on our beef?"

She scurried away. Cameron leaned in to Simon. "I didna' mean to show up the poor wee lassie. But at the Palace they're teachin' me how to wait at table."

Simon raised his glass. "You were right to say something. Lyons' Corner House needs to maintain standards. But she's relatively new and she seems to be awfully busy. She'll learn soon enough and we don't want to draw attention to ourselves if you've got top secrets to tell me."

"I feel embarrassed now. It's not really a top secret. Just a wee bit of news." Cameron raised his glass and clinked it against Simon's. "Slàinte mhath."

"Happy days." Simon drank from his glass. "Now that bordeaux's really not bad. Don't disappoint me. I was looking forward to some juicy gossip from the Palace." He smiled to see a look of consternation on Cameron's face. "But to be fair, Bill simply said you had some news. Tell me. What's happening?"

"Och, it's nothin' really." Cameron set his glass down. "I've been asked to look after a visitor who's stayin' wi' the Prince of Wales when he goes up to Sandringham for Christmas. It means I'm goin' wi' him to Norfolk in a few days."

"That sounds very grand. Christmas with the royal family."

"I know." Cameron was clearly excited. "Although it's nae exactly wi' the royal family. I wa' supposed to be catchin' the train to Scotland to stay wi' ma family. But it all changed today. It's a step up for me. I've nae been assigned to a member of the household before."

"Haven't you? You said you worked for the two princes at York House."

"Aye, but nae directly. I do whatever the keeper of the household tells me. Sometimes I do for the Prince of Wales if there's nae one else around. But when this gentleman arrives the day after tomorrow, I'm assigned directly tae him."

Simon raised his glass. "Congratulations. A promotion."

Cameron shook his head. "Nae. More of a try-oot. He's only staying with the Prince of Wales over Christmas and New Year. I'm back to ma auld job after that. But mebbe one day..." He smiled.

"And who is the gentleman?"

"The Duke of Saxe-Coburg and Gotha. His name's Charles Edward, and he's the king's first cousin. And Queen Victoria's grandchild."

"One of many. She must have had at least thirty grandchildren."

Cameron grinned. "Forty-two tae be exact. From her nine children. She wa' poppin' them out for the Prince Consort like shellin' peas."

"Come, come." Simon wagged a finger at Cameron in mock admonishment. "I don't think you're supposed to make comments like that. If the king hears you speak that way while you're at Sandringham, he'll send you to the Tower for treason."

"Ah, but he won't," Cameron began. At that moment the waitress arrived with their food and he stopped talking abruptly.

"Oi got you extra helpin's 'cos you're both so noice to me." She put the plates down on the table with a flourish. "Oi told chef you was respectable gentlemen what wanted feedin' up."

Simon laughed. "You're a delight, my dear. I'm sure you'll have a long and successful career with Lyons' Corner Houses."

"Oi don' wanna do that, sir." The waitress sniffed. "Oi'm goin' to be a dancer. I'm only doin' this to fill in until I get me another job in a theatre."

"I wish you all the luck in the world with that," Simon replied. "Does your mother know of your ambitions?"

The girl looked sheepish. "She don' know. Oi ran away last summer."

"From your accent, I'll wager you're not from London," Simon said. "Where are you from?"

"Oh, you wouldn't know it, sir. It's a tiny village in Kent."

"I might have heard of it," Simon replied. "What's its name?"

The waitress paused before she replied. "Well, it's called Aldington. But it's a tiny place on the way to the sea."

"Good grief." Simon almost spilled his wine. "What an astonishing coincidence. I'm motoring down to Aldington in a few days. Spending Christmas there in Noël Coward's house."

"Really, sir?" The waitress's face broke into an angelic smile. "You know Mr Coward?"

"Well, no," Simon replied. "But a friend of mine does and she's invited me to stay there for a few days." He could see the waitress was entirely star-struck since he had mentioned Noël Coward. "If you'd like to send something to your mother, I could take it down with me. When did you last speak to her?"

The waitress picked up the bottle of wine and topped up their glasses. "Last summer. When I left for London." Her voice was subdued. Simon decided his desire to be sociable might be considered unnecessary prurience. He took a pen and an old bus ticket out of his pocket.

"Well, my dear." Simon wrote his name and his address on the back of the bus ticket. "If you'd like me to take something to your mother for Christmas, bring it to this address before Thursday." He handed her the piece of paper. "What's your name?"

"Jenny." The waitress took the paper and stuffed it into the pocket of her apron. "Jenny Stockwell." She smiled, and her face lit up with the freshness of youth. "You're ever so kind, sir. But I'm not sure me mam would want to hear from me now. I'll leave you gentlemen in peace."

Jenny Stockwell disappeared into the back of the restaurant. Simon noticed Cameron staring at him.

"What's the matter?"

"Och, it's just tha' I've rarely met a gentleman as kind as ye," Cameron replied. "That wa' a lovely thing ye offered to do. For someone ye'd never met before."

"Poor girl." Simon picked up his knife and fork and cut into a piece of beef on his plate. "She looked so lost. And I admire her ambition. Foolhardy as I think it is. I'm sure Noël would have something discouraging to say about it. Bill tells me he gets strings of letters from mothers desperate for him to put their daughters on the stage." He pointed his fork at Cameron's plate. "Tuck in. It's awfully good. Tell me more about Sandringham. How exciting to be spending Christmas Day with the royal family."

"That's what I wa' goin' tae tell ye just now," Cameron said. "The king doesnae wan' the duke stayin' at Sandringham. From what the head of the household wa' sayin' today, the Prince of Wales is very angry. He's refusin' tae stay wi' the rest of the royal family at Sandringham. Instead, he and the duke are stayin' in a wee house elsewhere on the Estate."

"Good grief." Simon put down his knife and fork. He had heard rumours of ill-feeling between the king and the Prince of Wales before. The gossip columns had reported on several occasions that the king was unhappy at the prospect of Edward, Prince of Wales being the next king. He would become the eighth King Edward. But the prince was next in line and there was nothing the king could do about it.

"Why on earth would the king want that?" he asked. "Is it because this duke, whatever his name is, comes from Germany? How big is this 'wee house' you're staying in? It's going to be cosy, isn't it?"

"I'm nae stayin' there," Cameron replied. "They're puttin' me in the stables next door."

Simon smiled. "You're sleeping in a stable? At this time of year. How appropriate." He leaned across the table. Cameron leaned in further, their heads were almost touching.

"And where are you sleeping tonight?" Simon whispered. "Would you like me to show you the backstairs to my flat this time?"

Simon lay awake, watching the gentle rise and fall of the bedclothes over Cameron's sleeping form beside him. Simon had slept for little more than an hour after they had turned off the light. His mind was too full of thoughts and disturbances for him to settle. He considered going to the kitchenette to make himself a hot drink. But that risked waking Cameron, and the man was so peaceful in his repose.

Their lovemaking had proved passionate and satisfying. It was rare for Simon to find such immediate connection with a man. There was a real possibility he might see Cameron again, and that filled him with happiness.

Courtship was a strange affair for men of their type. It was, by necessity, hidden from public view. The usual social rituals of walking hand-in-hand, enjoying a first, chaste kiss in the street or in the park had to be foregone. The risk of criminal sanctions was too great. Instead, courtship was usually brief and led to a more immediate and often complete physical connection.

Of course, that required neither participant to be reviled by the physical activity in which they engaged. Society imprinted on men almost from birth that any sign of affection towards another man was to be abhorred. That any physical contact was sinful, shaming, and an abomination. Simon had been relieved when it had become clear Cameron found no offence in kissing him, nor did he resist engaging in other physical activities of passion.

At least it meant one aspect of Simon's life was taking a turn for the better. Even his friendship with the temperamental Bill was more settled than it had been. The prospect of five days on holiday with her for Christmas was both exhilarating and daunting. Exhilarating because Bill could bring life and excitement to any occasion with her wit and acid remarks. Daunting because she could equally destroy an occasion with a single, acid remark.

What unsettled him was his life at the BBC. He thought back to his run in with the Head of News that afternoon. He was confident in his own abilities as an investigative reporter, but they were being ignored. If he was still working for *The Chronicle,* his editor would have allowed him to do whatever was necessary to find the story behind the mysterious disappearance of the woman in the alleyway.

His move to the BBC was a big mistake. Maybe it was time he resigned. It would mean going back to the editor of *The Chronicle* and begging for his old job back. It would be humiliating. But it would be no worse than the constant humiliation of reading out poorly written news scripts whose content was devoid of controversy, and failed to uncover hidden truths.

He plumped his pillows and sat up further in the bed. He would resign, he decided. But not until the new year. Christmas was never a good time for such rash decisions. Meanwhile, he would carry out his own investigation into the woman's disappearance. He reached for the notepad and pencil he kept by the bedside. There was a faint glow from the gaslights in the street outside his window and, with difficulty, he could see to write. He wanted to avoid switching on the light and waking Cameron.

It was time to make a plan.

First, he would try to get to see Robbie at Scotland Yard. He might also try to book an appointment with the Commissioner at the same time. Then he would speak to his friend Betty Richardson at the Home Office. They had known each other since childhood and still remained great pals. Betty was now in charge of administration for the Registry Department at the Home Office. She was the ideal person to help him investigate recent arrivals from Germany. Perhaps there might be a file related to suspicious characters linked to Der Sturmabteilung.

Then there were the documents Bill's contact Anna was looking at. He would risk Bill's wrath to find out what progress had been made. He also wanted to have another attempt at revisiting the alleyway. Maybe the police, or whoever they were had finished their business. It was unlikely they had left anything for him to discover, but he would go back in the morning to check.

"Are ye awake?"

Cameron reached across with his arm and rested it on Simon's chest. His hand knocked the notepad and pencil, and he sat up.

"Are ye working at this hour?" he asked, rubbing his eyes. "Did ye want me tae go? I didnae know ye had business to attend to."

Simon put the pad and pencil back onto the bedside table and rolled over to face Cameron.

"No," he said. "It can wait."

9

Simon woke again a few hours later. It was still dark, but he could hear someone moving around the apartment. He reached out to the space next to him in the bed and found it unoccupied. Perhaps Cameron had gone in search of the bathroom. He rolled over, curled up with his pillow, and awaited his return.

At the point that the comfortable void of sleep was about to engulf him, he heard the front door open and close. He reached for the switch on the bedside lamp. The light dazzled him when he switched it on and he screwed up his eyes to peer at the time on the alarm clock. It was four-thirty. Reluctantly, he pushed off the bedclothes and sat up. It was cold. The building's heating system was yet to kick into action. He pulled the woollen bed cover around his shoulders, and headed out to the hallway.

The rest of the apartment was in darkness. He stood in the doorway of the sitting room, switched on the wall lights, and looked around. In the past, friends at the Fitzroy Tavern had told Simon horror stories about one-night-stands who waited until the host was asleep and then robbed them of anything they could find. It had never happened to Simon. Everything in the sitting room still seemed to be in its place.

He followed the hallway down to the kitchen and switched on the light there. A piece of paper lay on the dresser by the stove.

"Simon. Thank you for a wonderful evening (and night!) Sorry I have to leave, but they will sack me if I am not in by six to start my duties. I will go down the backstairs. C.

PS I took a pound note from the dresser. Will pay you back"

Bloody cheek, Simon thought. If only Cameron had woken him to ask, Simon would have been more than happy to give him the money. Perhaps he had to report early for duty, and took the money to pay for a bus. Then Simon remembered the hour of the morning. There would be no buses running at this time. Perhaps Cameron had gone to get a taxi from the rank at Marylebone Station. It would be quicker than walking to St James's.

At least in his note Cameron said he was taking the backstairs to leave the building. It would have been exceedingly awkward if anyone had seen him leave by the front entrance at such an early hour. All sorts of questions might be asked about Simon inviting men to stay overnight. If he was found out, at best he could be forced to forfeit the lease on his apartment. At worst he could go to jail for two years with hard labour.

It was time for a cup of tea, even at this hour of the morning. He decided to take it back to bed and do a bit more planning.

It was well after nine o'clock when Simon woke again. He had no need to go into work first thing that morning. Today he was scheduled to work late. In the evening after he finished reading the news at 6:30 p.m., he would stay on to announce the piano recital concert from the Wigmore Hall. As well as reading the opening and closing announcements, he would have to remain in the studio throughout the concert in case there were any technical difficulties. The usual announcer for the evening concert had been sick for over a week, and it was Simon's turn to deputise for him.

He went into the bathroom, filled the washbasin with hot water, and scrubbed up a lather on his shaving brush. He regarded his face in the mirror. He so wanted to grow a beard and stop this tiresome chore of shaving each morning. But the head of news disapproved of beards at the microphone, claiming they were unhygienic.

Simon was irritated by yet another example of the Corporation dictating how he appeared when communicating in a purely auditory medium. It was bad enough that he had to wear a bowtie and dinner jacket when he read the news. When he had first questioned the requirement, he was told it was to conform with his colleagues in music and entertainment who wore similar attire when announcing from concert halls. It resolved him further to resign in the new year.

The telephone rang. Simon left the lather on his face and walked to the sitting room to answer it. He saw no reason to be concerned about his appearance when no one could see him to judge. For that matter, he could answer the telephone in the nude and the caller would be none the wiser. Perhaps he should read the news in the nude. Although maybe that would perturb the studio managers.

"Marylebone 5411?" he answered.

"Morning, Mr Sampson." It was Pethers, the porter. "There's someone down here with a package for you."

"That's very kind." Simon was puzzled. The post was usually delivered much later in the day, and he was not expecting anything. "Can you take it, please? I'll call down for it later."

There was a pause while Pethers spoke with another person.

"The young lady asks if she might bring it up, sir."

"That's a bit awkward," Simon replied. He pulled the towel tighter around his waist. "I'm having a bit of a late morning. I haven't finished my ablutions yet. Who is it?"

"She says her name's Miss Stockwell, sir."

It was the waitress from the Lily Pond last night. Presumably she had decided to take him up on his offer to take a parcel down to her mother in Kent. It was a strange time to be calling, so early in the day. But perhaps she had to get to work and this was the only opportunity she had. All the same, she could have quite easily left the package with Pethers. Why was there a need for her to bring it upstairs?

"Pethers. This is rather embarrassing. I'm not long out of bed and I'm not dressed. Could you ask her to leave the package with you and I'll be sure to get it to her mother later this week?"

There was another pause while Pethers had a further conversation with Jenny Stockwell.

"Mr Sampson? She says she's very sorry to inconvenience you, but she would very much like to speak to you. She says she can wait in the lobby until you're ready."

The young lady's insistence on meeting him had piqued Simon's curiosity. He removed the towel from around his waist and wiped the lather from his face.

"Tell her to wait five minutes and then come up. Please warn her I'll be in my dressing gown."

Jenny Stockwell was a strange sight when she arrived at Simon's apartment ten minutes later. A large cloche hat was pulled low over her forehead and dark glasses covered much of her face.

"Goodness Miss Stockwell. You look like you're auditioning to portray Greta Garbo. Do come in."

He closed the door and led her into the sitting room. She held out a small package wrapped in brown paper. Her head remained bowed and he could only see the top of her hat. "Thank ye so much for offering to take this to Aldington," she said. "Oi 'ope it's still possible. But oi quite understand if you've changed your plans."

"Of course I'll take it." Simon took the package and placed it on the dining table. He attempted to peer at her face, masked by the hat. "Is everything all right Miss Stockwell? You seem far more subdued than you were last night. Has something happened?"

She turned away and walked over to the window. "Oi am sorry, Mr Sampson. Oi shouldn't have come. But you be so kind. An' after what 'appened last noight. Oi didn't know who else to go to."

"Why? What's happened?"

Slowly, Jenny Stockwell removed her hat and dark glasses. Simon was shocked by what he saw. An enormous bruise half closed her left eye, and there was blood caked in her hair.

"What happened?" Simon asked.

Miss Stockwell made no reply. She shivered. She opened her mouth to speak, but no sound came out, and she gasped for air. The dark glasses slipped from her fingers and fell to the floor. Simon hurried over to her, convinced she was about to faint. He put an arm around her waist and guided her to an armchair.

"Miss Stockwell. Jenny. Please, sit down. I'll get you some brandy and you can tell me all about it." He looked at the congealed blood matted into her hair. "Although I feel I should take you to a hospital. St Mary's at Paddington is not far away."

"No. Please don'." She lowered her head. "It's not as bad as it first looks."

Simon went to the drinks cabinet and took out a short-stemmed glass and a bottle of cognac. He rather fancied a drink himself, despite the early hour. But he thought it better he kept his wits about him.

"Here." He handed her the glass of brandy. "Drink this. Tell me what happened to you, and then you can use my bathroom to clean yourself up."

The glass was more than a third full, but Miss Stockwell rapidly drained the majority of it. She put the glass down on a side table and flopped back in the armchair.

"You're very kind, sir." She began. "Not all men are as kind as you. Especially the man who did this to me."

"Who is he?" Simon asked. "We must call the police and have him arrested."

"No." She sat forward and stared up at him. There was a look of fear on her face. "You mustn't. If you do, oi'll lose me job. An' oi need it to stay in London."

"But who is he?"

She slumped back in the armchair again.

"'e's me landlord. At the lodging house. 'e gets drunk sometimes. Last noight 'e got very drunk. That's when 'e wants me. An' when oi resist, sometimes this happens."

Simon kneeled down beside the armchair. "Does this happen often?"

"'e's only beaten me once before." She reached for her brandy. "It weren't bad that time. Oi was able to dodge out the way. 'e's too fat, see, an' can't move fast. But last night oi slipped and 'e got me."

Simon was shocked. He had heard of such attacks on women, but had never encountered one first-hand before. He realised he had been foolish to suggest calling the police. They would do little if anything to interfere. Whenever it was a woman's word against a man's, the woman lost. *The Chronicle* seldom bothered to report attacks on women. They were considered domestic incidents and not newsworthy.

"I don't understand. Why did you say you'd lose your job if we told the police?"

Jenny took the brandy glass from the side table. This time she sipped at it more delicately. "'e works there as well. 'e recommended me. That's 'ow oi got the job." She sighed. "How oi wish oi hadn't."

"Then you must leave the lodging house."

The young woman shook her head. "It's not as easy as that. Lodgin's don' come easy in London. Not at that price."

Simon stood and crossed to the hallway. "We'll see. You need to be safe. But first, I'll get you a towel and you can clean up. What time do you need to be at work? Will he be there?"

Jenny shook her head. "It's me day off today. And it's 'is too. That's probably why 'e got drunk."

"Then you can rest here." Simon went down the hallway to his bedroom. He took a clean towel from his wardrobe and returned to the sitting room. "The bathroom's across the hall. You'll find a few medicines and bandages in the cupboard if you need them. Please help yourself."

He held out his hand to help her out of the armchair. She stood and swayed slightly.

"Oh, my. Tha' brandy's gone straight to me head."

Simon led the way to the bathroom. At the doorway he handed her the towel. "I have to leave for work in a short while, but you're very welcome to stay for the day while you sort yourself out."

"Oh, but Mr Sampson—"

"I insist," Simon said. "Use the telephone if you want, and try to find yourself some new lodgings. I'll leave a key for you. Then if you find somewhere, you can go to check if it's suitable. I'm afraid I'll be back quite late so I can't help you any more than that."

"Oh, but you've been more than enough help already. You're not like other..." Her shoulders shook, and she appeared on the verge of tears. Simon had always felt awkward in the presence of female emotion. He patted her on the shoulder.

"There, there," he said. "You have a good wash, and I'll go and find that key for you."

Jenny Stockwell went into the bathroom and locked the door behind her. Simon went to the kitchen and reached for the spare keys hanging underneath the dresser shelf.

They were missing. He was sure they had been hanging there two nights ago because he thought he had shown them to Cameron. There was a small brass ring with both the front door key and the key for the outside door at the foot of the backstairs.

Cameron must have taken them. Perhaps he thought he needed the key for the backstairs door. It was not the case. The door at the foot of the backstairs could be opened from the inside without a key.

But if Cameron had taken the key ring, why had he not mentioned it in his note? Perhaps he was half asleep when he wrote it and had forgotten. Or perhaps he had thought about it afterwards.

Simon was annoyed with himself. Perhaps he was being more trusting than he should. It had been a wonderful evening with Cameron. But now the man had taken both the pound note and also the keys to his apartment. It was a thoroughly disagreeable start to the day.

10

"You did what?" Bill's voice exploded at Simon across her desk. "What the bloody hell were you thinking? Were you born yesterday?"

Simon said nothing. After telling Bill what had happened, it did sound as if he had acted naively. But he was not about to admit that to her. He could suffer his own judgment over his series of rash decisions. But not hers.

"Hang the key from a lamppost in the street, why don't you?" she continued. "While you're doing that, tie a card to it with your address on it, and a note reading '*help yourself*'?"

"Stop it, Bill," Simon said crossly. "You know you really can be infuriating sometimes."

"And you're not?" Bill sniffed. She took out a cigarette and lit it. "What are you going to do with this woman? She can't stay indefinitely. It's a lovely little flat, but there's only one bedroom. And are you even permitted to have her stay? I thought you said Bellman Buildings was very strict about guests staying over."

Simon folded his arms and stared out of the window. Bill's office was at just the right level to look towards the faded grandeur of the old Langham Hotel. It was a shame the building had been allowed to fall into such decay, Simon thought. It could only be a matter of time before it was closed down and demolished.

All Bill's questions were legitimate, and Simon struggled to find easy answers to them. But he had no regrets for what he had done. What little he knew of Cameron's thinking, Simon believed he had taken the spare key in the mistaken belief he needed it to get out by the backstairs. He was confident Cameron would return it when they next met. He was a young man who was occasionally thoughtless.

As for Miss Stockwell. She had been in such a distressed state, any human being would have done exactly the same in Simon's position. His was a decent act of compassion. Furthermore, he was confident the telephone calls she would make this morning would result in new accommodation and she would be gone by the evening. If he had time, he would pop in to check how she was getting on before his evening shift started.

When he had arrived at Bill's office that morning, it had not been Simon's intention to tell her about either Cameron or Miss Stockwell. Somehow she managed to get the information out of him even before he had settled in his seat with a cup of tea. It was time to steer the conversation back to the original purpose of his visit.

"Can we stop talking about this, Bill? I only intended a brief visit this morning. I wanted to discover if that German colleague of yours had made any progress with the text in that document."

"You mean Anna? She's Polish, not German. And I've no idea." She leant forward, scattering cigarette ash across her desk, and clicked the inter-office intercom. "Miss

Braithwaite? Could you pop down the corridor and bring Anna Forster here, please? Quick as you can." She flicked off the intercom.

"Forster?" Simon asked. "Doesn't sound very Polish to me."

"It's German-Polish," Bill replied. "And her name's really Forsterowa. But of course no one in England can manage that." She leaned back in her chair, and put her feet up on the desk. "So tell me. What's this Stockwell woman look like? Is she pretty?"

Simon thought hard. He always found it difficult to recall the appearance of women he had met. Perhaps it was because he was not attracted to them, and so he was not designed to retain their image in his mind. If so, it seemed awfully callous. He would prefer to think it was because, when he had been employed by *The Chronicle,* he was in the habit of noting down the descriptions of people he interviewed. Either way, it was a deficiency.

"She wants to be a dancer," he replied. "And I must say she's got the physical attributes to be one. She's tall and slender, with rather shapely legs. Her hair was a bit of a mess this morning because of the injury. And last night it was tied up under her little waitress cap. Her eyes were green, I think. Or maybe brown."

"You haven't the faintest idea whether she's pretty or not, do you?" Bill laughed. "I might as well ask the cat whether she finds the dog attractive."

"She was very pretty," Simon replied. "I might not be able to recall the colour of her eyes—"

"She can stay with me." Bill swung her legs off the desk, leaned forward, and stubbed out her cigarette in an ashtray. "If Miss Stockwell hasn't found anywhere by this evening, she can stay with me." She smiled at Simon. "Don't look so surprised. There is a heart beating underneath this jacket. Somewhere."

There was a knock at the door.

"Come in," Bill shouted.

The door opened and a woman carrying a brown folder stood in the doorway.

"Miss Miles?" the woman said. "You wanted to see me?"

"Anna," Bill replied. "Thank you so much for coming." She jumped up from her chair and strode across the office to the new arrival. Simon was astonished by Bill's sudden energy. It was as though she had drunk ten cups of coffee all at once.

"Anna. I'd like you to meet my colleague Mr Sampson. He works in the News Department as an announcer."

"Pleased to meet you." Simon stood and shook hands with Anna Forster. "And do call me Simon." This time he tried to make a conscious effort to take note of her appearance. She was roughly the same height as Bill, about five-feet-six. Her jet-black hair was cut into a stylish Eton Crop, and she had very brown eyes. She wore neither makeup nor jewellery and, like Bill, she wore a well-tailored trouser suit.

"I am pleased to meet you as well," Anna replied. "Are you a journalist or an announcer?"

"He's both," Bill replied before Simon had a chance to respond. "But not here. He was a very successful crime reporter for *The Chronicle*. And now he's stuck behind a microphone at the BBC."

"I am very impressed," Anna answered. "But why are you not also a journalist at the BBC?"

"Because the system's barmy." Bill closed the door of her office and ushered Anna to the other chair by her desk. "But it's up to us to change it. And Simon will be both an announcer and a journalist before long, just you wait and see." She sat on the corner of her desk and pointed to the folder in Anna's hand. "Is that the translation?"

Anna shook her head. "I started to translate your document. But it makes no sense. It must be in some kind of code." She turned to Simon. "Are you the gentleman who found it?"

"I knew I was right." Simon nodded. "I thought maybe I'd forgotten my German all of a sudden. Can I see what you've done?"

Anna handed him a sheet of typed paper from the folder. It was as he remembered it when he first scanned the document. The collection of words made no sense at all:

"Over day ring forward operation in ham in and Christmas to sand taken speak to on up message..."

And so it continued for nearly a page. He handed it to Bill. "The question is, do we decode it in German? Or translate it to English and then decode it?"

"Oh, that's easy," Anna replied. "Unless the German translation is a deliberate distraction, then this is some kind of German word substitution code. You'll have to decode the original German."

"Does it make any sense in the context of the other pages it was with?" Simon asked.

"What other pages?" Anna looked confused.

Simon turned to Bill. "You mean you only gave her the last page? How was she expected to make head or tail of it in isolation?"

"I told you I was going to keep them." Bill went behind her desk, opened a drawer, and took out the manila folder Simon had trusted to her safe keeping. "When you were so keen to get me off the telephone yesterday, I was trying to explain that I thought I might know what these diagrams and so on are all about."

Bill took the remaining four photo-duplicated pages from the envelope and spread them across her desk. She picked up a leather-bound manual and opened it to a page marked with a slip of paper. She lay it on the desk and pointed to a drawing on the open page.

"See? I've not been wasting my time like some, taking in waifs and strays."

Simon looked from the drawing in the book to the diagram on the third sheet of paper. They were virtually identical. He picked up the manual and turned to the title page. It was called:

BBC broadcast circuits for long wave transmitters. 1932 edition. INTERNAL USE ONLY

"How on earth did you know it was this?" Simon asked.

"I've told you before." Bill lit another cigarette. "I'm the BBC's head of libraries. I'm expected to know everything." She blew a smoke ring in Simon's direction. "I did get a little help from Cynthia Pemberton, that sweet young administrator in the engineering offices in the basement—"

"You showed them to someone else?" Simon interrupted. "I don't think that was wise, old thing. This seems to be evidence that someone in the BBC is selling engineering secrets—"

"You don't know that they're selling anything yet," Bill countered.

"Someone inside the BBC is up to no good," Simon continued. "For all you know it could be Miss Pemberton. And now she knows she's been found out."

Bill roared with laughter. "You are ridiculous, Simon. There's absolutely no question about Cynthia's loyalty to the

BBC. If you cut her in half you'd find BBC carved through her like a stick of rock."

Simon was undeterred. "What if she tells someone else, and that someone is the one leaking these documents? They'll more than likely be in the engineering department."

"Cynthia Pemberton gave me her word she would keep this absolutely confidential." Bill leaned back against the wall behind her desk. "And I'd trust Cynthia with my life." She pointed at Simon with the two fingers gripping her cigarette. "You need to understand something, dear Simon. In this world there are women like me, women like Miss Forster here, and women like Miss Pemberton. We know we can trust each other. Totally and absolutely." She looked at Anna. "Isn't that right, my darling?"

Anna nodded.

"You see," Bill continued. "Society has cast us out because we don't fit in. We're not destined to be conventional. Not destined to marry a man, settle down and have children. We live an *other life*, rather like you, Simon dear. And being *other* naturally draws us together."

It was a moment of surprising candour from Bill. In all the time Simon had known her she had remained tight-lipped about her other life. She knew a great deal about Simon's network of friends and acquaintances in his other world. He had introduced her to many of them and she knew how helpful they could be when Simon sought information, or introductions, or ways to get through doors that were normally closed. Bill's network of women was clearly just as useful.

"You need say no more," Simon said. "That was very well put. Let's get our heads together and see how we can crack this code."

"I can help," Anna said. "That's what I worked on before I joined the BBC."

"Really?" Simon asked. "Where was that?"

"In Poland," Anna replied. "At the Cipher Bureau. I worked in the support office."

"Fascinating," Simon said. "What made you leave Poland and come to work for the BBC?"

"I saw an advertisement. They wanted people with languages to work on the new Empire Service, and it sounded interesting."

"Tell Simon how many languages you speak," Bill interjected.

"Five fluently," Anna replied. "Polish, German, English, Russian and French. Then I have a reasonable knowledge of Lithuanian, Latvian and Estonian. Plus a little Danish."

"Good grief," Simon said. "Sounds like we're lucky to have you."

"We are." Bill gathered up the pages from her desk, put them back into the manila folder, and handed them to Anna. "See what you can do. But don't let it interfere with your work. I don't want you getting into trouble."

"Oh, it's no trouble," Anna replied. "I don't think it's a very complicated code. I'm certain I can decipher it in a few days."

"Excellent." Simon looked at the clock. He stood and held out his hand to Anna. "It's been a pleasure meeting you. Sorry I have to dash. I'm popping in on Betty Richardson at the Home Office, and then I've got an appointment with some underling at Scotland Yard."

"Good grief." Bill lit another cigarette and let it hang from the corner of her mouth. "When will you have time to fit in your announcing work?"

11

Big Ben was ready to chime midday when Simon stepped off the bus in Parliament Square. He walked towards Westminster Bridge, stood under the clock tower, and took out the pocket watch his grandfather had given him on his twenty-first birthday. It was a diversion he enjoyed indulging whenever he came to Westminster.

Although grimy with soot, the Palace of Westminster was a beautiful building. Each time he visited this part of London, Simon would see a new detail in its Victorian architecture. And the clock tower housing the bell called Big Ben was very special to him. Several years ago, the BBC had placed a microphone inside the tower, permanently connected by a cable to Broadcasting House. When Simon broadcast the news each night, he would wait for the live sound of Big Ben to chime before he started reading. Each time he heard it chime, adrenalin coursed through his body, preparing him for the live broadcast.

The first chime of midday sounded and Simon confirmed that his pocket watch had neither gained nor lost time since he had set it that morning. He turned to head for the grand building housing the Home Office. As he turned the corner onto Parliament Street, he spotted a large woman hurrying along the pavement towards him.

Even with her head down, the size of the woman's hat made it obvious it was Betty Richardson. He remembered first seeing Betty in an outsize hat when they were both ten years old. They had been at her parents' home in Wiltshire, and she had walked down the grand staircase like a debutante at her first coming out ball. Her obsession with oversized hats had continued through the years, even when the fashion was for little cloche hats, or berets. Betty refused to follow the crowd and presented herself to the world in headgear that grew larger on each appearance.

"Betty," Simon called. "I was just coming to see you."

Betty Richardson looked up and pushed back the brim of her hat. "Good God, what are you doing here?" Instead of stopping when she drew level with Simon, she walked past and called over her shoulder. "Can't stop. I've been summoned to the House. The PM needs some urgent information. Walk and talk, darling."

Simon turned and hurried to catch up with her. "I thought you were grand enough to send one of your people for errands like this?"

Betty glanced sideways and gave him a hard stare. "Can't trust this kind of mission with some office junior. If you want a job done well, then do it yourself. Why were you coming to see me? It's not my birthday."

The jibe was not lost on Simon. Their meetings were confined to moments when Simon needed a favour, as he did this lunchtime. He had failed to be a reliable friend to Betty in the past few years. He hoped she would be a in a decent mood to help him out today.

"Sorry Betty, my darling," he replied. "I was hoping we could get a drink in before Christmas—"

"Of course you do," she interrupted. "And what favour do you want in return for that?"

Betty was giving no ground and it was going to be a struggle to enlist her help.

"It's about the Sturmabteilung."

Betty stopped walking. "Well. Now you've got my attention. Why on earth are you mixed up with that shower?"

"I'm investigating an assault on a woman two nights ago. Possibly a murder, but certainly an abduction."

"Really?" Betty looked puzzled. "I haven't read anything about it in the Fleet Street rags. No offence darling. You used to work for one, didn't you? I mean newspapers. Where did this happen?"

"An alleyway round the back of Oxford Street," Simon replied. "You won't have read about it. I think the police are trying to hush it up."

Betty snorted and resumed walking. "Whether the police have or haven't 'hushed it up' as you quaintly put it, I'd still know about it. The Home Secretary is always kept informed on such matters. And I know for a fact he hasn't been."

"Does that mean you're confirming that the police do hush up crime reports?"

Betty glanced sideways at him under the brim of her hat. "I couldn't possibly comment. But where the hell have you been all these years? I know full well you weren't born yesterday."

Simon smiled. "Thank you. And it's good to have it confirmed from such an impeccable source."

Betty waved a gloved hand at him. "I'm never quotable. You know that full well. You haven't told me what this woman's got to do with the brownshirts."

"When I found her—"

"You found her?" Betty stopped walking again and turned to face him. She held her side and caught her breath. "You didn't mention that. How was it you came to find her? Where was she, and why didn't you report it to the police?"

"I did report it," Simon replied. "I found her in an alleyway in Bloomsbury. She was in a bad way and I told her I was going to summon a policeman. But when I returned with the officer, she was gone."

"It's pretty obvious to me what happened." Betty resumed walking and turned left onto George Street. "She was a prostitute. Her client attacked her and left her in the alleyway. You come along, tell her you're going to get the police, and she scuttles off before they arrive."

"I'm certain she wasn't a prostitute." Simon replied. Betty's stride had increased and he had to break into a half trot to keep up. "She was very expensively dressed. Sophisticated. I'd say not English, more Continental."

"High-class prostitute then."

Simon persisted. "When I knelt beside her to tend to her, she dropped a button into my hand. It must have come from her attacker." He reached into his pocket and retrieved the metal button. "I've got it here. It's got the marks of the Sturmabteilung on it."

They had reached the entrance to the Palace of Westminster. Betty stopped, took the button from Simon, and examined it. "So it has," she muttered. "How very interesting." She handed it back to him and looked up at the clock tower.

"And you want me to delve into Home Office files and tell you how many members of the brownshirts are currently operating in Britain?"

Simon shoved the button back into his pocket. "I know you're awfully busy—"

"I am." Betty lifted the bulging leather case she had been carrying and waved it at Simon. "And these papers are due with the PM right now. I'll see what I can do." She strode off towards the entrance gates. "And that's more than a bloody drink you owe me."

Because his meeting with Betty had been far shorter than he had planned, or hoped for, Simon had plenty of time to walk the short distance to Scotland Yard. He stopped at the bronze statue of Boadicea, standing majestically in her chariot facing the river with her arms outstretched. He had hurried past this statue many times on his way to meetings. Today he paused to examine the beauty of the artwork. A plaque on the plinth read:

Boadicea, Queen of the Iceni. Who died A.D. 61 after leading her people against the Roman invader.

Queen Victoria, another strong woman leader of Britain, had commissioned the work. Simon looked back at the Houses of Parliament and felt a flash of anger. In his opinion, Betty Richardson had one of the finest minds in the world. And yet there she was scurrying about at the behest of the prime minister. A man who presided over a National government of more than six hundred Members of Parliament, only fifteen of whom were women.

He reread the plaque on the plinth beneath the statue of Boadicea. Nearly nineteen hundred years had passed since she had died, and yet her legacy was still not truly reflected in the country's government. Simon relished the company of strong women, and despised the company of privileged men. Men who got to positions of power through clubbable connections that began when they were sent to all-male boarding schools.

At the age of eight, Simon's parents had dispatched him to such a school. He had hated it. He had hated the older boys' bullying, the abuse and beatings from the masters. But most of all he had mourned the absence of his mother's affection throughout each term. It had taken Simon a long time to find friendships at the school. Robbie Mountjoy, the man he was going to see at Scotland Yard that lunchtime, had been in the year above him. Robbie became the older brother Simon never had. He had defended Simon against the school bullies, and in return, Simon had helped Robbie with his schoolwork.

When Simon was thirteen, Robbie's parents moved their son to another school. Simon's parents had been told that Robbie had been moved because there were suspicions of "*an unnatural relationship*" between the two boys. They had been summoned to the school and had been warned that he would be expelled if he were foolish enough to indulge in such sinful activities again. Of course Simon's protestations that nothing had happened had been ignored. His father had been furious and never forgave him for bringing shame upon the family. Simon's final years at the school had been miserable.

Big Ben sounded the half hour. Simon walked back to Victoria Embankment and headed for Scotland Yard.

"Hello, hello." Simon announced breezily at the front desk. "I'm here to see DI Mountjoy."

"Is he expecting you?" The desk sergeant's voice was mournful, like that of an undertaker greeting a client.

"I'm an old friend of his," Simon replied. "I thought he might be free for a drink before we both break up for Christmas."

"They're all very busy." The flat monotone of the desk sergeant's voice was unshaken by Simon's joviality. "These union demonstrations are taking up most of our time. I'll see what I can find out." With no sense of urgency, he reached for the telephone and spoke into the receiver. "Hello Mavis. Gentleman here wants Mountjoy in CID." He paused to listen to someone at the other end. "I told him that. But these folks never listen."

Five minutes later Detective Inspector Robbie Mountjoy bounded down the stairs two at a time.

"Simon, old friend." His voice boomed in the cavernous entrance to the building. "What an unexpected pleasure."

They shook hands and Robbie grasped Simon's shoulder with affection.

"I was told you were probably far too busy to see me." Simon nodded towards the desk sergeant who was watching them intently.

"Oh, don't listen to Gloomy Godfrey," Robbie replied. "He tells you the world's about to end most days of the week." He leant towards Simon and spoke into his ear, loud enough for the desk sergeant to hear him. "He's one of those strange religious coves. Hoping the Book of Revelations will be enacted in Bloomsbury. You know. Where all those artistic types hang out. Fancy a quick one at the Red Lion?"

"As long as you've got the time."

"I've always got time for a pint." Robbie ushered Simon towards the main doors. "Come on. I'm sure you know the way."

They headed down Richmond Terrace towards Whitehall where they heard the distant sound of shouting and cheering. As they reached the end of the Terrace, the reason for the noise became clear. A crowd of several hundred people was marching down from Trafalgar Square towards Parliament. The protestors, all men, as far as Simon could tell, carried banners with the words *Greater Britain* written in large, uneven letters. Male voices chanted "jobs for the British", followed by a variation on the nursery rhyme 'Old MacDonald Had a Farm' that was highly uncomplimentary about Prime Minister Ramsay MacDonald.

"This is Oswald Mosley's new fascist lot, isn't it?" Simon shouted to Robbie as they walked down Whitehall towards the Red Lion.

"Is it?" Robbie asked. "I can't tell them apart. Communist. Fascist. All the same to me. All troublemakers that should be locked away. Who's Oswald Mosley anyway?"

They arrived at the Red Lion and Simon held the door open for Robbie to go inside. "Failed MP who couldn't decide which party to go with," Simon replied. "First Conservative, then Labour, then he set up his own and didn't get elected. Now he spends his time writing about how this fellow Mussolini has got it all sorted in Italy and how we ought to do the same. The *Daily Mail* is right behind him. That's why *The Chronicle* is taking the opposite view."

Simon pushed his way through the crowded pub behind Robbie to get to the bar. "I'll get these, Robbie. I'm looking for a favour so it's the least I can do."

"I might have guessed," Robbie replied. "On the sniff of some gruesome crime again, are you? Wanting inside knowledge? You know I've got to be careful what I say, or the powers that be will jump on me from a great height." Robbie looked around the bar. "This isn't the best place for me to be seen talking to *The Chronicle's* chief crime reporter. I wouldn't be surprised if the Home Secretary himself was propping up the other end of the bar."

"Good Lord, Robbie," Simon replied. "Is it that long since we last spoke? I'm respectable now. I'm a news announcer with the BBC. What are you drinking?"

Robbie laughed. "'Respectable'? I'm not sure you'll ever earn that title, Simon Sampson. Seeing as you're after a favour, and seeing how it's nearly Christmas, make it a double Scotch."

12

Simon collected their drinks from the bar and saw Robbie leaning against a wall in a quieter spot at the back of the pub. The place was raucous, packed with groups of workers from the surrounding government offices starting their celebrations early for Christmas. As Simon made his way through the crowd, he nearly lost control of the glasses in his hands as he was jostled by boisterous drinkers.

"Cheers, Robbie." Simon raised his glass. "Here's to old friends."

"Old friends," Robbie repeated. "So, you've left *The Chronicle* to be an announcer on the BBC? I'll say this. You've got the voice for it. I always thought you'd go on the stage. But I suppose the wireless gets you a bigger audience. What's it like now you've given up your life of crime reporting?"

Simon set down his glass on a narrow wooden ledge next to them. "I must admit I get a real thrill when the red light goes on and it's just me and the microphone. But I miss *The Chronicle*. I had planned to do reporting as well. But my head of department isn't interested. He's got journalists who do little more than rehash government announcements."

Robbie nodded. "I can't say I listen much. Are you going to stay?"

Simon shrugged. "If things were to change I would. But that's partly the reason I wanted to see you."

"Go on. Out with it." Robbie smiled. "You warned me you wanted a favour."

"Information really," Simon replied. "There's something pretty rum going on. I was trying to get into Fortescue Place, W1 yesterday. It's an alleyway in Bloomsbury. But it was roped off by your chaps. They wouldn't tell me anything. Referred me to Scotland Yard. But it's my suspicion they're investigating an assault, possible murder, of a woman in the alleyway there."

Robbie shook his head. "I don't think so. I'd know if there was a murder inquiry on. And there hasn't been one for West London in the past week. I'm certain. What makes you think that?"

Simon told his story to Robbie. From his first encounter with the woman in the alleyway, to his meeting with Constable Smith, finishing with the events of the previous day when he had discovered the alleyway roped off and the detective loading bags into a van. He decided against telling Robbie about Cameron and how they had found the envelope of documents. He wanted to protect Cameron from any prurient police questions, and there was no need for Robbie to know about the documents for now.

Robbie took a drink from his glass. "What did this fellow look like? You say he was a detective?"

That's the odd thing," Simon replied. "He didn't say he was exactly. But the constable in uniform treated him as though he was, and the man claimed to know you when I mentioned your name. Only I deliberately got it wrong to test him. I said your name was Robbie Mountcraft, not Mountjoy."

"Maybe he thought you'd got it wrong and couldn't be bothered to correct you."

"I don't think so," Simon replied. "Because he repeated the wrong name back to me. And there was another thing. He was loading these bags into the back of a black van. But it didn't have a number plate. Do you ever take the number plates off for covert operations?"

Robbie shook his head. "We don't. And neither does Special Branch as far as I know. It's counterproductive. It's illegal not to display a number plate in England, so it would draw more attention to what we're doing. It's easier to use a false one."

"Would you know if it was Special Branch?" Simon asked.

"Not necessarily." Robbie took a drink of whiskey.

"But could you find out?"

Robbie put his glass back on the ledge. "I could make a discreet enquiry. But I need to be careful. What about the policeman who was with him? Did you get his number?"

Simon took a notebook from his pocket and flipped open a page. "Here you are. Do you think you could check him out?"

Robbie took a diary from his pocket and noted down the number. "Shouldn't be difficult. I'd be surprised if he was a fake. Although it's happened once before. In the Hatton Garden jewellery robbery three years ago. The gang that did that got hold of four uniforms." He stuffed the diary back in his pocket.

"Thanks Robbie." Simon reached into his coat pocket and took out a paper bag. "I did manage to retrieve a few clues from the alleyway that night." He took out the metal button he had showed Betty earlier. "The woman had this in her hand. She could have torn it off her assailant's coat." He offered it to Robbie. "Look. It's got the symbol of the brownshirts on it."

Robbie took the button. "What's the brownshirts?"

"They're the Fascists, Robbie," Simon replied. "Similar to that lot we saw causing a rumpus in Whitehall." He opened the paper bag to show Robbie the blood-stained box of matches. "I also found this at the spot where the woman's body had been after she disappeared. It's got a couple of fingerprints on it. The person who last had it had blood on their hands."

Simon reached into his coat pocket, took out the small, black clutch bag and put it on the ledge.

"Been Christmas shopping, have you?" Robbie asked.

"I also found this at the scene," Simon explained. "It could have belonged to her."

Robbie held up his hand. "Hang on, hang on. You say you found this woman's body in an alleyway in Bloomsbury?"

Simon nodded. Robbie pushed the bag back towards Simon.

"And what else was there in this alleyway?" Robbie asked. "All sorts, I imagine. How do you know it's hers?"

Simon held up the bag and opened it. "It's got the initials S and C engraved on the clasp. It might help identify her."

"*If* it belongs to this woman." Robbie shook his head. "I really don't have time for all this."

"Can't you at least get the fingerprint boys to look at the matches?"

"You don't ask much, do you?" Robbie took the paper bag from Simon and peered into it. "It's going to raise a lot of questions if I ask them to do a bit of work for me. They'll want a crime reference number and all sorts. I'm not sure I can help. I don't want to risk drawing that much attention to myself. I've got my career to consider."

"Would another Scotch help?" Simon asked.

By the end of their conversation that lunchtime, Simon was certain the man he had met in the alleyway the day before was neither a detective, nor a member of one of the covert police operational groups. Robbie was guarded in the answers he gave, but he knew most of what was going on at Scotland Yard. An event like a serious assault or a murder in Bloomsbury would not have gone unnoticed by him. He promised to make further enquiries and give Simon any information he felt safe to confide with him.

Robbie was more concerned about the presence of Miss Stockwell in Simon's apartment. Like Bill, he accused Simon of being naïve. He made the point on more than one occasion during their conversation. By the time they parted outside the Red Lion, Simon wanted to put his own mind at rest. He would go back to the apartment before the six o'clock broadcast, and check that Jenny Stockwell had not ransacked the place.

As he headed towards Trafalgar Square to catch a bus, he experienced once more the flush of excitement he used to have when working on a story for *The Chronicle*. He now had multiple lines of enquiry underway. It was time to be patient and wait for one of them to produce a lead. Robbie would do some investigating about the fake detective and the possibly fake police constable. Meanwhile, Betty Richardson was going to do some snooping at the Home Office and find out if the *Sturmabteilung* were operating in Britain.

At the top of Whitehall, he stopped by a telephone box. It

was a little after two o'clock. Plenty of time to check on the other line of enquiry he had set going.

"Your ears must be burning." Bill's voice crackled in the earpiece. "How did you know I've been acting as your social secretary again? Or do you simply assume it's what I spend my day doing?"

"I didn't," Simon replied. "But you're an absolute brick. I've just come from a jolly interesting drink with Robbie Mountjoy."

"Who's he? And why should I care?"

Simon smiled as he pictured Bill with her feet up on the desk, puffing on her umpteenth cigarette of the day. "I told you about him. Detective Inspector Mountjoy at Scotland Yard. Old school chum of mine. My hunch about that dodgy detective is right. Now I need to find out who's really doing what."

"Fascinating." Bill sounded less than fascinated. "Do you want your messages now?"

"It's not Cameron, is it?" Simon asked. "I'm so sorry. I did tell him the other night not to call you again."

"Well, he did call me," Bill replied. "To be fair, he said he tried your flat and the news department. I was his last hope. He's got some important information that might have a connection with the woman in the alleyway."

"Wonderful news. And what is it?"

Bill's explosive laughter rattled the handset. "He didn't tell me, my dear Simon, I'm a mere woman. Why would he trust me?"

"Didn't he leave a number?"

"Apparently the Palace won't allow it. Very strict."

Simon was intrigued. If only he and Cameron had made arrangements to see each other again before Christmas. He looked to his left through the grimy panes of glass of the telephone box, and saw Admiralty Arch at the entrance to The Mall. Less than half a mile up that road Cameron was working in St James' Palace. And now Simon knew he possibly had a vital lead that could open up his investigation. He contemplated walking up to the main gate of St James' Palace and asking to speak to Cameron.

It was a fanciful and short-lived daydream.

"Thank you, Bill," he said. "I'll have to hope he calls me again after the broadcast."

"Oh, that's far too vague," Bill replied dismissively. "I've told him to meet you at the Fitzroy Tavern at nine. The *Radio Times* says the concert finishes by eight forty-five, so you should be on time if you walk fast."

Simon was elated. He would get to meet Cameron again. Plus, there was another possible lead for his investigation.

"Thanks awfully, Bill," he replied.

"But I'm sure that's not the reason you were calling." There was the sound of a match being struck and Bill inhaling on a cigarette. "Not unless you've suddenly turned psychic, which I very much doubt. It's a sensitivity beyond the wit of most men."

"Actually," Simon began. "I was ringing to see if Miss Forster had made any progress—"

"Well really," Bill exclaimed. "Some of us around here have real jobs to do. And that includes Anna. She's up to her eyes with all the work to be done for the Empire Service over Christmas. Give the poor woman some time. You only left here a couple of hours ago."

"I know, I know." Simon regretted mentioning it. He should have finished the call with the news from Cameron, but his flush of enthusiasm for the investigation had got the better of him. "Those plans are a vital clue in this whole mystery. If she can decode them, we might be able to prove there's an international plot to steal secrets from the BBC. Although why anyone wants to do that, I have no idea."

"If you're in such a hurry," Bill replied. "Why don't you take all this information to the police? Or at least the top brass at the BBC, seeing as it's a plot against them. They'd have far more resources than little old you and a few well-meaning friends tossing in favours."

Simon had been half expecting this reaction from Bill. It was not that she was the type to side with the Establishment. In her combative way she was more inclined to challenge the Establishment, particularly if she sensed any form of Old Boy Network conspiring against her. But when it came to Simon's approach to investigating stories, Bill was more conventional. During his last investigation for *The Chronicle,* Simon had masqueraded as an insurance investigator to uncover compelling evidence about shipping fraud in the London Docks. Bill had strongly disapproved and argued Simon should have handed his evidence to the police first, not have it published on the front page of *The Chronicle*. Her suggestion to tell the BBC's senior management was based on the same argument.

"I *did* tell the police," Simon protested. "I tried to report it to that ludicrous Constable Smith the first night. And I've spent the last two hours telling Detective Inspector Robbie Mountjoy about it. It's not my fault the police aren't doing anything."

"Of course," Bill replied. "The fact that you might get an exclusive story out of it all is entirely coincidental."

"Bill—"

"I'm joking, my darling." Simon could hear Bill's throaty chuckle down the line. "I'll pop along and see how Anna's doing. I must confess I'm as intrigued as you. What are you up to now?"

"Thank you for everything, Bill dear." Simon was relieved to hear she was still on his side. "I'm off to the flat first, and then back to Broadcasting House. I want to check everything's okay."

"Finally." Bill coughed loudly on her cigarette. "You're doing something sensible."

The front door to Simon's apartment was unlocked. He cursed himself for trusting Miss Stockwell with the key.

"Hello? Is anyone there?"

Simon closed the door of his apartment behind him. There was no answer to his call. Perhaps she had found new lodgings and moved on. It was a relief if she had. Simon had begun to doubt his decision to leave the woman alone in his flat after first Bill and then Robbie had questioned his actions. Her absence was a form of vindication that he had done the right thing.

He hung up his coat and scarf, walked down the corridor to the closed sitting room door, and pushed it open. It took him a moment to comprehend the mess and destruction he saw. Everything had been swept off his bookshelves and onto the floor. Several of the drawers of his desk had been pulled out and tipped upside down. Even more shocking were the ripped-open cushions on the couch and armchairs. He stood in the doorway, considering his next move. Was this the work of Miss Stockwell? When he had left her this morning, she had not seemed in the state of mind to make a frenzied attack on his property. Was this caused by her landlord? Perhaps the man had discovered where she was and had come after her.

More likely it was a burglar. Although burglaries in Bellman Buildings were rare. The security of the reception and a porter permanently on duty made sure of that. If it was a burglar, then he or she could still be in the apartment. And because Simon had called out Miss Stockwell's name when he arrived, they now knew he was there.

Simon pushed the door of the sitting room fully open against the limit of its hinges. There was no one hiding behind it, and there were few hiding places left in the room. The only possible spot was behind the couch. To the right of the doorframe stood a long-handled shoehorn, with a round silver knob for a handle on one end. Simon picked it up and weighed it in his hand. It was not much of a weapon, but it was better than nothing.

As he walked towards one end of the couch, he saw first a pair of women's high-heeled shoes, and then the woman's legs stretched out. He froze. His stomach churned and he swallowed as he felt bile rise in his throat. He took a deep breath and stepped forward to confirm what he expected. The body was that of Miss Stockwell. Simon dropped the shoehorn and went behind the couch to see if she was still alive.

Jenny Stockwell lay face down on the parquet floor. A pool of blood spread out from under her body. Simon leaned forward to find out if she was still breathing

A cloth covered his mouth and nose and the acrid smell of chloroform penetrated his nostrils. He grabbed hold of his attacker's arm and tried to pull it away, but his strength was diminishing by the second, and his head felt like he had drunk an entire bottle of whisky. The last thing he noticed before the room faded from his vision was the handle of a stiletto knife, jutting from the side of Miss Stockwell's neck.

13

It was dark when Simon regained consciousness. He was lying on the floor of the sitting room. His body felt stiff and painful, as if he had been beaten. He tried to sit up, but neither his arms nor his legs would respond to his attempts to move. His mouth was dry and he coughed as he tried to swallow.

"Mr Sampson," said a man's voice in the darkness. "You're awake."

Simon coughed again, and summoned up the energy to speak. "Who are you?" he asked hoarsely.

"This is indeed very fortunate." The man spoke with an aristocratic English drawl, as if he was bored and Simon was an inconvenient interruption to his day. "Now we have a more imaginative way to stop your interference. And there's no need for me to have the untidiness of killing you. I'll be gone in a short while. But before I go, there's one question I must ask. Where are the documents you stole from us?"

Simon had a keen ear for accents. Even now, in his pained state, he detected the hint of a rural county in the way he pronounced his vowels and the letter R. Wiltshire? Possibly Gloucestershire, the county where Simon had been born.

"I'm trying to place your accent," Simon replied. "I've narrowed it down to one of the western counties. I don't think you're from as far as Dorset or Devon. Nevertheless—"

"Don't waste my time." The man was irritated. "It's been an unnecessarily long day for me, Mr Sampson. I'm tired and I have more important people to meet than a dreary little journalist who sticks his nose into other people's business. Let me ask you again." A brown boot appeared in Simon's field of vision and he felt its weight on his neck. "Where are the documents?"

Simon choked as the pressure on his neck increased. It was impossible to speak. After what was probably no more than a few seconds the boot was lifted and reappeared inches from Simon's face. He coughed, and struggled once more to move his arms. They felt like dead weights, as if they were no longer part of his body.

"I imagine you're wondering why you can't move," the owner of the brown boot said. He bent down, and Simon could vaguely see the outline of his head, but he struggled to focus on the detail of his face.

"A little injection in your neck," Brown Boot continued. "It should wear off in half an hour. By which time I'll be gone."

The man straightened and the boot disappeared from Simon's field of vision. A moment later he felt it press on his neck once more. He choked and struggled to breathe as his windpipe sealed up.

The telephone rang.

The weight on Simon's neck was lifted and he gasped in a lung full of air. Before he could take another breath, Brown Boot kicked him hard in the stomach.

"Don't think about leaving," the man said mockingly. He walked away and answered the telephone.

"Yes. He's returned. No. He's not. I'll continue to—"

He paused as a voice spoke at the other end of the phone.

"Are you sure?" Brown Boot asked. "And you think she has them?"

He paused again for a reply.

"Yes," he said at length. "That's a good plan. I'll do it now."

He hung up and walked back to Simon. He took hold of Simon's hand, thrust a metal object into it and wrapped his fingers around it.

"You're now holding the knife that killed this woman, whoever she is. While you were unconscious, I took the trouble to put your fingerprints on her neck and arms. Of course, my fingerprints are nowhere to be found in this apartment."

He squeezed Simon's fingers around the handle of the knife one final time and stood. "No one saw me entering your apartment. And you can be certain I'll not be observed when I leave. After I've left, I'll make an anonymous phone call to the police. I'll tell them that a woman's been murdered here. They'll arrive and conclude, very logically, that you're the prime suspect."

Brown Boot chuckled. "It's a far better plan than our original one. It was fortunate for us that this woman was here. Not fortunate for her of course. And now, not fortunate for you either, Mr Sampson."

"Who the hell are you?" Simon struggled to speak. His dry tongue felt like an alien object in his mouth.

"I'm the person who's had the tedious task of trying to recover those documents you stole. As you can see, I searched your apartment thoroughly. I was on the point of leaving when you arrived. I'd considered killing you, but this is a far better way to stop you interfering in our business."

He stood and kicked Simon hard in the stomach. Bile rose in Simon's throat but he was still unable to move. A trickle of sweat ran down his face. This man could kill him if he chose and there was nothing Simon could do about it.

"Out of curiosity I'll ask you once more," Brown Boot said. "Where are those documents?" He kicked Simon in the stomach again. This time the bile erupted into Simon's mouth and he felt as if he was going to suffocate. He choked and tried to spit out the foul-tasting contents of his stomach.

"They're not here," he said in a hoarse whisper. "They're locked away. In a BBC office."

The man kicked him again. This time Simon's body reacted to the blow. The muscles in his chest clenched and spasmed. He felt a surge of pins and needles shoot down both his arms. Perhaps the shock of the blows was combatting the effects of whatever drug had been injected into him.

"We believe we know otherwise." Brown Boot cleared his throat noisily. "And we have ways to explore that line of inquiry tomorrow morning. By then, you'll be safely locked in a police cell."

He walked to the sitting room door.

"Goodbye Mr Sampson. I look forward to reading about your arrest in the morning's papers. Ironic, isn't it? The former crime reporter of *The Chronicle*, arrested for murder."

Simon heard footsteps recede up the hallway and the front door open. It slammed shut and the man was gone.

Simon took long deep breaths and tried to flood his lungs with oxygen. He hoped it would help his body counter the effects of whatever drug had been injected into him. After several minutes he felt light-headed and stopped. The weight of his head pressed his ear against the floor and he could hear his blood rushing through his veins.

A muscle in one of his fingers wrapped around the knife twitched. It gave Simon sufficient encouragement to resume his deep breathing. At the same time he concentrated on moving the other fingers on the same hand. He had no idea how long it would be before Miss Stockwell's murderer called the police. He had to get out of the apartment as soon as he could. He would work out what to do after that. His only other option was to wait for the police to arrive and tell them the truth. He had no intention of doing that.

The telephone rang. A reflex action caused Simon to twist his head around. The fact that he could move meant some sense of control must have returned to his muscles. He flexed his fingers and knocked the knife away. His legs remained useless, but he could haul himself up onto his elbows and drag himself towards the desk. Each move was painful, as if his whole body was alive with pins and needles. As he reached the desk the phone stopped ringing. The effort exhausted him, but Simon persevered. He hooked his arm over the chair and pulled with all his strength to rest his chest on the seat cushion. The phone rang again. It was a few inches away from his head. He reached for the receiver.

"Hello," said a woman's voice at the other end. "Are you there, Simon?"

It was Bill.

"I'm here," Simon called out. The effort caused him to overbalance on the seat cushion. The chair slipped on the polished parquet and he fell flat on the floor.

"Simon? What's going on?" Bill's voice crackled from the receiver. "Why the hell are you still there? You're supposed to be in the studio by now. They're hunting all over for you. Simon? Speak to me." Even through the distortion of the telephone handset, Bill's voice was imperious and commanding.

"I've been attacked," Simon shouted. He struggled to regain his grasp on the chair. Sensation was returning to his legs and he found he could wedge himself in an upright position with his head alongside the telephone receiver, which now lay on the edge of the desk. "What time is it?"

"Just after six," Bill replied. "What do you mean you've been attacked?"

"Listen, Bill. Can you get a car?"

"What? Now? I can probably get a taxi. Do you want me to call the police?"

"No, don't do that." Simon felt his grasp slip on the chair and he struggled to keep his balance. "I've been attacked and drugged. I can hardly walk. I need you to come and get me, Bill. But whatever you do, don't call the police."

There were times when Bill seemed to know it was best not to ask questions. Fortunately, this was one of them. "I'll go down now and get a cab from the rank in Portland Place."

"Thanks, Bill," Simon replied. "Have you still got that key for the rear stairs I gave you? It's best if Pethers doesn't see you come in through the front entrance."

There was silence at the end of the phone. Simon wondered if Bill had hung up.

"Are you there, Bill?"

"What the hell have you got yourself involved with?" she asked. "Yes, I have. I'll be there in ten minutes."

There was a loud *click* and the line went dead. Simon became aware of an eerie silence in the apartment. All he could hear was the pounding of his heart and his rapid breathing. He rested his head on the edge of the desk and waited for several minutes while he recovered from its exertions.

He looked across the room. Jenny Stockwell's body lay in the corner behind the couch and he was the prime suspect for her murder. Bill was right to ask the question. What *had* he got himself involved with?

He thought about what Jenny Stockwell's killer had said shortly before he had left. Something about knowing who Simon had given the documents to, and that he would investigate in the morning. Did he mean Bill? If so, she was no longer safe either. He would have to warn her when she arrived. Yet another opportunity for her to chastise him.

The feeling of pins and needles in Simon's body had lessened. It was time to test his legs. He grasped the arms of the chair with both hands, took a deep breath, and levered himself into a kneeling position. He exhaled and flexed the muscles in his leg. The pain in his stomach was excruciating, but he chose to ignore it. He wedged his feet against the frame of the desk, held onto the chair, and pushed down. With his body arched, he shuffled his right foot forward, followed by his left and pushed himself into a standing position. He felt light-headed and swayed like a toddler taking its first steps.

"If this is what it's like to feel old," Simon muttered to himself. "I'm not looking forward to it in the slightest."

Plan. He had to make a plan. It was impossible to remain in the apartment. The police would be there within the hour. But neither could he stay at Bill's, even if she agreed to it, which he doubted. He could go to his parents in Wiltshire. But it was likely that the police would catch up with him there at some point. And when they did, his parents might face charges of accessory to murder for hiding him.

Simon had never thought that one day he might be a fugitive from justice. In a perverse way he felt proud of the label. He was an outsider, battling against the forces of darkness attacking England's civilised society. Whatever or whoever those forces were.

His career looked to be in tatters. The BBC was probably about to sack him for failing to turn up to read the news that evening. Right now, that was the least of his worries.

He stood from the desk and turned to rummage in the top drawer, left hanging open by the intruder. Some of its contents had already been scattered over the floor. Simon reached into the back of the drawer and sighed with relief when he found his passport. Leaving the country might be his only option. Next to the passport was a bag of foreign currency. It contained the French Francs and German Reichsmarks he had left over from his travels. He had no idea what the current rate of exchange was for either currency, but there would be little more than a few pounds in total.

If he was to leave England's shores, where would he go? He had made a few friends in Germany on his two visits to Berlin. He exchanged letters with them from time to time. But he was doubtful they would welcome him into their homes when he turned up unannounced. And they would be even less welcoming when they found out he was wanted for murder in London.

Robbie. He had to somehow get in touch with Robbie at Scotland Yard and explain what had happened. Would his friend trust him? He had to believe he would, even if the evidence in the apartment left by Jenny Stockwell's murderer was stacked against him. His friendship with Robbie went back a long way.

Simon put his passport and the foreign currency on the desk and turned to the bottom drawer. It too was open and most of its contents had been tipped out. Simon bent down and found the large satchel he had used when travelling in Europe. It was lying against the side of the desk where the intruder had discarded it. Simon picked it up and discovered the package Miss Stockwell had given him to take to her mother in Kent had fallen behind it. He retrieved it and put it into the satchel. As he did, he checked the hidden pocket in the lining of the satchel. Inside was the black leather clutch bag Simon had concealed there. It might have no significance. But for now, together with the metal button and the blood-stained matchbox he had given to Robbie, it was one of the few pieces of evidence remaining from that night. He closed the hidden pocket again and stood. The swimming sensation in his head returned and he held on to the edge of the desk for a few seconds and waited for it to subside.

"I damn well hope I can make it to the taxi without collapsing," he muttered.

Simon gathered up his passport and the foreign currency and shoved it into the satchel. He turned and made his first shuffling steps towards the hallway. His muscle control was better than he expected and he grew more confident with each step.

The doorbell rang. After a few seconds it rang again, longer and with an annoying insistence.

"All right, Bill," Simon muttered to himself. "I'm coming as fast as I can."

He walked unsteadily down the hallway, resting his hand lightly on the wall to stop himself from falling. He got to the hat stand, retrieved his coat and scarf, and opened the front door.

"You didn't have to—" Simon began to say, but Bill interrupted him.

"As quick as you can," she whispered. "I thought I saw a police car turning into the street when I slipped round to the back stairs. We've got no time to lose."

14

"Scott Ellis Gardens, St John's Wood," Bill announced to the taxi driver as they climbed into the cab. She slammed the door behind them and sat beside Simon, who leaned forward to speak to the cabbie.

"Do you mind taking us around Regent's Park first?" Simon asked. "The Outer Circle route."

"No skin off my nose, guv'nor," the cabbie shouted back to him. "More pennies in me pocket at the end of the day."

The cab lurched forward and Bill and Simon were thrown back into the seat.

"Why are we going around the Park?" asked Bill. "Isn't it a bit dark for sightseeing?"

Simon looked through the rear window. "I want to make sure we aren't being followed before we head back to yours." The cab turned left onto Gloucester Place and headed towards Regent's Park. A cream-coloured Rover Meteor pulled out and followed them. Simon was certain the same car had been parked in the street behind Bellman Buildings when they had got into the cab. He turned and leaned forward to the driver.

"I say, cabbie," he said. "I think that car behind is following us. Any chance you could lose him?"

The cabbie turned and grinned. "You've made my evenin', mate. Sit back an' 'old tight."

The taxi turned sharp left into a side street, right into another street, and then right again into a mews where it screeched to a halt.

"Keep yer 'eads down an' I'll turn me lights off," the taxi driver said over his shoulder.

Simon and Bill bobbed their heads below the level of the rear window. A moment later a car roared past the end of the mews. "'Old on boys an' girls," the driver shouted. He reversed back into the street, swung the cab in the direction from which they had come, and sped off down the street. A moment later they turned first right and then left and then right again. Simon collided with Bill several times as they slid back and forth on the wide leather seat.

"Know these streets like the back of me 'and," shouted the cabbie. "I think we've lost 'em. But I'll pull into the Park and stop in the shadows away from the street lamps for a few minutes to make sure."

Simon turned to Bill. "Are you all right?"

Bill smoothed down invisible creases on her trousers, reached into her jacket for a cigarette, and lit it. "You should congratulate me on my choice of cabbie," she said. "It's just as well I anticipated you needed an experienced getaway driver."

Simon chuckled. He patted her thigh, but withdrew his hand hastily when the light from a streetlamp showed the look of disdain on her face.

"Don't patronise me, Simon Sampson." She inhaled on the cigarette and blew smoke back at him. "I'm not one of your bright young things. Which reminds me." She knocked ash from the end of her cigarette into the ashtray in the armrest. "I presume you'll not be seeing young Cameron this evening? He'll be very upset you stood him up."

"I don't know." Simon knew it could be dangerous to return to the Fitzroy Tavern, but he wanted to see Cameron. "Perhaps I can still go."

"Are you mad?" Bill shook her head. "After a car chase through north London and God knows what else that's happened to you? The Fitzroy Tavern is going to be a little too public for..." she leaned towards him and whispered. "a man on the run from the police."

"Nonsense," Even as he said it, Simon knew Bill was right. It would be a risky rendezvous with Cameron. But the man had said he had information relating to the case, and it was too important a lead to ignore, despite the danger.

"Remember what Jonny said the other night?" Simon continued. "He paid off someone high up in the Metropolitan Police last year. They haven't had a visit since. It's going to be fine."

Bill laughed. A deep, throaty laugh. "Simon Sampson. I do believe you're in love."

"Nonsense." Simon wished he sounded more convincing. "I'm in a bit of a sticky situation. If Cameron's got information that might help me clear my name—"

"Oh, tosh." Bill stubbed her cigarette out in the ashtray, and without pause reached for her cigarette case to light another. "If it's that important I can go on your behalf."

"He might not talk to you," Simon replied. Perhaps he was a little too quick to dismiss her offer. "I mean, he only met you briefly that night. I've seen him a bit more than you have. He knows me better."

"A great deal better by the sounds of it."

Simon leaned forward to speak to the cab driver. "Any sign of that car that was following us?"

"No, guv'nor," replied the driver. "We've been sat 'ere with the lights off for a few minutes now. I'll give it another couple and then go out the top entrance of the Outer Circle. I reckon we've lost 'em."

"I'm so grateful to you," Simon replied. "I'll be tipping you double when we get to St John's Wood."

"Thank you, guv'nor," the cabbie replied. "Much appreciated at Christmas time. What with the kids an' all."

Simon leaned back in his seat, and took out his pocket watch. "It's coming up to seven," he said to Bill. "We should be at yours before half-past. It's still a couple of hours before I'm due to meet Cameron. Let's talk about what's best to do later."

He undid the last few buttons of his shirt and slipped his fingers inside to feel his abdomen. It was very tender and he winced when he encountered the areas where he had been kicked. Bill watched him and wrinkled her nose.

"Too much liquid lunch with your Scotland Yard friend today?" she asked.

"No, Bill," Simon replied. "I've been kicked in the stomach. Several times."

The disdain dropped from Bill's voice. "Oh, darling, let me take a look."

She gripped her cigarette in the corner of her mouth and went to unbutton his shirt further. Simon could see the cab driver watching them in his rear-view mirror.

"Not here, Bill," he hissed. "We'll get thrown out of the cab."

Bill glanced up at the cab driver and smiled in a way Simon was not used to seeing. "Please excuse us, young man," she said. "My husband was set about by ruffians earlier this evening. I need to examine him and make sure we don't have to take him to a hospital."

"Don't mind me, missus," the cabbie replied. "Was it them blokes in the car?"

"Quite possibly," Bill replied.

"I got its number plate if it helps yer with the police." The cabbie scribbled the number on a piece of paper and handed it back to them.

"Thank you, dear man." Bill took the scrap of paper and gave it to Simon. "See?" she whispered. "You don't have to be a hero all on your own. Now show me those injuries. I did teach first aid in the Girl Guides you know."

She opened the rest of Simon's shirt, untucked his undershirt and slid it up to reveal his chest. Simon lay back on the seat and closed his eyes. Much of the time Bill could be contrary to the point of bloody-mindedness, but right now he was grateful she had come to his rescue. He winced as she applied gentle pressure to his abdomen.

"The problem is if any of your vital organs have been damaged." She pressed hard under his ribcage and for a moment Simon felt nauseous. "But I think you'll live." She rolled his undershirt back down and pulled the two halves of his shirt back together. "Here. Make yourself decent again."

"Is that it?" Simon asked. It seemed a very cursory examination.

"What do you expect?" Bill removed the cigarette from the corner of her mouth and tapped off the ash. "I can't do a thorough examination of your internal organs in the back of a taxi cab. And I know exactly why you don't want to go to a hospital. They'd alert the police straight away. If you start passing out, we'll have to think again." She turned to look through the rear window. "I'm getting bored sitting here in the dark in the middle of winter. Can we go home now please?"

Simon fastened the last of the buttons on his shirt and tucked it into his waistband. "Excuse me," he called out to the driver. "Could you take us to Scott Ellis Gardens, please? Number 17. I think we've lost our tail."

The cabbie restarted the engine and turned on his lights. The taxi pulled out onto the Outer Circle and headed north towards St John's Wood. There were several cars parked outside the expensive villas that lined the street, but no other vehicle was on the road, apart from their taxi.

"And are you expecting to stay at mine, my darling?" Bill asked. "Only I haven't ordered enough milk for the morning."

Simon shook his head. "We need to talk about this. It's not safe for me to stay. It puts you in danger."

"I don't think there's—" Bill began, but Simon held up his hand to silence her.

"More to the point," he continued. "I may have already put you in danger. That despicable man at my apartment was after the documents you've got."

"Anna's got," Bill corrected.

"Good point," Simon replied. "After he gave me a good kicking, I told him they were locked in a BBC office, and he gave me the distinct impression he knows who has them and how to get them. I presumed he meant you. But he could mean Anna."

"He's bluffing."

"Maybe," Simon said. "But the fact remains he, or his cronies may come after you. And if they managed to find out where I live, I'm sure they'll have no difficulty tracking you down."

Bill said nothing. She leant her head against the window

and stared out into the night, her face fleetingly illuminated at regular intervals by passing street lamps.

"I'm sorry, old girl," Simon began. "I didn't mean to—"

"Quiet," Bill snapped. "I'm thinking."

Simon lay back in the seat and watched as the smart mansions on the northern edge of Regent's Park passed by. The taxi turned into Avenue Road and then on to Prince Albert Road, heading for Lord's Cricket Ground. The streets were more crowded here. There was a hot chestnut seller on the corner, a few customers huddled around his brazier for warmth. Farther along the road a group of people waited to enter St John's Church. A notice board announced a special Christmas carol concert was taking place that evening.

It was evidence that normality still existed in the world, even if Simon's own world had lost all sense of normality. Bill was deep in thought. He felt a pang of guilt for involving her in something that had become so dangerous. Perhaps it was best if he simply got on a train to Portsmouth tonight and took the ferry across to France. He was fluent in French and could make his way back to Germany and Berlin. It was not fair of him to put her life at risk.

The taxi turned into Scott Ellis Gardens and pulled up outside a mansion block of flats. Bill turned to Simon.

"Out you get, then," she said to him. "I'm going to take the taxi on to Patsy Prendergast's and pick up her motor. You know where I hide my spare key don't you? You can let yourself in. I should be back by nine. If not before."

Her brusque instructions took Simon by surprise. She had clearly been hatching a scheme while she stared out the window. "What are you planning, Bill?"

"It's obvious," she replied. "Quite rightly you say we can't stay here. I've no intention of living in fear of being murdered in my bed by whoever roughed you up this evening. I'll get

Patsy's car and we'll motor down to Noël's place in Kent tonight. No one will think of looking for you there."

"Brilliant," Simon said. He would have kissed her if it were not for the consequences he knew he would suffer if he did so. "You're a brick, Bill. But what about work? Won't you get into trouble if you don't turn up tomorrow?"

Bill gave him a withering look. "My darling, I'm senior management. They wouldn't dare criticise me for taking the little extra holiday they already owe me. I'll phone in first thing in the morning and tell them I've started Christmas early. I'll also tell them that you were stricken with appendicitis this afternoon and rushed to hospital. It might buy you a little more time. At least until the police start making inquiries."

"Even more brilliant!"

This time Simon felt no inhibition. He reached across and kissed Bill on the cheek. She brushed him away in the manner a young child would reject the attentions of an elderly aunt.

"Stop it," she said, although Simon thought he detected a note of tenderness in her voice. "One of us around here has to be sensible, or we'll both end up dead before Christmas."

"Are you two lovebirds getting out?" the cab driver called over his shoulder.

"Here." Simon took out his wallet and gave Bill a pound note. "Make sure he gets a generous tip." He opened the cab door on his side and stepped out.

"Goodnight my darling wife!" he announced loudly, and slammed the door before Bill had a chance to reply.

15

"Gin or vodka?" Bill was fixing martinis for them both. It was eight o'clock and she had not long returned from Patsy Prendergast's mews flat in Chelsea with a car. While she had been away, Simon had spent the time soaking in the bath. The warm water had eased the pains in his abdomen, and when he walked into Bill's sitting room wearing her silk robe, he felt almost human again.

"Gin, of course," he replied. "I can't abide vodka. There's no taste to it."

"How very narrow-minded of you." Bill picked up the cocktail shaker and waved it at him. "I'll make it with gin, but you're having it shaken whether you like it or not. Harry, the barman at the Savoy, insists on martinis being shaken and not stirred. He says it's the only way to combine the vermouth. Lemon or olive?"

Simon dropped onto the large leather couch and swung his legs onto the cushions. "Olive, please my darling. Lemons are for lemonade."

"And don't get comfortable there." Bill shovelled ice into

the cocktail shaker. "We have to pack and be ready to leave in less than an hour."

"Pack?" Simon wrapped the robe around himself and snuggled down into the cushions. "I have nothing to pack. All I have are the clothes I arrived in and my satchel hanging in the hall."

"Then you're going to stink to high heaven in a few days." Bill added generous measures of gin to the cocktail shaker followed by the merest anointing of vermouth. "How tall are you?"

"Six foot. Why?"

"Perfect." Bill put the lid on the cocktail shaker and gave it a noisy shake. "Same height as Noël. You can use some of his clothes."

"Wouldn't he mind?"

"Of course he would." Bill removed the lid of the cocktail shaker and strained the liquid into two glasses. "But he's not there, so he won't know. Here. Take your drink."

She handed Simon a gin martini. "Bottoms up." To his astonishment she burst out laughing. "I'm terribly sorry," she snorted. "Noël always thinks that's killingly funny. He said to me once: 'It's what men like us call an invitation to copulation'."

Simon grinned. "You never introduced me while you worked for him. And now I'm going to be living in his house and wearing his clothes."

"Oh, but darling." Bill stopped laughing abruptly and there was a look of concern on her face. "You must never tell another soul."

"If I get out of this alive," Simon replied. "I might just tell the whole world." He took a sip of his cocktail. "Heaven. Thanks most awfully."

"Poor Noël." Bill sighed, and sat beside Simon.

Simon set his glass on a small round table beside the couch. "Why 'poor Noël'? The lucky chap is spending his Christmas partying in New York."

"Yes," Bill replied. "But he's very distracted by his brother's illness. He told me when I rang him yesterday about the arrangements. It's thanks to young Erik being so unwell that we can flee to Goldenhurst."

"Why?"

"Erik's been living there with their parents, and dear old Aunt Vida of course, ever since he became ill."

Simon nearly spilled his drink as he reached for the glass. "Good God, they're not going to be people there? We can't possibly go."

"That's what I'm trying to tell you." Bill sighed heavily. "Erik was taken to the Royal Victoria Hospital in Folkestone a week ago. He's convalescing there. Arthur and Violet—"

"Who?"

"Noël 's parents." Bill tutted. "Do try to keep up, darling. Arthur and Violet have gone to stay with Noël's Aunt Ida in Folkestone."

"I thought you said she was called Vida?"

Bill glowered at Simon. "Are you being deliberately obtuse? Aunt Ida is Arthur's sister. She lives in Folkestone. Aunt Vida is Violet's sister. She lives with Arthur and Violet at Goldenhurst."

Simon took a sip of his cocktail, and felt relief as the cold gin assaulted his brain. "Are you saying there is going to be somebody to greet us at Goldenhurst, or not?"

"Not." Bill stood, picked up her glass, and walked over to the door. "Now drink up and get ready. I've got to drive you to the Fitzroy Tavern first to meet young Cameron."

"Are you sure? You're going to be driving through the night at this rate to get all the way down to Kent."

As soon as Simon asked, he knew it was a redundant question. Bill had most likely long ago decided on the plan. And he was pleased she had.

"Don't ask questions when you already know the answer," she replied. "I'll wait outside the Tavern in the motor and be your getaway driver. If things go wrong, you can dash outside and we'll make our escape." She raised her glass in salute to him. "I seem to have gained employment with Marylebone's very own Al Capone. How ripping."

Patsy Prendergast's motor was a bright red MG sports car. It had a flimsy canvas roof and the sides were open to the cold night air. Bill drove at high speed down Charlotte Street. She turned left into Windmill Street with a squeal of tires and parked at the side of the Fitzroy Tavern. Simon peered through the windscreen. All was quiet in the street. A stray dog trotted past and stopped by a rubbish bin to mark its territory. Simon shivered as a gust of cold wind blew through the open sides of the car.

"You're going to freeze sitting out here," he said to Bill. "Why don't you come in with me?"

Bill shook her head. "If we do have to make a quick escape, at least I'll have the engine running." She patted the steering wheel affectionately. "Her heater works better when we're stationary."

Simon turned to look through the car's small window. As far as he could see no one had followed them. The Fitzroy Tavern would be closing soon, and then there would be a flood of people emerging from the pub. He knew it was risky for him to be seen in such a public place after what had happened earlier that evening. He turned up the collar of his coat and pulled his hat low on his head.

"What's the matter?" she asked. "Cold?"

"Yes," he replied. "But I'd also prefer it if as few people in the Fitzroy recognised me when I go in there."

"Don't be silly." Bill laughed. "All you need is for Jonny to spot you from the bar and he'll call out your name and ask where you've been. I told you I should go in."

"Certainly not." Simon pushed open the passenger door and stepped out of the car. He leaned back in to whisper to Bill. "I'll be as quick as I can. It's going to take at least two hours to get to Kent. Are you sure you'll be all right driving at this late hour?"

"Do I have a choice?" Bill asked. "Go now. And try to look a little less furtive."

The bar of the Fitzroy Tavern was packed. A thick cloud of cigarette smoke hung over the heads of the patrons, and the noise of early Christmas celebrations ricocheted off the walls. Simon eased himself into the crowded space and paused while his ears adjusted to the intensity of the sound. He peered through the smoky haze to try to see Cameron without drawing attention to himself. There was no sign of the man. He was reluctant to push through the crowds and go on a tour of the pub to find him, but there seemed no other option.

The door swung open and Cameron walked in. He towered over the other customers as he scanned the room. Simon reached out and tapped him on the arm. Cameron turned and his face lit up when he saw Simon.

"There you are!" he shouted. "Sorry I'm late. Last minute panic before—"

Simon raised a finger to his lips and held up his hand to stop Cameron talking. "It's absurdly crowded in here," he said. "If you want me to hear your Palace secrets, you'll have to talk so loud that half the damn pub will hear. Let's go outside."

Cameron nodded and went out into the street again. Simon followed. The door slammed shut behind them and the level of noise dropped immediately.

"That's better." Simon walked a couple of paces to the end of the building and stopped at the corner of the side street Bill had parked in and the main street. The car was a few yards away with the engine running. Simon could see the orange glow of Bill's cigarette through the windscreen. "So, what's this all about?" he asked. "And have you got my spare key? I don't mind, really. Only I needed them this morning."

Cameron looked puzzled. "I have nae got yer key."

"Oh," Simon replied. "Only I thought you took it when you took the pound note this morning."

"Look, I'm sorry." Cameron stared down at his feet. "I left a note. I needed the money to get back to St James's on time. Otherwise they'd ha' kicked me 'oot." He looked up. "But I didna' take yer key."

Now Simon was puzzled. If Cameron had not taken the spare key, who had? He recalled the open front door when he returned to the flat that afternoon. There was no sign of a forced entry. Perhaps his assailant had got hold of the key and simply let himself in. But who had given it to him? It was something he would have to think about later.

Cameron peered at Simon's face. "Are ye nae well? Ye look as if ye're waiting at death's door for the devil tae open it."

"It's been a difficult day," Simon replied. This was not the time to reveal he was a wanted man. "Tell me what this is about. Bill said you had some information for me."

"Aye, it's mighty strange," Cameron replied. "It's tae do wi' that German duke I'm tae look after."

"Charles Edward," Simon said. "Duke of Saxe-Coburg and Gotha. Has he arrived?"

"Aye, he has. I have tae say, he's nae to ma' likin'. He's nae polite like the Prince o' Wales. But the two of them are as thick as thieves. Non-stop talking since the foreign duke arrived."

"What about?"

Cameron paused and looked around, as if expecting to see someone listening in to their conversation. The street was empty.

"Ye'll nae tell anyone I told ye this, will ye?" Cameron asked. "I'll get intae awful trouble if they find oot I've been blabbin'."

Simon shook his head. "You can trust me."

Cameron took out a packet of cigarettes from his pocket and lit one. He put it to his lips and closed his eyes as he breathed in the smoke. His hand was shaking.

"Are you sure you want to tell me?" Simon asked. "If you'd rather not, I completely understand."

It was not entirely true. He needed something to help him unravel the mystery in which he was entangled. Cameron's information might give him an opportunity to unlock the puzzle before he had to go into hiding in Kent. But he felt responsible for Cameron, and he had no desire to get the young man into trouble with the Palace.

"I think they knew about the woman you found in the alleyway," Cameron said.

Simon leaned back against the wall of the pub. He felt the

pain from the bruises on his abdomen throb, and a wave of nausea washed over him.

"The duke knew about her?"

"Not just him," Cameron replied. "The Prince o' Wales as well. I'm sure they were talking about her this lunchtime. I was helping His Grace—"

"You mean the duke?"

"Yes." Cameron inhaled on his cigarette and the tip glowed orange in the dark. "I'm nae tae call him His Royal Highness, despite him bein' related tae the royal family. I didnae know he wa' disgraced."

Simon nodded. "I thought it strange when you told me the other day he was flying over from Germany to join the royal family for Christmas. He's very unpopular in England. The blighter sided with the Germans against us in the Great War, even though he was born here. Thoroughly bad show." He smiled. "I didn't think it was a good idea to tell you then. Didn't want to prejudice you against him before you'd met the chap."

"That's why ye cannae tell anyone I told ye this." There was fear in Cameron's eyes as he pointed his cigarette at Simon. "No one's tae know he's even in the country. If newspapers get wind of it—"

"I've already said." Simon laid his hand on Cameron's arm, and he felt the young man move closer. "You can trust me. What were they saying about the woman in the alleyway?"

"They didnae say it wa' her directly." Cameron took a final drag on his cigarette and threw it to the ground. "As I said, I wa' helpin' his Grace get his bags ready for the journey to Sandringham tomorrow. The Prince o' Wales came intae the room and they began talkin'. They spoke about one of their agents eliminatin' a woman called Kristina in London two nights ago. They described her as 'A rogue recruit sabotagin' vital documents'."

"'Rogue recruit'?" Simon repeated. "Did they give any more clues as to her identity?"

"Not much," Cameron replied. "I think his Grace the duke called her 'Agent K' at one point. And he said she'd be missed because it hae taken nearly a year tae recruit her and have her placed in King Charles Street."

"Really?" Simon interrupted. "But then she must have been in the Foreign Office. Or even the Home Office. I wonder if Betty knew her? And they said all of this in front of you?"

"Aye." Cameron shrugged. "Well, not as such."

"What do you mean?"

"His Grace sent me tae get some clothes from his dressing room next door. After I left, I heard the Prince o' Wales come in. They couldnae know I could hear them, but I wa' only in the other room. I heard it all."

"This is marvellous," Simon said. Cameron was so close he could have kissed him, if not for the fact they were in the street and anyone could have seen them. "Did they say anything else?"

"They had a bit o' a barney," Cameron continued. "The Prince o' Wales said that wi'out the information in the documents it couldnae go ahead."

"What couldn't go ahead?"

Cameron shrugged. "They didnae say. But the duke was insistent. He said it ha' to happen, and their agent in Norfolk ha' enough information."

"In Norfolk?" Simon said. "They must mean Sandringham."

There was the roar of an engine. Simon turned to see a black police van screech to a halt outside the Fitzroy Tavern.

"Damn it," he said to Cameron. "Looks like the Busys are going to raid the Fitzroy. Thank God we weren't inside. Follow me. Bill's in the car."

He ran across to the car and threw open the passenger door. Cameron remained on the corner. "What are you waiting for?" Simon shouted. "Jump in."

Cameron turned and ran across to the car, a look of terror on his face. "I'll lose ma' job if tha' police catch me wi' ya."

"They won't," Simon said. "Now get in quickly."

Cameron squeezed his large frame into the back of the tiny sports car. Simon climbed in, and slammed the door.

"What's he doing here?" Bill asked.

"Don't ask questions," Simon replied. "Just drive."

He leaned out of the car to look behind and saw two policemen appear at the corner.

"Drive!" he shouted again.

16

The little red car skidded onto Tottenham Court Road. It narrowly missed an omnibus and turned the corner into Great Russell Street. Three gentlemen dressed for the opera stepped off the pavement a few yards in front of them. Simon closed his eyes as the car screeched to a halt. There was a loud thumping noise and Simon reopened his eyes to see that all of the gentlemen were in one piece, but one of them, who had a large cigar wedged in the corner of his mouth, was hitting the bonnet of the car repeatedly with his silver topped cane.

"Maniac!" he shouted.

Bill leaned out of the window. "Get away from my car, you ruffian! And stop hitting it."

To Simon's surprise Cigar man did as he was told. His two companions were very drunk, and watched the argument from the safety of the pavement. They had broad smiles on their faces. Their friend walked around to Bill's side of the car and rapped on the doorframe with his cane.

"Madam, you're a lunatic," he barked. "And a perfect

demonstration of why women should never be allowed behind the steering wheel of a motorcar."

Before Bill could respond, Simon leaned across her, pushed her back in her seat, and addressed the man.

"I'm most terribly sorry," he said. "My wife's rushing our friend here to hospital. He's having a heart attack."

Cigar man peered into the cramped space behind Simon and Bill to see Cameron wedged with his legs contorted under him. He lifted a hand and waved.

The drunk man stood away from the window. "Errand of mercy. Of course. Don't let me hold you up. Foolish of us to get in your way." He saluted them and the upper part of his body swayed in a circular motion. He was as drunk as his friends.

"Drive on, my dear," Simon said to Bill. "And this time, perhaps we might be a little more sedate in our progress."

Bill pushed Simon away from her and turned to the man.

"Idiot," she said.

The car lurched forward and accelerated towards the British Museum.

"Bill, you don't have to drive this fast," Simon protested. "The police had only just got out of their van and were going to raid the Tavern. They're hardly likely to come chasing after us."

"An' I think I'm goin' tae be sick," said a voice from the back. "Do ye think ye can let me out?"

The car slowed, turned into a narrow mews, and came to a halt. Bill turned off the headlights, opened her door and climbed out.

"If you're going to be sick," she said to Cameron, "could you possibly not do it in the car? Patsy would be furious with me."

Cameron struggled to extricate himself from the back of

the car. He rolled clumsily onto the road and hauled himself onto all fours. Simon pushed open the passenger door, got out, and walked over to crouch down alongside him.

"Are you all right, my dear chap?" he asked.

Cameron coughed and raised his head. "Does she always drive like that?"

"I've no idea," Simon replied. "It's the first time I've been a passenger with her."

He thought about the long drive ahead of them to Kent. If only he had thought to pick up his hip flask before he left the flat. He could have anaesthetised himself against the potential trauma of the journey.

Bill had walked across to a set of garages and was trying the handles one by one.

"What on earth are you doing?" Simon asked.

"I'm certain that Ottoline's motor is kept in one of these," Bill replied. "I wanted to see if she's got it here in London, or whether they've already gone off to Oxfordshire for Christmas."

"Lady Ottoline Morrell?" Simon exclaimed. "You can't go stealing her car." He pointed to the little red sports car. "Anyway. What are you going to do with this one?"

"I wasn't going to steal it." There was a note of impatience in Bill's voice. "I thought I might check if it was here first before I go bothering her at this time of night."

Cameron had got to his feet. "Who's Lady Ottoline Morrell?"

Bill tried to open the last of the garage doors without success. "A very good friend of mine." She walked back to rejoin Simon and Cameron. "Well, she's been seeing a good friend of mine who introduced me. She and Dora have been together for a little while."

"Do you mean 'seeing' in the sense of having tea

together?" Simon asked. "Or 'seeing' in the sense of..." He struggled to find a euphemism.

"They're intimate, if that's what you mean." Bill lit a cigarette and leaned against the car bonnet.

"But I thought she was married," Simon said.

"She is." Bill removed the cigarette from her mouth and exhaled smoke into the night air. "To that absurd little former MP who keeps having children with other women. What else was darling Ottoline expected to do?"

She looked at Simon and laughed. "Don't pull a face like that. Honestly, you men." She turned to inspect the bonnet of the car. "That dreadful person with his walking stick has dented poor Patsy's bonnet. I'll have to pay for the repair when all this is over."

"Why do you want to change cars?" Simon asked. "Do you really think the police are going to come after us? Just because we were parked outside the Tavern when they came to raid it, doesn't mean we're automatically wanted criminals."

Bill shrugged and rubbed the dented surface of the bonnet. "They probably took a note of the number plate," she mumbled.

Simon waved in the direction of the end of the street. "Why don't you try Virginia Woolf while you're at it? Tavistock Square is just round the corner."

"Don't be absurd," Bill replied sharply. "Ginnie doesn't drive. She finds it hard enough to use a letter opener."

Simon took out his pocket watch. "It's already eleven. We really should get going." He turned to Cameron. "We'll take you back to the Palace and then we'll head off to Kent."

Cameron backed away. "I'm fine," he said. "I can walk from here. Don't let me take ye away from yer long journey."

It was perfectly clear Cameron had had quite enough of

Bill's driving for one night. Simon smiled. This was the moment they would have to say goodbye. They had only met a few days ago, but he had already developed a fondness for him. When might they meet again? There was no telling. If Simon had to leave the country, it might be never.

He remembered the night he and Cameron had dined at Lyons' Corner House, and the pleasurable hours it had led to afterwards. It was during that meal that Jenny Stockwell had served them. The waitress who now lay dead on Simon's sitting room floor. What if Cameron was to pick up a newspaper tomorrow and see Simon's picture and the headline *Wanted for the Murder of Jenny Stockwell*? Before they parted, he needed a few minutes alone with Cameron to tell him what had happened. He turned to Bill.

"I say old girl."

Bill looked at the two men. Cameron's shoulders were slumped. Simon's hand rested on his arm. She took one last drag on her cigarette and threw it to the ground.

"Don't mind me. I'll go up there and be your lookout. In case the busys decide to come down this way." She walked away from them towards the end of the mews.

"Is it wrong for me tae say she terrifies me?" Cameron asked.

"Not at all," Simon replied. "She puts the fear of God into me."

Cameron laughed. He pulled his shoulders back and Simon's hand slipped away from Cameron's arm. A sparkle had returned to the young Scotsman's eyes, and he seemed to have recovered his composure after the nausea-inducing car ride.

"But ye seem awful close. Are ye sure ye two are nae...?" Cameron left his sentence unfinished.

"Good God, no." Simon shook his head vigorously.

"Nothing more certain to cause me to lose the lead from my pencil than to think of Bill and me in an amorous connection. Impossible. Anyway, she bats for her home team. Like I do."

"I cannae understand, but I think I understand." Cameron chuckled.

"Cricketing term, old boy," Simon replied. "Don't suppose you chaps up in the Highlands play it that much."

Cameron smiled and stared at Simon. Expectantly. It was dark, save for the dim glow of a light from a small upstairs window at the far end of the street. Simon was less than two feet away from Cameron. They were in a public mews in Bloomsbury, and Simon was within touching distance of forbidden fruit. Forbidden by a society that considered men like Cameron and Simon, and women like Bill, to be perverted. They, and others like them, risked judgment, shame, and criminal prosecution if they dared show their love for each other. Simon felt a flood of indignation at the unfairness of it all.

"Will I see you again?" Cameron asked.

"I hope so." Simon leaned forward and kissed Cameron on the lips.

He put his arms around Simon's waist and pulled him closer.

Simon was lost in the bliss of the moment. The injustice of the world faded into the darkness of the night. All that existed in that instant was Cameron. The sweet taste of his lips, the man's arms around his waist, and the warmth of his face. The world and its petty rules and judgments could go hang. Simon's mind filled with thoughts of rebellion. To be a member of so-called decent society he had been forced to suppress his true self and wear a mask of conformity throughout his adult life.

Damn them. Damn them all. He was determined he

would do it no more. He had always been an outsider. Now that he was on the run from the police for a crime he had not committed, he was even more of an outsider. He had nothing more to lose, and everything to gain.

He would fight. Fight to prove his innocence, fight to avenge the murder of poor Jenny Stockwell, and fight to expose whatever plot was being hatched that had caused the death of an unknown woman two nights ago in a grubby west London alleyway, and probably involved a German duke and the Prince of Wales.

"I will see you again," he whispered to Cameron. "I'll make damn sure of it. But I have to go away for now. Before I do, there's something you must know."

He told Cameron about the man who attacked him in the apartment, the death of Jenny Stockwell, and how he was being framed for her murder. When he finished the story, Cameron was silent. His arms remained around Simon's waist and his fingertips gently massaged Simon's back.

"I wanna help ye," he said at last. "Everything's connected, isn't it? Yon woman in the alleyway. The documents we found. Even His Royal Highness the Prince of Wales." He released Simon from his grip. "An' I can help ye. I'll be with the duke and His Royal Highness for the next seven days. I can go through their things. Investigate for ye."

"No." Simon shook his head. "It's too dangerous. If they find out, you could lose your job. You may even be arrested."

"I dinnae care." Cameron's eyes sparkled, even in the gloom. "They willna even know. Remember, I wa' trained as a hunter by ma father. I can be stealthy an' silent. They'll never see me comin'."

It was too good an opportunity to allow to slip away. If Charles Edward, Duke of Saxe-Coburg and Gotha was implicated, Cameron was best placed to gather evidence. If only he was not going to be hundreds of miles away in the wilds of rural Norfolk.

"All right," Simon conceded. "But be careful. Is there a telephone you can use while you're at Sandringham?"

"We're no' staying at Sandringham. The duke's nae allowed tae stay with the royal family. We're in a set of lodge houses on the Estate."

"I thought you told me you were sleeping in a stable?" Simon asked.

Cameron laughed. "Aye, well I am. They tell me the duke's in the house and I'm in the stable next tae it." He shook his head. "It's nae goin' tae be easy tae get tae a phone. But mebbe I'll find a way. Can ye gi' me a number?"

Simon turned and called to Bill. She paused to finish her cigarette, threw it to the ground, and strolled over to them.

"Have you two finished your tearful goodbyes?" she asked.

"Farewells," corrected Simon. "We'll both be back in London before too long. You'll see. Now. Is there a telephone at Noël's house?"

"Of course there is, darling," replied Bill. "He's the last person to live in the dark ages."

"Good. Give the number to Cameron."

Bill reached into her pocket, took out a pen and a slip of paper, and scribbled a phone number on it. "How sweet. The love birds can whisper sweet nothings to each other before they go to bed each night." She handed the paper to Cameron. "And don't give that to anyone else, or Noël will have you deported to Australia when he returns from America."

The crunch of approaching footsteps made Simon look up. A policeman was walking towards them. Cameron released his grip on Simon's waist and they stepped apart. Simon hoped the constable had not witnessed their embrace.

"Damn it," Bill whispered. "We should have left sooner."

"Don't worry," Simon whispered back. "We can deal with it. Get in the car and be ready to start the engine."

He turned to Cameron and held out his arm to shake hands. "Thank you so much, young man," he said in a loud voice. "I thought we were never going to get the car started. I won't detain you any longer. You must be getting home."

They shook hands and Cameron walked off towards the advancing policeman. Simon got into the car.

"Evenin', officer," he heard Cameron say with forced cheeriness. "It be a cold night, b'aint it?"

"What's going on here?" asked the policeman.

The sound of the voice confirmed Simon's suspicions. It was Constable Smith, the same officer who had been so unhelpful in the alleyway three nights ago.

"Start the car," he whispered to Bill. The engine roared into life and its headlights lit up Constable Smith and Cameron. The gearbox made a grinding sound as Bill selected first gear and edged the car forward until the driver's side drew level with them. She leaned out of the window.

"Thank you so much, dear man," she said to Cameron. "Send my regards to the king."

She stamped on the accelerator and they shot forward before Constable Smith had time to speak.

17

The smart houses on Belgrave Road in Pimlico flashed past as the little red sports car headed south to the river. Simon opened the glovebox and searched among a collection of rags and half empty cigarette packets crammed into it.

"What are you looking for?" shouted Bill above the noise of the engine.

"A map," Simon shouted back. "Do you have to drive so fast? We're less likely to get stopped by the police if you drove a bit slower."

Bill snorted, but she lifted her foot from the accelerator. "Why do you need a map?"

"To get to Kent of course." Simon abandoned his search and struggled with a metal catch to close the glovebox. He swung round in his seat to look in the back of the car.

"We don't need a bloody map," Bill shouted.

She spun the car onto Vauxhall Bridge Road, slammed on the brakes to avoid hitting a tram, and waved a fist at a driver who had the temerity to flash his lights at her. "Bloody trams," she said. "Why do they have to clutter up the roads?"

"Have you driven to Noël's place before?" Simon asked.

"Once," Bill replied. "I'm sure I'll remember the way."

"In the dark?"

The tram screeched to a stop to drop off passengers and Bill brought the car to an abrupt halt behind it. She drummed her fingers on the steering wheel. "The problem with you, Simon Sampson, is that you worry too much."

Simon located a battered book of maps hidden in the recesses of the Spartan rear compartment of the car and waved it at Bill in triumph.

"Voilà." He turned the well-thumbed pages until he found Aldington in Kent. "I say, old thing, it's an awfully long way."

"Three hours at least." The tram accelerated away and they followed a few feet behind. Simon was certain they would run into the back of it if it stopped suddenly again. Bill looked across at the map on Simon's knee. "Forget about that. I'm perfectly capable of getting us there. Why don't you get some sleep and stop fretting, my dear? You need to rest after what you've been through today."

Simon pushed the map book onto the floor and closed his eyes. At least it was better when the imminent dangers of Bill's driving were no longer visible to him. He tried to ignore the cold air blowing through the car's open sides and its spasmodic lurches as Bill inched along in the traffic. If only he could clear his mind, he might get some sleep.

But it was spinning too much with a thousand different thoughts and ideas. He could still see Jenny Stockwell's body lying on the floor behind his couch. When Bill had arrived earlier and he had staggered from the sitting room to the hallway, he had wanted to stop and examine Miss Stockwell's body, in the forlorn possibility that she might still have been alive.

He wished he had. But it had taken him all his strength to get to the doorway. And when Bill had announced she had seen the police car arriving outside Bellman Buildings, there was no time to go back and check if Miss Stockwell was still breathing. He felt sad and guilty for the poor young woman who had been caught up in this series of terrible events. She was the innocent victim of a sinister plot, the aim of which Simon was yet to uncover.

The latest information from Cameron was enough to keep him awake on the journey. It was a sobering shock to think the Prince of Wales himself was somehow involved. He knew His Royal Highness had a reputation for womanising. The prince was never out of the gossip columns and, from what Simon had heard, the king was deeply unhappy with his son's much-publicised activities.

But it was one thing to be a serial philanderer, it was quite another for the Prince of Wales to be plotting an intrigue with his German relative. If the two royals were involved, what were they plotting? And how was the BBC involved? Cameron had said they mentioned the name Kristina, and called her Agent K. Simon thought that the woman he had discovered in the alleyway had a more continental style about her. It was partly because of the elegant way she was dressed. And now he remembered her voice when she tried to speak to him. What was it she tried to say? *Curling in cover*? Although she had difficulty making any sound at all, he remembered her accent was possibly foreign. Perhaps she too was from Germany.

Simon opened his eyes and reached for the satchel at his feet. He fumbled in the secret compartment until he found the black leather clutch bag he had retrieved from the alleyway.

"Is there a light in this contraption?" he asked.

Bill laughed. "You're lucky to have a heater, my darling. Why? I told you we don't need the map."

"I've got an idea about this bag I found the other night," Simon replied.

Bill took one hand off the steering wheel and reached towards the dashboard. "Here. Use this." She handed Simon her silver cigarette lighter. "But try not to set fire to us."

Simon took the lighter and illuminated the gold frame of the leather clutch bag in its flickering flame. The two engraved letters were clearly visible: *S* and *C*.

He closed the cap of the cigarette lighter with a snap. "Saxe-Coburg," he announced.

"What?" Bill asked.

"These two letters engraved on the clutch bag I found. S and C. I think they stand for Saxe-Coburg. That links the woman in the alleyway with this German duke who Cameron's been assigned to over Christmas while he's with the royal family in Norfolk."

"I wasn't aware he was," Bill replied. "You've told me nothing since your Bloomsbury canoodling with young Cameron."

A taxi pulled out from the kerb in front of them. Bill swerved around it, narrowly avoided hitting an oncoming tram, and leaned on the car horn. Simon shoved the leather bag back into his shoulder bag, lay back in his seat, and closed his eyes.

"I'll tell you later," he said. "You concentrate on getting us there in one piece."

The dream was a familiar one. But this time it had a new twist.

It was two minutes before six in the evening. Simon was outside the studio door in the basement of Broadcasting House, a script for the six o'clock news in his hand. The door was locked and he was throwing all his weight against it to force it open. He could hear the chimes of Big Ben echoing along the corridor, as though he was in the Westminster clock tower itself. The disembodied voice of the Head of News resounded in his ear.

"Where are you, Simon?" he was saying. "Why aren't you at the microphone? It's time Simon. It's time."

At that moment the studio door fell open. Simon stumbled inside to find Jenny Stockwell lying on the studio floor. The script had turned into a knife and it dripped with blood. He tried to throw it away, but the knife remained stubbornly in his grasp. Again, he heard the voice of the Head of News.

"What have you done, Simon? I knew the BBC was not the right place for a grubby little Fleet Street reporter like you. Get back to the gutter where you belong."

The floor opened up to reveal a dark chasm and he felt a hand on his shoulder. He twisted to shrug it off and lurched forward, falling headlong into the void before him.

"Wake up, sleepyhead. We're here. Welcome to Goldenhurst."

Bill was at his side whispering in his ear. Simon shook his head and opened his eyes wide. His heart pounded and he panted as if he had just run a marathon.

"I don't know what you were dreaming about," Bill continued. "But I'm awfully glad it wasn't me. Are you all right?"

Simon lay back in the car seat and forced his breathing to

slow down by inhaling long, slow gasps of air. The car's headlights lit up a pretty farmhouse built in the Elizabethan style. The white-painted stucco of its facade was interspersed with exposed timber beams. It was a two-storey building with three dormer windows on the upper floor under a tiled roof. Despite its size, the house looked cosy and inviting.

Bill switched off the engine and there was almost complete silence, save for the mournful hooting of an owl. Swiftly moving shadows around the roofline of the house indicated there might be bats flying. The tranquillity and calm were in sharp contrast to the noise and bustle of London. Simon's heart rate had slowed and his breathing was no longer frenetic. He turned to Bill.

"This is where you're going to conceal a wanted man for the next few days, is it?" he asked her. "In case the police get to me before we have time to celebrate, I'd like to wish you a very Happy Christmas, old thing."

"You do come out with the most ridiculous nonsense," Bill retorted. "No one's going to find you here. And before you know it, Anna will have cracked the code in that document, we'll be able to prove you're no murderer, and then we can get our lives back to normal."

She pushed open her door and got out of the car. "Now stop dawdling and help me unload. Patsy's very kindly filled the boot with a hamper of goodies for Christmas. So at least we shouldn't starve if we can't find what we want in the local shops."

Simon took out his pocket watch. It was nearly three o'clock in the morning. How quickly his life had changed in a day. Twenty-four hours ago, he had been asleep next to Cameron in his flat. Since then he had been drugged and beaten up, forced to go on the run from the police and hide in Noël Coward's country home. On top of that he was soon to be jobless. He had not slept well during the drive and now he felt almost drunk with tiredness. He desperately needed sleep to clear his head, ready to put together a plan of action. Thank God Bill was with him.

He went to the back of the car to find her struggling with a wicker hamper.

"Here," he said. "I'll take that. You go and get the house unlocked. The sooner we can get to bed, the sooner we can be up and ready tomorrow."

"Good man," Bill replied. "Once we've unloaded, I'll park the motor out of sight, just in case the police put out an alert for it. We can use Noël's Bentley if we need to go out."

"A Bentley?" Simon was beginning to enjoy being a fugitive from justice. It would be almost a shame to return to normal life.

If he ever managed to return to normal life.

He grasped the handles on either side of the hamper and lifted it from the car. Bottles clinked loudly against each other as he walked towards the house.

"That's a good sound to hear," he said in loud whisper to Bill. "I presume it's champagne. Get the door for me, my darling."

The front door of Goldenhurst opened into a small entrance lobby. Bill led the way into a low-ceilinged sitting room and switched on the wall lights.

"Just leave it here." She indicated a space on the carpet next to a table and headed back to the entrance lobby. "We can unpack it in the kitchen in the morning. I'll go and get our bags and move the car."

Simon bent his knees to set the hamper down on the carpet and felt a stab of pain across his chest. He leaned heavily on the wicker basket, and waited for the pain to pass. Across from him was a grand piano. The lid was closed and the keyboard covered. Simon levered himself into a standing position, crossed to the piano and sat on the stool. He slid his hand over the surface of the polished wood and felt a frisson of excitement. This was where the master composed. What a privilege it was to be able to touch the very instrument at which he had written *Cavalcade*, and more than likely a host of songs. He felt the wooden lip of the keyboard cover under his fingers and lifted it with reverence.

"Don't you dare touch that." Bill's authoritative tone cut through the silence in the room. Simon hastily lowered the wooden cover back into place. "If you so much as scratch Noël's piano, I'll hand you into the police myself."

Bill dropped her suitcase and Simon's satchel by the door, walked across to the couch and flopped down. "God, I could do with a gin."

The telephone in the far corner of the room began ringing. Bill sat up and looked over to Simon.

"Who the devil can that be at this time in the morning?" she asked.

"Noël?" Simon queried.

"Hardly," Bill said. "He thinks I'm coming down tomorrow. Anyway. He must be far too busy to be calling little old me."

She stood and walked over to the phone. "Should I answer it?"

Simon shrugged. "It's the only way you'll find out who it is."

"But what if it's the police?"

"Then you'll tell them the truth," Simon replied. "That you've been invited to spend Christmas here at the invitation of Noël Coward." He stood and walked over to join her. "Go on. Pick it up."

Bill lifted the receiver and held it to her ear so that Simon could hear as well.

"Hello?" she said.

"Is tha' you, Bill?" came a man's voice at the other end. "It's me. Cameron. I've been callin' for the last twenty minutes. I've found oot something I think ye both need tae know."

18

"Where are you?" Simon asked.

"Oh good, you're both there," Cameron replied. "I'm in a phone box near Green Park. I'm nae in the Palace if tha's what ye mean."

Sensible man Simon thought. If Cameron had made the phone call from the Palace, he would have not only risked being overheard, but one of the Palace telephone operators might have listened in to the call. The young man was smarter than Simon gave him credit for.

"Why call so late?" Bill asked. She looked at the electric clock on the sitting room wall. "I mean, early, I suppose. Aren't you supposed to be in bed?"

Cameron chuckled. "I'll get ma sleep, don't ye worry, missy. Tomorrow we're travelling tae Norfolk. I wa' worried I'd nae have time tae call ye then."

"What have you found out?" Simon asked.

"After I left you, I got back tae the Palace aboot eleven-thirty," Cameron began. "And I wa' in big trouble. The Head of the Household gave me a right tellin' off. He said I ha' no right tae leave without tellin' anyone while the duke wa' visitin'. He told me tae go tae the duke and apologise."

"I thought you told me you were finished for the day when we met?" Simon asked.

"Aye, tha's wha' I thought," Cameron replied. "No one told me I couldnae leave the Palace. Anyway, I know now. So, I went along to the duke's rooms and the door wa' open into the corridor. I heard him arguin' wi' the Prince o' Wales. He wa' really goin' for him."

"What was he saying?" Bill asked.

"Somethin' aboot the plan bein' crucial to the joint futures of Britain an' Germany. He said it wa' time for two great Empires to unite. And he said if the king wouldnae support it, then the Prince o' Wales had tae take over."

"Take over what?" Simon asked.

"Tha's wha' I don' know. But it's ganna happen at Sandringham. And the duke said somethin' else that wa' strange. He said it must happen because Adolf Hitler insisted. 'It ha' gone as high as that' is what he told His Royal Highness."

"Adolf Hitler?" Simon was shocked. He knew the democratic government of the Weimar Republic in Germany was lurching from crisis to crisis. Germany's Chancellor had been replaced yet again in the last few months. Simon had also read that Adolf Hitler was manoeuvring his Nazi Party into power. But an alliance with Britain? It was too ludicrous to contemplate. The two countries had been at war fourteen years ago. He waited for Bill's response, but she was busy refilling her cigarette case.

"This is getting out of hand," Simon said. "There's going to come a point very soon when we'll have to let the government know about this."

Bill looked up from the cigarette case, and snorted

derisively. “They wouldn’t listen to you for a moment. Do you think they’d believe some cock and bull story from a man wanted for murder?”

“What if it was you who told them instead of me?”

“Tell them what?” Bill took out a cigarette from the case and lit it. “We don’t know enough. And anyway, I’m too closely linked with you now. They probably wouldn’t trust me either.”

“I’ve got tae go.” Cameron’s voice interrupted their discussion. “The duke ha’ retired for the night. But if he wakes up an’ finds I’m nae there, I’ll nae ha’ a job anymore.”

“Of course. Off you go.” Simon said. “And good work. Don’t take any unnecessary risks. Call us when you can, once you get to Sandringham. But keep your head down, my dear.”

The line went dead, and Bill replaced the receiver on its cradle. She inhaled deeply on her cigarette and blew a smoke ring into the air.

“What do you make of that?” Simon asked. “This could be the biggest story of the year, and I’m stuck in deepest Kent, unable to do damn all about it.”

“What do you want to do about it?” Bill asked.

Simon held up his hand and counted off a list of tasks on his fingers. “We desperately need that code cracked. I’ve got to speak to Robbie at Scotland Yard—”

“Are you mad?” Bill interjected. “He’ll send a fleet of police cars after you straight away.”

“Not if he doesn’t know where I am,” Simon replied. “Thank God I didn’t tell him about us coming down here when we had that drink yesterday. I also need to talk to Betty at the Home Office.”

“Just as mad.” Bill shook her head. She thought for a moment. “Do you fancy a trip to the seaside tomorrow?”

Simon furrowed his brow. "Do you think I've got time for that? I've got far too much to do here."

"Exactly," Bill replied. "If you're going to make all these phone calls, I won't have you making them from Noël's phone. I don't know whether it's true or not, but somebody in Engineering Department told me the police can trace phone calls if they really put their minds to it. We're not going to risk that."

She pointed to a framed water colour on the wall. "Hythe. Charming little market town on the sea. Noël loves going there. We can motor down in the Bentley, and you can make all your phone calls from the phone box on the front."

"I'm going to have to find a disguise of some sort," Simon replied. "If the police put out a wanted notice with a photograph, people might recognise me"

"You're in Noël Coward's house, darling," Bill said. "You'll have no difficulty at all finding something theatrical." She yawned and stretched. "Hythe. Did you know it means haven? Rather appropriate, don't you think?"

When Simon reached the foot of the staircase the next morning, he could hear a wireless being tuned somewhere in the house. It was a comforting sound. He had slept deeply and when he awoke, he lay in the warmth of the bed and listened to the birds chirruping outside. They were usually drowned out by the roar of the traffic in London. He realised there would be no newspaper waiting for him. He was anxious to get out and find one. Simon was annoyed at his own impatience. He had been in Kent no more than a few hours and already he felt cut off from the rest of the world.

Bill was in the breakfast room, leaning over a large

wooden wireless set. The hiss of radio static gave way to a woman's voice speaking in German.

"What are you listening to?" Simon asked from the doorway.

"Radio Luxembourg," Bill replied. "They're doing test transmissions. Should be starting next year. Damn it. Wish I understood German."

The BBC's Head of News was dismissive of the plans by the Duchy of Luxembourg to broadcast English language programmes directly into Britain, but Simon knew that senior management saw the new broadcaster as a threat to the BBC's sovereignty on the airwaves. The British government had made strong representations against the proposals, claiming it would undermine the authority of the BBC. So far their protestations had been ignored.

Bill pointed at the speaker grille. "That's my friend Eva. Eva Siewert. We met in London a few years ago and we've corresponded ever since. She's one of us you know. A sister."

"Is there anyone you know who isn't?" Simon smiled.

Bill wrinkled her nose. "No one of any consequence, I imagine," she replied. "Eva's the editor-in-chief there. God how I envy her. They're so much more forward-thinking about putting women in decent jobs on the continent."

The announcement in German ended. There was a brief pause, followed by a male voice speaking in English.

"And now here is a news test transmission from Radio Luxembourg. Broadcasting to you from our studios in the Grand Duchy of Luxembourg."

"Bingo," Bill said. "Let's hear what real radio news sounds like."

"I say, old girl. That's a mean thing to—" Simon began, but he was silenced by a wave of her hand.

This was the first time Simon had heard any of the test

transmissions from Radio Luxembourg. The programme carried by the Long Wave signal was very clear, and the news content was much more varied than the dry reports Simon was given to read each evening. The stories were international, with a strong emphasis on news from continental Europe, but there was also a story involving the new trade union legislation being debated in the Houses of Parliament.

The only report about Germany concerned the progress of the coalition government, headed by the new Chancellor Kurt von Schleicher. There was no mention of the Nazi party. The English test transmission ended, and Eva Siewert spoke in German again. Bill sighed and retuned the wireless set. After a few moments they heard the sound of a church organ playing.

"And this is all the BBC can offer." She pointed to the clock on the wall which showed it was already twenty past ten. "Nothing to listen to before ten in the morning. And then they start off with a church service. No news report until after six in the evening."

"That's because the government won't allow the BBC to compete with the newspapers." Simon was surprised by Bill's sudden attack. "If you're so impressed by this foreign upstart, why don't you go and join them?"

"I might well do that." Bill tapped the end of her cigarette into an ashtray on the wooden cabinet of the wireless set. "Perhaps you should think about it as well. You might find yourself less employable very soon."

"You know you can be damned unhelpful sometimes when you make comments like that." Simon walked back to the hallway and stood at the foot of the staircase. "You could at least show me a little more support in my hour of need."

"How dare you." Bill slammed the lid of the wireless shut.

"Haven't I done enough? I rescue you from the murderous clutches of an assailant in your flat. In the middle of the night. I drive you to this sanctuary to keep you hidden from the police. I've already called Miss Braithwaite and told her about your fictitious appendicitis—"

"Look, Bill old thing," Simon interrupted. He knew immediately he had made a clumsy remark. But Bill was not to be stopped. She stalked over and stood glowering at him.

"Don't 'Bill old thing' me," she continued. "I've also telephoned Anna about decoding that German text, managed to find Noël's bloody dressing-up box for your disguise, and to cap it all I made a pot of tea." She inhaled deeply on her cigarette and blew a cloud of smoke into Simon's face. "I'm not your little housewife you know."

"I'm sorry, old girl." But Simon knew it was an inadequate apology. He had overstepped the line with his careless remark, and Bill was the last person he wanted to fall out with as his own life disintegrated around him. "I'm a complete ass. You've been wonderful, Bill. I should be thanking you, not moaning on. I'm truly sorry."

There was a long pause. Bill stared at him and shook her head.

"You men," she said. "You're all the same. At the first sign of trouble, you look for someone to blame." She pointed the glowing end of her cigarette at him. "Don't you dare say I don't 'support you in your hour of need' again. Or I'll call the police myself and turn you in."

She sighed and turned to stare at a watercolour landscape hanging on the wall. The storm was subsiding. Bill was not the kind of person to prolong an argument. She was far too intelligent for that.

"I'll make you some breakfast," Simon offered by way of a feeble apology. Then I'll find a fake moustache and dark glasses from that dressing-up box, and we can toddle off to the seaside for our day out. Just like you said."

"Dark glasses? In December?" Bill gave Simon a withering look. "That's a sure-fire way to draw attention to yourself." She pushed him out of the way and stood on the first step of the staircase. "Go and fix breakfast and let me sort out a disguise for you. I won't say no to a boiled egg and toast soldiers. You'll find it all in the kitchen. I got the local farmer to drop off some eggs and bread for us last night before we arrived."

Before Simon could thank her, the telephone rang. Bill turned from the staircase and walked back into the sitting room. Simon followed her.

"Aldington 503." Bill's voice was deep as she spoke into the mouthpiece. She held the handset for Simon to hear as well.

"Hello?" said a woman's voice. "Miss Miles? It's Anna Forster here."

"Hello, Anna," Bill replied. "Is everything all right?"

"Yes. Well, I mean, no. No, it's not all right. It's very bad. Very bad indeed. I've managed to decode the first part of that German text. If I'm right, the king is in terrible danger. You must tell someone right away."

19

Anna Forster's voice was high-pitched and agitated. Her Polish accent was much more pronounced than when Simon had first met her in Bill's office.

"There is not much time," she said. "It will happen tomorrow."

Simon took the phone from Bill. "Hello, Anna. It's Simon Sampson here. Please keep calm. Tell me exactly what the text of the message is."

He covered the mouthpiece and whispered to Bill. "I need paper." He uncovered it again as Anna started to speak. "Wait two ticks my dear. Bill's getting me something to write on."

Bill handed a sheaf of paper to Simon. "Take this. The housekeeper uses Noël's old scripts for scrap paper."

Simon handed the phone to Bill and took the crumpled sheet of paper from her. It was a page from a script with *No! No! No!* scrawled across it in black ink, He assumed it was in Noël Coward's handwriting. It would be worth a fortune if he took it to London to sell.

"Go ahead, my dear," he said. "What does it say?"

Simon scribbled as Anna read out her translation.

"They will replace the king's first radio broadcast to the Empire with a message to pledge support for Herr Hitler and the Nazi Party. The assassination will happen on 24 December at Sandringham. Their agents will be in place on 23 December. The Prince of Wales will make the broadcast in place of his father. The prince has merely been told the king will be—"

She stopped. "That's all I've been able to translate. The next section is in a different code."

"Why?" Simon asked. "Why switch codes?"

"Intelligence services often do that. It reduces the risk of an entire message being cracked." Anna's voice became calmer. "I think this note was a briefing to a foreign intelligence service."

Simon remembered the woman's accent when she had struggled to speak to him in the alleyway.

"Presumably it's intended for the Germans," he said.

"Maybe," Anna replied. "But it could be the Austrians. Or the Swiss. And as you found it in London, it could even be for your own intelligence services."

"But the document's written in German," Bill interjected. "Surely MI6 would have used English?"

"Not necessarily," Anna said. "If an agent's first language is German, they would probably use their native tongue to avoid confusion in the translation."

"There's nothing confusing about this message." Simon recalled the words the woman in the alleyway had spoken to him. He remembered it sounded like '*Curling in cover*'. He told Anna what he had heard.

"Are you sure it wasn't *König in gefahr*?" she asked.

"Of course." Simon shook his head when he realised the mistake he had made. "I'm such a fool."

"I'm happy to agree with that statement," Bill said. "But

why particularly this time?"

Simon glowered at her. "Because *König in gefahr* happens to be German for *king in danger*."

"Ah," Bill replied. "So this women tried to tell you several nights ago and we only just find out now. Anna, my dear. How long will it take you to translate the rest of the message?"

"I don't know." Anna's voice rose again. "I need help. I can't do it alone. I thought I could, but I can't."

"Don't distress yourself," Simon said. "We need to try to get you to someone we all can trust."

He thought back to the fake detective he had met on his return visit to the alleyway two days ago. He wanted to tell Anna to take the documents to a police station. But how could he be sure of her safety? There were only two people he felt he could trust. Robbie Mountjoy at Scotland Yard and Betty Richardson at the Home Office.

"Are you at the BBC?" Simon asked.

"Not yet," Anna replied. "I've been given some time off because of all the hours we put in when the Empire Service started on Monday. I'm supposed to go in later."

"Well, sit tight there," Simon said. "I'm going to call a chum of mine at Scotland Yard. His name's Robbie Mountjoy. Detective Inspector Mountjoy. I'll get him to pop round and you can hand him the documents. He's completely trustworthy."

He covered the mouthpiece again to speak to Bill.

"I presume this means that breakfast is cancelled," she said.

"I'm afraid so, my darling," Simon replied. "How long will it take us to get to Hythe? I need to make this call as soon as possible."

"Twenty minutes," Bill replied. "Less if I put my foot down."

Simon recalled the terrifying high-speed drive through London the night before.

"Twenty minutes is fine," he said.

The wide promenade alongside Princes Parade on the seafront in Hythe was deserted when they arrived forty minutes later. It was hardly surprising. Heavy grey clouds rolled overhead. An icy east wind whipped the waves of the ashen sea into foamy crests, and a dust storm of sand swirled over the empty beach.

Bill parked the gunmetal grey Bentley a few feet away from two red telephone boxes. There was an elderly man in one of them and a young woman in the other. Simon nervously fingered the moustache Bill had glued to his upper lip.

"Stop doing that or it'll come off," Bill commanded.

"It itches," Simon complained. He peered through the windscreen. "These surely can't be only telephone boxes in the whole of Hythe?"

"They're the two I know about," Bill replied. "Do you want me to drive around all day searching for another one? I'm sure one of them will come free in a minute. People in Hythe can't have much to talk about."

Simon pulled out his pocket watch. "We're wasting valuable time. Isn't there a town hall or something? I'm sure there'll be a phone box there."

"As a matter of fact, there is," Bill replied. "It's right next to the police station. Do you want me to take you there? Then you can get arrested straight away."

The door of one of the telephone boxes swung open and the elderly man stepped out. He staggered as the door threatened to spring shut on him and he leaned against it heavily.

"There you are." Bill revved the engine and drove the Bentley forward to draw alongside the phone boxes. "Patience is the virtue of women, while impatience is the curse of men."

"Who said that?"

"I did." Bill pulled hard on the hand brake and took her cigarette case from the dashboard. "Go on. Jump out. I'll shoot into town and get a couple of newspapers. I want to see if you've made the headlines yet."

Simon shivered. Her comment was an unwelcome reminder of the reason why they were parked on the promenade in a seaside town in December, over seventy miles from London. He took out the gold-framed spectacles Bill had found in the dressing-up box and put them on. The lenses were made for someone with a mild astigmatism, and the world became a distorted mass of coloured shapes that squashed and stretched like images in a fairground mirror as he turned his head.

"I can't wear these." He pulled the spectacles off again. "I'll fall over or bump into something."

Bill lit her cigarette and shrugged.

"Up to you. But they do a damn good job of hiding your face."

Simon took out a pair of dark glasses from his pocket and put them on instead. "What do you think?"

"Ridiculous." Bill pointed to the spots of rain that had appeared on the windscreen. "Why don't you go the whole hog and put on a bathing costume as well? People will assume you're an eccentric Londoner in search of a winter swim."

Simon removed the sunglasses, shoved them back into his pocket, and perched the gold-framed glasses on the end of his nose. He could peer over the top of them instead. He pulled a flat cap low on his head and pushed open the car door. The icy wind caught it and wrenched it from his hand.

"Don't be long getting the paper," he said. "I'm going to feel very vulnerable until you return."

"I won't," she replied. "And don't you be long with that phone call. I gave up my breakfast for this, remember?"

Simon stepped out of the car and slammed the door. Bill accelerated away down Princes Parade. Simon strode towards the phone boxes. The elderly man was still leaning against the open door.

"Are you all right?" Simon inquired.

The man looked at him with watery blue eyes.

"You're not from round here, are you?" he said. "I was holding the door open for you. I saw you and your missus waiting. Where are you from? London?"

Simon took hold of the phone box door but the man continued to lean against it.

"Thanks awfully," Simon said. "Don't let me keep you."

The man stared at him and tilted his head to one side. "Maybe you are from round here. You look familiar."

"A lot of people say that," Simon pushed the glasses up his nose and his world became blurred again. The whiskers of the fake moustache fluttered in the wind and Simon touched it nervously. "I've got a very common face."

"Maybe you have." The man heaved himself away from the door and leaned on his walking stick. "And maybe you haven't. But I don't forget a face quickly. I'll remember soon enough." He shook his head and shuffled off down the promenade. "Merry Christmas to you, young man."

Simon stepped into the phone box and the door swung shut behind him. He leaned against the glass-panelled side and breathed heavily. The conversation with the elderly man had unnerved him. Was his photograph already in the newspapers? Had he been recognised? He would know soon enough when Bill returned with the paper. He pulled out a handful of pennies from his pocket and placed them in readiness on the shelf under the phone. He dialled the number for Scotland Yard and prayed that Robbie was in that morning. A few minutes later came a welcome voice.

"Mountjoy."

"Robbie. It's me. Simon."

There was silence from the other end of the phone.

"Robbie? Are you there?"

"I'm here all right," Robbie replied. "Where the hell are you? Half of Scotland Yard is looking for you."

"I can't tell you," Simon replied. "But I've got urgent information for you about the king."

"Whoa, hold on there," Robbie said. "Why don't you start by answering my question?"

"Oh, come on Robbie," Simon replied. "You don't for a moment think I killed that woman, do you? I'm being set up. You've *got* to believe me."

"From what I've heard, the evidence is conclusive," Robbie replied. "Are you going to tell me your side of the story?"

Simon sighed. It was going to be a long phone call. "I will. But only if you—"

"Not another favour." Robbie was exasperated. "I don't think you're in any position to ask favours."

"It's not a favour," Simon protested. "I told you. I've got important information about a threat to the king."

"Later," Robbie replied. "You can start by telling me why Jenny Stockwell was discovered dead in your flat."

"All right." Simon took a deep breath and started to recount the story. "I left Jenny Stockwell in my flat when I went off to work yesterday morning," Simon began.

"What was she doing there?"

"She came to me for help," Simon replied. "Her landlord had attacked her the night before and she needed to find somewhere to live."

"But why you?" asked Robbie. "I didn't think you were interested...I mean. Women aren't your thing, are they?"

Simon smiled as Robbie stumbled over his words.

"That's right, Robbie," he said. "But Miss Stockwell is... was, a nice young lady. And when I first met her, I'd offered to help deliver a Christmas present to her mother. She brought the present round to my flat yesterday morning. When I saw her injuries, I asked what happened. She told me about her landlord, and that's when I offered to stay until she could find somewhere else to live."

"So how did she end up with her throat cut on your sitting room floor?" Robbie asked.

Simon winced as he heard Robbie describe Jenny's cause of death so casually.

"After I'd met you for drinks at the Red Lion yesterday lunchtime, I went back to the flat—"

"What time?"

"It must have been about three." Simon thought for a moment. "Yes, it was definitely three. Pethers was just coming on duty."

"Pethers?"

"The porter in my building. When I went into the

sitting room, I found it in a terrible state. Ransacked. Then I saw Miss Stockwell lying behind the couch. Before I could get to her, someone chloroformed me. When I woke up, I was on the floor, unable to move. The man had drugged me and my muscles were paralysed."

"This man," Robbie said. "Can you describe him?"

"It was very difficult to see him because I couldn't lift my head. All I saw were his boots. At one point he bent down and I vaguely saw the outline of his face. It was a long face. Clean-shaven I think."

"Anything else," Robbie asked. "Can you describe his boots?"

"Brown." Simon paused to recall the moment he first saw them. "Now I come to think of it they were rather splendid. Tall boots. Brown leather. And I remember now. They laced up at the front."

"Interesting," Robbie paused and Simon imagined he was making notes. "Did he speak to you?"

"Oh, yes." Simon remembered the chilling tone of the man's voice. "But first he beat the bally stuffing out of me."

"How did he sound?"

"Very cultured accent, but not Home Counties. Gloucestershire I'd say, or maybe Wiltshire."

Robbie chuckled. "You always had an ear for the way people spoke. Even at school. Did he say what he wanted?"

"You remember I told you about the woman I found in the alleyway?" Simon asked.

"I do," Robbie replied. "I've drawn a blank on that so far. No reports at all."

"Nothing?" Simon was surprised and disappointed. "Never mind. There was something I didn't tell you yesterday."

"Oh, really." It was not a question. Robbie's tone was sarcastic.

"After that useless constable left, I discovered an envelope hidden behind a metal sign in the alleyway. There were copies of BBC engineering documents in it and a coded message in German."

"Why the hell didn't you tell me yesterday?"

It was the response Simon expected. "It doesn't matter. I'm telling you now. That's what this dreadful man wanted. Very insistent he was. Then, all of a sudden, he seemed to change his mind. He put the murder weapon in my hand to put my fingerprints on it..."

"Very clever."

"Yes," continued Simon. "Evil. But clever. You've got to find him. But first, you need to get those documents from Miss Forster."

"What's so special about them?"

Simon rapidly described what was in the documents and read out Anna Forster's translation.

Robbie gave a low whistle. "Is this the truth, Simon?"

"I swear on my mother's life."

Robbie chuckled. "That doesn't mean much. I know you can barely tolerate her."

The man knew him too well.

"It's the truth, Robbie. Even I couldn't make up a story as fantastic as this. You've got to get those documents now. And you must warn Sandringham as quickly as possible. The king's going to be assassinated."

"I'll lose my job," Robbie replied. "If they find out that a wanted murderer told me a cock and bull story about a plot to murder the king. I need proof."

"Exactly. And if you get over to Miss Forster's you'll have all the proof you need."

There was silence at the end of the phone. Simon said nothing, waiting for Robbie to speak next.

"I can hear seagulls," Robbie said at last. "You're by the sea, aren't you? Where the hell are you, Simon?"

"Not in London," Simon replied. "That's all I can say. Look. If you won't do this, I'll get on to the editor at *The Chronicle* and tell him DI Mountjoy was tipped off about an assassination attempt on the king and refused—"

"All right," Robbie interrupted. "I must be bloody mad. Where can I contact you?"

"You can't," Simon replied. "I'll be in touch later. Let me give you Miss Forster's address."

20

Simon gazed through one of the small panes of glass on the side of the phone box. There were more people walking around on the promenade than when he had first arrived. Still no more than a handful, mainly elderly couples, braved the spattering of rain to get some fresh air. He looked up and down the road but there was no sign of Bill. The longer he stayed in this glass prison, the more exposed he felt. He gingerly touched the fake moustache. It felt insecure, as if it might peel off at any moment. His stomach rumbled to remind him he had forsaken breakfast that morning.

His next phone call was to Betty Richardson at the Home Office. He wanted to find out if she had any more information about the activities of Der Sturmabteilung in the British Isles. He picked up the receiver, pushed two pennies into the slot and called Betty's office.

Two small boys, no older than seven or eight, ran up to the phone box and banged on the door. Simon turned away to shield his face from them. He heard a woman's voice shouting outside.

"Eric! Douglas! Come back here and leave that poor man in peace."

Simon dared not look round to see what was happening. He feared the moustache might droop even further. A telephonist on the Home Office switchboard answered and Simon pushed the button to connect the call.

"I'd like to speak to Miss Betty Richardson."

"Who shall I say is calling?"

"Tell her it's March Hare."

"I beg your pardon?" the telephonist asked.

"My name is Hare," Simon repeated. "Mr March Hare. I'm a close friend of Miss Richardson."

"One minute please, caller."

March Hare was the name Betty had given Simon when they played together as children. One day he had put on one of her oversized hats. Betty had giggled and said that if she was the Mad Hatter then she was going to christen him Mr March Hare. On occasional drunken reunions she still used the name.

"You've got a nerve." Betty's booming voice rattled the earpiece. "Don't expect me to get you out of the mess you've got yourself into this time. I've read the papers this morning. My favours only extend so far, Simon."

"I'm not asking you to," he replied. "And don't believe everything you read in the papers."

"Especially when you've written it," Betty retorted. "Oh, I forgot. You're *respectable* now. Working for the BBC. What do your new employers think about you making front page news this morning?"

"I've no idea," Simon replied. The bulbous bonnet of a large grey car loomed in his peripheral vision. He cautiously looked out and saw the Bentley come to a halt a few yards away.

A man walked past holding a folded newspaper. Simon turned his face away from the windows. Was his photograph on the front page? The telephone box felt more and more like a goldfish bowl. It put Simon on display to anyone who walked by. Perhaps he should cut short the call with Betty.

"Why have you called me?" Betty asked.

"It doesn't matter," Simon replied. "I was going to ask if you'd had time to follow up what I told you about Der Sturmabteilung yesterday. But I'm sure you're busy right now—"

"As a matter of fact, I have," Betty interrupted. "You piqued my interest. My God." There was a pause and Betty took a sharp intake of breath. "That's not what this newspaper story is all about is it? I hope not, for your sake, Simon."

"I'm afraid it is, old thing."

The two boys banged on the sides of the phone box again and made Simon jump. He felt an urgent need to hang up and get back into the car with Bill as rapidly as possible.

"I really ought to go, Betty. Let's talk another time."

"Not so fast March Hare." Betty sniggered. "Goodness, it's years since I called you that. Takes me right back to those days in The Grange in Littlecote. Do you remember? We used to—"

"Betty, I don't have time."

"Of course." Betty coughed loudly. "Foolish of me. Listen. I'll be quick. You know the gist of what Der Sturmabteilung is about don't you?"

"Fascist group in Germany. Also called the brownshirts. Devout followers of that bugger Hitler. Run by another man with a ridiculous moustache called... Röhm, is it?"

"Very good," replied Betty. "You've got a good memory. Ernst Röhm. Very close friend of Hitler. Very close indeed, by all accounts, if you get my gist. But the brownshirts are more than a group. Did you know they've got over a million members? They're the troublemakers. Involved in street brawls. Stirring up the workers to strike. But they're much more than that. They want their chap Hitler to take over the reins in Germany. And if that happens, it'll be the end of the Weimar Republic."

"Is that such a bad thing?" Simon asked. "It's all a bit of a mess there from what I've heard."

"Yes, but at least it's a democracy," Betty replied. "Imperfect, yes. But if the fascists take over, it'll be a dictatorship."

"Ah, democracy," Simon replied. "Some have argued that democracy is simply the sleight of hand to make the preordained appear to be the will of the people."

"That's extremely cynical, Simon," Betty said sharply. "If you don't mind me saying. There are people in our government who are very concerned about what's happening in Germany. They fear it could lead to another war."

"Really? I thought the Great War put paid to that. Germany surely doesn't want another beating?"

"People have short memories, Simon. And the fascists have got a lot of friends over here. You've heard of that man Mosley, haven't you?"

Simon recalled the demonstration he and Robbie had seen in Whitehall the day before. "He's running the new British Union of Fascists, isn't he? I saw their particular brand of thuggery only yesterday."

"Absolutely. That's the blighters." Betty's voice rose with her enthusiasm. "Our secret services have been tracking their meetings with Germany's brownshirts. And what's more, there are people in very high places who want to see them succeed. What if I was to tell you—?"

Someone banged on the side of the telephone box. Simon looked out to see the old man he had been speaking to standing outside once more. He held a newspaper in his hand and shouted something angrily.

"I've got to go, Betty old thing," Simon said.

"But, Simon—"

The old man tugged the door open.

"I knew I'd seen you somewhere before," he shouted and waved the newspaper at Simon. "It's you, isn't it? You're him."

Simon slammed the telephone receiver back in its cradle, pushed the man aside and ran back to the Bentley.

"Hey!" shouted the man. "I haven't finished with you."

But Simon had already reached the car, and was relieved to find Bill had the engine running. He wrenched open the passenger door, clambered in, and slammed the door shut behind him.

"What's going on?" Bill asked.

"Drive," Simon commanded. "I've been spotted."

The tyres screeched on the damp road and the car shot forward. Bill spun the steering wheel and Simon clung onto the door handle as they skidded up a side street. Bill reached behind her and threw a newspaper into Simon's lap.

"I'm not surprised you've been spotted," she said. "You're almost front-page news."

Simon unfolded the crumpled copy of *The Daily Mirror*.

"Page three, my darling." Bill threw the car down a side street and immediately right onto a road leading away from the sea front. Simon was tossed from side to side as the car slipped across the wet roads.

"How many times must I ask you to slow down?" he shouted above the roar of the engine. "You're only drawing attention to us."

Bill snorted her annoyance but did as Simon asked,

possibly because a horse-drawn milk cart pulled out in front of them from a side street.

"You've got no sense of fun," she grumbled. "First opportunity I've had to drive a motorcar in almost a year. I get to drive two in two days and you behave like a hysterical nun." She patted the newspaper. "Very fetching photograph, darling. They must have got it off *The Chronicle*."

"Traitors," Simon said. "Is there no honour left in Fleet Street?"

He opened the newspaper to page three and his black and white face stared out at him from the bottom of the page. The headline above it was: *From Sleuth to Suspect*.

"Is that the best they could come up with?"

Bill glanced across. "What would you prefer? Murderer at the Microphone? Killer Pansy?"

"Don't," Simon said sharply. "God help me if someone spills the beans to them about that particular aspect of my private life. Who knows who might speak out? I'm fair game as far as they're concerned."

"I think that's the least of your worries," Bill replied. "I would concentrate on avoiding the gallows for the moment. If you manage that, think of it as an achievement."

"But if the papers expose me as—other—I'll never get any work again."

"Nonsense," Bill replied. "Everybody knows about dear Joe Ackerley, but he broadcasts quite happily on the BBC."

"Yes, but he's not got his face plastered across all the newspapers." Simon dropped the newspaper into the footwell of the car. "It's so unfair. Perhaps I should go back to Berlin. They're so much more accepting there."

"Not according to my friend Eva. Why do you think she moved from Germany to Luxembourg? She knows something's coming. The net's tightening on us yet again."

Simon leaned back in his seat and watched the neat little rows of houses on the outskirts of Hythe give way to the countryside once more. What was he going to do? On reflection, the journey had been foolhardy. Even wearing a disguise, he had been spotted. The old man at the phone box was very likely to report him to the police, and it would only be a matter of time before they came knocking on the door of Goldenhurst. Robbie had guessed Simon was near the sea because of the cries of seagulls in the background. The police would not take long to put the two pieces of information together.

The car was also a liability. He was sure Noël Coward's Bentley was well-known in the area. If the old man reported the number plate to the police, it was further evidence to help them come looking. This morning it had seemed such a good idea not to use Patsy's sports car, in case the London police had put out a report about it to other forces across the country. He and Bill had no more than a few hours of safety left at Goldenhurst.

"We're going to have to move on," he said to her.

"I was thinking the same thing," she replied. "But we're running out of options."

"Maybe it's finally time for me to slip across to France and make my way to Berlin," Simon said. "I could be there in a couple of days." He shook his head. "But then the police will arrest you for being an accomplice to a suspected murderer. I can't leave you on your own to face that."

Bill patted his knee. "You're very sweet, dear boy. But I'm all grown-up now. Even though you think of me as a weak and feeble woman."

"I didn't say that," Simon protested. "Honestly, Bill. Are you saying that I can never say the right thing?"

There was no answer from Bill.

"I'll take that as a 'no'," Simon said crossly.

"Don't sulk, darling," Bill said. "I didn't answer your silly question because I'm thinking. Germany's not a good idea. If you want to clear your name, you're better off staying here. What did your chum Detective Inspector Mountjoy say to you?"

"I thought Robbie was going to give up on me to start with," Simon replied. "But I persuaded him to go round to Anna's and pick up the documents."

"Good."

"Yes. But he refused to alert Sandringham about the assassination attempt. Said he needed evidence."

"Which he'll get when he picks up those documents," Bill replied. "Still. It doesn't help you to clear your name. We need to find that beastly man who damn near killed you. Is there nothing else about him you can remember?"

Simon closed his eyes and tried to picture the moment the man had bent down to look at him. His face had been in silhouette, lit from behind by the lamp in the corner of the sitting-room. It was impossible to determine his features. But the man had turned his head, and something in his eye had glinted as it caught the light.

"A monocle." Simon opened his eyes and turned to Bill triumphantly. "He was wearing a monocle. I'm certain of it. If only I'd remembered when I was talking to Robbie."

"No matter," Bill said. "I'll call Anna when we get back and she can pass on the description to him. That's if he's not been and gone already."

The Bentley accelerated along the narrow country lane. Tall hedges made it impossible to see into the fields on either side, and the road twisted and turned. Bill threw the car into a blind corner with no attempt to slow down. Simon closed his eyes and prayed another vehicle was not headed towards them around the bend. The road straightened and the car slowed. Simon cautiously reopened his eyes to see the gates to Goldenhurst appear up ahead.

"Do you know you're the most frightful passenger, Simon Sampson?" Bill swung the Bentley through the gateway and into the wide gravel driveway in front of the house. "It looked like you were going to wrench that door handle from its fastenings just now."

"That's because I thought I was about to die." Simon felt the side of his neck. It was stiffening with tension from the short journey. "Can you let me out now?"

"Not yet."

The Bentley rolled up the drive, around the side of the house, and stopped outside a large wooden barn.

"Hop out, my darling," Bill said. "We need to do what we can to hide the Bentley in here. If the police come visiting, at least we'll make it difficult for them to find the car."

"And me?" Simon asked.

"Ah," Bill replied. "I've had a thought about that."

21

The two large wooden doors of the barn hung open, revealing a cavernous parking area. There was ample space to park the Bentley. Simon walked up to the entrance and peered into the gloomy interior. In the far corner was a pile of ruby red fabric adorned with gold trim.

"I say," he called back to Bill. "I think I see some theatre curtains back there. Where did they come from?"

Bill climbed out of the Bentley and joined him at the entrance to the barn.

"Another of Noël's impulsive ideas," she said. "He was going to build a little theatre here at Goldenhurst. I don't think he even managed to get any plans drawn up. The idea came to him when he rescued the curtains from the Albery when they were refurbishing."

"Let's use them to cover Patsy's car and the Bentley," Simon suggested. "If the police come knocking, we can claim they've been in mothballs all winter while Noël's in New York."

"Good idea," Bill replied. "But it's going to be me who tells them that, not you. You'll be hidden somewhere safe. Mind out the way. I'm going to drive the Bentley in."

She went back to the car, revved the engine, and inched it forward behind Simon, who walked inside the barn. His eyes became more accustomed to the dark interior and he could see, propped up against the back wall, a very shiny motorcycle with sidecar. He walked over to examine the machine. It was virtually unused, and in beautiful condition.

The Bentley came to a halt behind him and Bill switched off the engine.

"I never thought of Noël Coward as a motorcycle kind of chap," Simon said.

"He's not." Bill got out of the car and closed the door. "He'll have bought it for one of his young men. Possibly young Alan Webb, who he's been seeing for a while. Who knows? There've been so many others."

"Good for Noël," Simon replied. "To be so famous, and yet have a private life that's worth living." He smoothed his hand lovingly over the curves of the petrol tank.

Bill tutted. "Stop caressing it like some young man's buttock and give me a hand with the curtains." She walked over to the drapes and tugged at them. "These are damned heavy. I'm not sure we're going to be able to move them."

"Out of my way, weak and feeble woman." Simon reiterated the words Bill used to chide him with during the car journey, and smiled as she sniffed disapprovingly. He walked over to the pile of cloth, grabbed the curtain resting on top of the pile, and unfolded it onto the floor.

"It's better if we open it out first," he said. "Give me a hand and take that end. Once we've done this, it'll be easier to drag it over the Bentley."

Bill sniffed again, but did as he suggested. Within ten

minutes both the Bentley and Patsy's sports car were wrapped in a rich swathe of maroon and gold.

Bill lit a cigarette and leaned against the doorpost. "Having them all wrapped up like that isn't going to help us if we need to make a quick getaway."

"We can always use the motorcycle," Simon suggested.

"You're not getting me on that thing for all the gin in Bloomsbury." Bill turned towards the house. "I'm going inside to fix us a couple of drinks and give Anna a call."

"Drinks? We haven't had breakfast yet."

"If you remember, you promised to make it." Bill gave him a smile that was anything but a smile. "Close the doors, will you my dear. And don't take all day. I'm starving."

She walked back across the drive towards the house. Simon struggled to close the barn doors, which creaked on their hinges as if they were about to disintegrate. After much pushing and shoving he coaxed them shut, and slotted a rusty metal bar into two U-shaped hasps that would keep them from falling open again.

When he got back to the house, Bill was already in the sitting room with a decanter of gin in her hand.

"Fetch the ice from the kitchen, will you darling?" she asked. "I'm making a couple of Gin Fizzes for us."

"Perfect." Simon headed for the kitchen. "What were you saying about a hiding place for me?" he called. "Is there some kind of priest hole in this ancient house?"

"Almost as good," Bill shouted in response. "I'll show you when you come in here."

Simon collected a tray of ice from the icebox and returned to the sitting-room. Bill stood to one side of the enormous fireplace, leaning against the mantelpiece with an electric torch in her hand. She pointed to two glasses on the cocktail table.

"The drinks are on there. Shove the ice in, will you?"

Simon emptied the tray of ice into a black and silver ice-bucket and added a few cubes to both glasses. He carried them over to Bill and handed one to her.

"Cheers, my dear," he said. "Good choice. So refreshing after you've been hounded from the Hythe seafront by an old man armed with a newspaper. Now. What have you got to show me?"

Bill pointed to the fireplace opening. "Stick your head in there and take a look to the left."

"What am I looking for?" he asked. "Father Christmas?"

Simon took the torch from Bill, switched it on, and crouched down to peer into the darkness of the chimney. He flashed the light from side to side and it revealed a soot-blackened seat built into the side of the fireplace behind the mantel. It was a cramped, dirty space, but there was probably enough room for a man to hide. Simon pulled his head back from the opening, stood, and checked his face in the mirror above the fireplace for soot smuts.

"What on earth's that doing there?" he asked.

Bill lit a cigarette and shrugged.

"No one knows. Noël threw a summer party here two years ago and we all ended up very drunk playing hide and seek of all things. Dear little Joyce Carey found it. She was so tipsy she forgot about the soot. Looked a frightful sight when she finally emerged. Noël was most unhappy about the soot stains on the hearthrug. But he forgave her of course. She's such a darling."

Simon switched off the torch and put it on the mantelpiece. "I suppose it's better than nothing. As long as no one lights the fire."

Bill carried her drink across to the telephone. "Fugitives

can't be choosers," she said, and dialled a number. "Let's see if your Scotland Yard chum has arrived at Anna's yet."

Simon wandered over to the window and stared at the rain drizzling down on a small copse of conifers on the far side of the lawn. Even in the gloom of winter the garden at Goldenhurst was a rich, verdant green. If he had to be a fugitive, this was not a bad place to retreat to.

"Simon." Bill's voice interrupted his daydreaming. He turned to see her with her hand over the telephone mouthpiece. "No slacking. You should be in the kitchen making that breakfast you promised us." She glanced at the clock. "Or should I say brunch?"

"Slave driver." Simon walked out of the sitting-room to return to the kitchen. He put his drink down on the farmhouse table next to a basket of provisions left by the local farmer. It was generously filled. As well as bread and eggs, there was milk, butter, sugar and a packet of tea. When Simon took out the loaf of bread, he found a half a dozen sausages wrapped in a butcher's paper. It would be a magnificent brunch.

"Your farmer chap has left us a veritable feast," he called out to Bill.

"He's a damn fine chap." Bill appeared in the kitchen doorway. "I'll take some money over to him in a while. Do you need a hand?"

"I thought you were calling Anna," Simon replied.

"There's no answer." Bill picked up the loaf of bread, ripped off a hunk, and waved it at Simon. "I'm starving." She took a bite from the bread and began chewing. "You know, it's very strange."

"Why strange?" Simon opened several cupboard doors looking for a frying pan. "We haven't eaten since yesterday evening."

"What are you looking for?" Bill crossed the kitchen to stand at his side. "I mean, it's strange there's no answer."

"Perhaps Robbie's arrived and they're talking," Simon suggested. "Where does Noël keep his frying pans?"

"In there." Bill pointed at a cupboard next to the gas cooker. "But Anna lives in a boarding house. It's in Pimlico. The telephone's in the hallway. There's usually someone around to answer it."

"It is the Friday before Christmas." Simon opened the cupboard door. He pulled out an enormous frying pan and put it on the stove. "Perhaps they're all out at the shops getting their Christmas gooses."

"Geese," Bill corrected.

The phone rang.

"There you are." Simon went back to the table and picked up the eggs and butter. "That's probably her now. Answer it will you, my love? I'm being creative in the kitchen. Fried or scrambled?"

"Scrambled. And don't make too much mess." Bill turned and headed back to the sitting-room. A few moments later she returned.

"It's for you," she said. "Cameron."

"Already?" Simon nearly dropped the frying pan. "I thought he'd be hours."

"Apparently the royal family likes to leave at the crack of dawn when they're traveling," Bill replied. "Hurry up. He says he hasn't got much time."

"Take over, will you?" Simon put the frying pan back on the stove and pointed to an enamel bowl on the table. "I've beaten the eggs and the butter's melting in the pan. You need to slice the bread for the—"

"Just leave," Bill gently pushed him to one side. "Go and talk to your young man. He's clearly pining for you."

"And me for him."

Simon walked into the sitting-room and picked up the telephone receiver.

"Cameron? Is everything all right?"

"Aye, it is." Cameron's strong Highland voice was loud and clear in the earpiece. "But I saw the newspaper. They've got a picture of ye. What are ye goin' tae do?"

"Don't worry about me," Simon replied. "I've got a good friend who's high up at Scotland Yard. He's going to help me sort this out." Even as he said it, Simon wondered how much he could trust Robbie to clear him of a charge of murder. "Where are you?"

"I'm in the Lodge House at the entrance to the estate," Cameron replied. The Lodge Keeper ha' kindly let me use the telephone tae call ma aged grandfather, who I havnae seen since I left Scotland."

"And have you called him?"

"Did ye nae get it?" Cameron chuckled and lowered his voice. "It's you. I cannae go into the village for a telephone box. It's too far. So, I spun a little white lie."

"Are you sure it's safe?" Simon was concerned Cameron would be overheard.

"Dougal's gone out tae feed the dogs. He'll be gone a wee while, and there's no one else here."

"Dougal?"

"Aye, Dougal McAllister," Cameron replied. "He's the lodge-keeper."

"Can you give me the number?"

Cameron hesitated. "I nae think tha's such a good idea. Ye cannae expect Dougal tae come lookin' for me."

"It's just for emergencies," Simon replied. The opportunity to have a phone number at the Royal estate in Sandringham was too good an opportunity to miss.

"Well, all right then." Cameron still sounded doubtful. "It's Dersingham 219. But dinnae use it unless ye ha' tae."

Simon noted the number down on a scrap of paper. "I won't," he said. "What's it like there?"

"The duke an' the Prince o' Wales ha' gone for a wee walk. They've gi'n me an hour tae ma sel'. Tha's why I'm mekkin' this call."

"What's the accommodation like?" Simon asked. "You said you were staying in the stable block."

Cameron laughed. "It's a ver' swanky stable block. I've got my own bedroom wi' a sitting-room as well. There's a big bathroom, which is just as well. As well as the staff, an extra gentleman's arrived. The Prince o' Wales says he's tae take care o' the duke's security. He wasnae expected. The Head of the Household is ver' upset."

"Is he from Germany like the duke?" Simon asked.

"Nae," Cameron replied. "He's English. Ver' English. Old-fashioned. Wears these big lace-up boots and a monocle."

22

"Are ye still there?" Cameron asked.

Simon realised he had been silent for several seconds. He needed to warn Cameron. "He's the man who killed Miss Stockwell," Simon replied. "The one who roughed me up."

"Are ye sure?"

"Pretty well certain. The monocle. Those boots. I can't believe there are many other men fitting that description wandering around."

"Och, I dinnae know," Cameron said. "These nobility types wear all sorts."

"What's his name?" Simon asked.

"They introduced him tae me as Admiral Newman. But the duke calls him Freddie."

"He's dangerous. Very dangerous indeed." Simon decided it was time to tell Cameron about the message Anna had decoded.

"We've managed to decode part of the German text in that —" Simon began. But Cameron interrupted him.

"I can see Dougal comin'" he said. "I've got tae go."

The line went dead.

Simon stared at the receiver for several seconds before replacing it in its cradle. He worried for Cameron. In twenty-four hours, probably less, there would be an attempt on the life of the king. He might be shot, poisoned, or suffocated while he slept. But if Cameron got in the way, even unwittingly, his life might be in danger too. Simon wandered back into the kitchen.

Bill looked up from the stove. "It's not good news, is it?"

Simon shook his head. "That blighter who was in my apartment is there. He's posing as the duke's security man. Says his name's Admiral Freddie Newman."

"'Admiral'?" Bill repeated. "Navy chap, then." She took the frying pan off the stove and unloaded its contents onto two plates on the table. "But you don't think he is who he says he is, do you?"

Simon shrugged. "What's he doing wrapped up in a plot against the king? It's treason."

"What if he's a German, like the duke? But masquerading as an Englishman."

Simon shook his head. "I know I was pretty befuddled when I was knocked out. But I'm pretty good at placing accents. I didn't get any hint of foreign in the way he spoke. Gloucestershire or Wiltshire I'd say."

Bill dropped the frying pan into the sink and pulled two sets of cutlery from a drawer.

"Breakfast is served," she announced. "You don't mind eating in here, do you? Only I don't want to mess up the dining room if we don't have to."

"I'm ravenous." Simon pulled out a chair and sat at the kitchen table. "I'll eat on the roof if I have to."

"Tuck in." Bill sat opposite him. "You know there's an easy way to check if he's bona fide or not."

Simon put a large piece of sausage in his mouth. "How?"

"Don't talk with your mouth full," Bill chided. "It's revolting. It's very simple. If he's an admiral he'll be in *Who's Who*. We just need to look him up."

Simon swallowed the piece of sausage before he next spoke. "Are you suggesting we take another jaunt down to Hythe and pop into the local library? Haven't we risked enough exposure for one day?"

"Of course not." Bill set down her knife and fork, stood, and walked to the kitchen door. "Noël always has a copy of *Who's Who*. He corresponds with them semi-regularly about the inaccuracy of their entry for him. I'll go and get it."

She disappeared down the corridor and headed for the library. Simon continued with his breakfast. It was very good, and fried bread was one of his favourites.

"Simon!" Bill shouted down the corridor. A moment later she reappeared in the kitchen doorway. "There's a police car coming up the drive. Thank God I saw it. You've got to hide. Now."

Simon shot to his feet and his chair fell back. He picked up his near empty plate, carried it to the kitchen dresser and hid it in the cupboard underneath.

"Don't worry about that," Bill said. "I'll do a quick scout round. Have you left anything of yours in the hallway or sitting room?"

"There's my coat and hat in the hallway," Simon replied. "But I don't think there's anything in the sitting-room."

"I'll check. Now go and hide. You know where."

Simon shook his head. "I'm damned if I'm messing up a perfectly good pair of trousers scrabbling around in that chimney. I'll go upstairs."

"But what if the police want to search up there?"

Simon smiled. "You've brazened it out in far tougher

circumstances than this, my darling. I'm sure you'll send them away with a song in their hearts."

There was a pounding on the front door. Simon crossed to the hallway and headed for the staircase while Bill went into the sitting room. Directly in front of him at the top of the stairs was the spare room he had been sleeping in. He looked in through the doorway. The bed was made and he could see no personal possessions to betray his recent occupancy.

To his right at the far end of the landing was the closed door to Noël Coward's room. It was a better place to hide. It was above the kitchen, and if Bill did allow the police into the house, she was most likely to show them in there. If they insisted on coming upstairs, Simon was confident she would find a way to intimidate them and prevent them from searching the master's room.

There was another knock at the front door.

"I'm coming," Bill called. "Let me finish getting my clothes on, darlings."

Simon smiled and hastened down the landing. Bill could always be relied upon to play a dramatic role to the full. He opened the bedroom door, stepped in, and closed it behind him without a sound.

It was immediately obvious why Noël Coward had chosen this room for his bedroom. It was more than twice the size of the one Simon had slept in. There was a large, diamond-paned window revealing the beauty of the Kent countryside. Simon crossed to the enormous bed that dominated the room. A counterpane hung down on either side, almost to the floor. Simon got onto his knees and lifted the cover to peer under the bed. There was ample space for him to hide. He crawled underneath, made sure the counterpane had fallen back into place, and made himself as comfortable as possible.

He pressed his ear to the floorboards to try to catch Bill's conversation with the police.

The wrought iron latch on the front door rattled and the door creaked open.

"Good afternoon, officers." Bill's voice was loud and imperious. "I hope there's a good reason for you disturbing the peace of my first day off in months."

A man responded. His voice was subdued and Simon found it difficult to hear everything he said.

"Good afternoon, ma'am. I'm sorry....you. My name is Detective Sergeant ... and this is Constable ... Do you own a....motorcar, registration....?"

"I do not," Bill replied. "But Mr Coward does. This is his house you know."

"Yes, I ... We've had reports...." Simon pressed his ear closer to the floorboard as he tried in vain to hear the policeman's words.

"Ridiculous." There was no mistaking the forcefulness of Bill's response. "The cars have been under wraps all winter since Mr Coward's been out of the country. You can go and look for yourself if you want."

The police officer appeared to be lowering his voice, even as Bill raised the volume of hers. If it was his attempt to calm her righteous indignation, it was not succeeding. His next response was completely inaudible.

"A man?" Bill laughed. "I wish. No, officer. I'm all alone here. You're welcome to come in and check if you like. But don't take all day. I was about to go out for a walk. If you waste any more of my time the daylight will have gone."

Good move Bill, thought Simon. *Call their bluff and hope you intimidate them enough to send them on their way.*

It failed.

"Very well," Bill said. "But your constable can wait out here. I'm not having two sets of muddy feet on Noël's floors."

There was the sound of footsteps in the hallway and the slam of the front door. Simon's guess about where Bill would take the police officer was wrong. He heard the sitting room door close and now the voices of both Bill and the detective were impossible to hear. He thought about creeping out to the landing to listen, but dismissed the idea immediately as an unnecessary risk.

Simon sighed and turned his head with difficulty in the cramped space to relieve the tension in his neck. He rolled onto his back to stretch out. His lower arm connected with a heavy metal object on the far side of the bed. He twisted his hand around to explore it with his fingers.

It was a gun, quite small, and looked like a service revolver, although Simon was no expert on guns. Robbie had shown him a few guns during previous visits to Scotland Yard, and he knew how to check if they were loaded or not. He picked up the weapon lying beside him and examined it. He flipped open the barrel and saw five bullets loaded and ready to fire. He placed the gun back on the floor carefully to avoid making any noise.

What was Noël Coward doing with a gun under his bed? Did he keep it in the unlikely event that burglars might break into this isolated house? Possibly. Was it actually his? If not, whose was it? Simon would ask Bill when he managed to get out from his uncomfortable hiding place.

His musings were cut short by the sound of Bill's voice. At first Simon thought she had come out of the sitting room. But then he realised she was talking on the telephone, and must have raised her voice because it was a bad line. Simon pressed his ear to the floor once more.

"He is," she said. "No, he doesn't know. Should I tell him?"

There was a pause.

"Very well. Look. This detective wants to speak to someone other than a mere woman like me. Can't you put him in the picture? Or get him to go away. It will make life a great deal simpler."

There was another pause, followed by the indistinct voice of the police officer. After several minutes, the door of the sitting room opened, Simon heard footsteps in the hallway, and the front door creaked open.

"Good day, officer," Bill said. "What a shame you've had a wasted journey."

"Merry Christmas, ma'am," the detective replied.

The front door slammed shut. Simon lay on his back in the darkness, trying to understand what he had just heard. Who was Bill talking to on the telephone? How had she managed to get the police officers to leave so promptly after the call? He reached for the revolver beside him, but an instinct made him decide to leave it where it was. There was something not right, and for the moment he was not sure what it was.

"Simon?" Bill called from the foot of the stairs. "They're gone. You can come out now."

Simon heard the creak of the first few steps of the wooden staircase. Bill was coming upstairs. It was better she remained unaware he had hidden in Noël's room. Simon hauled himself out from underneath the bed, crossed to the bedroom door and opened it. He stepped out onto the landing, closed the door quietly behind him, and hurried along the narrow corridor. He reached the guest room where he had slept and rested his hand on the door knob. Below him, Bill appeared on the half-landing at the bend in the staircase and stopped.

"They won't be coming back," she said. "I've made sure of that."

"Who were you on the phone to?" Simon asked.

"Phone?"

"Just now. While you were in the sitting room. You called somebody and got them to speak to the detective. Who was it?"

Bill dismissed his question with a wave of her hand. She turned on the half-landing and went back downstairs.

"Come down and see if your breakfast is still edible," she called behind her. "I'll make some coffee for us both."

23

The eggs were cold when Simon retrieved his plate from the kitchen dresser. And so was the last remaining sausage. He dutifully chewed through the detritus of the spoiled breakfast, as though finishing a plate of school dinner to avoid a beating from the refectory master. His throat felt tight and he swallowed with difficulty.

"Well?" he asked.

"Well, what?" Bill had her back to him at the sink. She filled the kettle. "I'm not sure there's any more coffee after all that. I think I had the last of it—"

"Bill," Simon interrupted. He was disconcerted by her failure to answer his question. "Who did you call?"

Bill slammed the kettle down on the drainer and turned to face him.

"If you must know, I just did you a favour, Simon Sampson." She took a cigarette from a packet that rested on the plate warmer above the stove and lit it with a match. "And I may have jeopardised my friendship with Noël as a result."

She put the cigarette to her lips, inhaled deeply, and blew out an enormous smoke ring. "I was getting nowhere with that damned detective. So I called the Chief Constable. I know him because Noël invited the man to one of his parties here last year. He says it's always good to keep in with the local bigwigs. We were introduced and, bizarrely, got on rather well. He was actually flirting with me. Even though his ghastly wife was standing not ten feet away at the time."

Bill shoved the cigarette in the corner of her mouth, picked up the kettle, and turned to fill it from the tap. "Happy now?"

It was plausible, except Simon remembered something from the conversation he had partially heard through the floorboards that failed to fit with the explanation.

"Why did you say, 'should I tell him?'" Simon asked. "Tell who what?"

There was a small explosion under the kettle as Bill lit the gas.

"What is all this, Simon? Don't you trust me all of a sudden?" She turned to face him with a furious look on her face. "I've just saved your skin. Again. And yet you're questioning me like Tomás de Torquemada in fifteenth-century Spain."

She took the cigarette from the corner of her mouth and pointed it at him. "You know what your problem is? You don't know you're born half the time. After everything I've done for you. Why on earth do I bother?"

"Then don't," Simon snapped. "Not if you're going to hold it against me like some mounting debt that has to be repaid."

He picked up his plate, carried it over to a bin in the corner of the kitchen, and scraped at its congealed contents with a force that threatened to remove the glaze.

"I think it was a mistake to come here anyway," he continued. "I feel so powerless. There's a threat to the king's life, and I'm doing damn all about it. I should be in Norfolk right now."

"Oh, really." Bill stubbed out her cigarette in the sink. She seemed to push so hard Simon feared she would drill a hole in the porcelain. "And what would happen if you bowled up there? You, a wanted murderer? You'd be arrested before you had time to open your mouth."

"And so I meekly sit here and wait to read of the king's assassination in the newspapers?" Simon took his plate over to the sink and stood face-to-face with Bill. "Or maybe I should tune in to listen to your chum on Radio Luxembourg announce it. And then I can ring Robbie and say, I told you so."

"Oh, for God's sake." Bill snatched the plate from Simon's hand, dropped it into the sink, and turned on the tap. Water sprayed everywhere and she struggled to turn it off again. "Now look what you made me do."

"You still haven't answered my question." Simon was determined to stop Bill deflecting him. He suspected her righteous anger was fake. "Who did you have to tell what?"

"Noël." Bill reached for another cigarette and lit it. She pointed to the sink. "Wash that plate, will you? I need to sit down."

She walked over to the table, dropped into one of the chairs, and rested her arm on the back of it. "It was Noël. Erik's not so good. The Chief Constable told me. He happened to speak to Arthur this morning and that's how he found out. I asked if he wanted me to tell Noël, and he said it was up to Arthur."

She put the cigarette to her mouth, inhaled, and blew the smoke out through her nostrils. "He's right of course. But I feel terrible. Fortunately, Noël's highly unlikely to call here. He's so tied up with the preview of *Design for Living.* It's opening in some God-awful place called Cleveland just after the new year. I won't be forced into the difficult position of talking to him while at the same time withholding bad news about his brother."

Her head twitched and she gave him a defiant look. "Happy now?"

A piece of congealed egg had become welded to Simon's breakfast plate as though part of the glaze. He turned back to the sink and scrubbed the plate hard with the dishcloth. Water splashed and the cuffs of his shirt became soaked.

He hated these arguments with Bill. She always seemed to emerge the innocent victim and he the needless attacker. Of course her explanation made sense. But why had she not told him straight away? After all, Bill was a forthright person. On occasions her directness threatened to intimidate him. But this time it felt as if he had to force the explanation from her.

The yellow stain of the egg began to dissolve. Simon gave the plate one last triumphant wipe and placed it on the drainer. Perhaps the strain of the last twenty-four hours was distorting his view on events, twisting them out of proportion. He dried his hands on a towel and stared out of the window. The rain had stopped and there was a hint of blue sky between the grey clouds.

"Am I happy?" he asked. "A man wanted for murder, with the knowledge that the king's in danger and being absolutely bloody powerless to do anything about it?" He walked over to the kitchen door. "I'm blissful, my darling." He looked back at Bill. "I'll go for a little walk. I need some fresh air."

Drops of rain greeted Simon when he stepped outside. The patch of blue sky he had seen from the kitchen window had betrayed him. The rain was light, but in his haste to leave the house Simon had forgotten his hat. He thought about going back to retrieve it but rejected the notion as a humiliating retreat. Was he being childish? Probably. But the drizzle would cool his hot head and give him a chance to restore a sense of rationality.

Without thinking much where he was going, he followed the drive around to the back of Goldenhurst and arrived at the barn where they had hidden the cars. Dark clouds erased the last remaining patch of blue and the raindrops grew larger and more persistent. It was not a good time to leave the shelter of the house. Simon felt cold, wet and miserable.

It was easy to lift away the metal bar that secured the barn doors. But the doors themselves were stiff and it took Simon several minutes to coax one of them open just far enough for him to slip inside. A nesting pigeon flapped its wings above his head and startled him. He pushed the door open farther to allow more of the limited daylight to illuminate the inside of the barn. The flash of a reflection from somewhere near the back wall caught Simon's eye.

It was the motorcycle. Perhaps it was the reason something in Simon's subconscious had drawn him to the barn. His passion for motorcycles had begun when he was sixteen when his uncle bought him a Trusty Triumph model H. It was a favourite of dispatch riders in the Great War. A reliable machine, apart from its tendency to leak oil. He had not ridden it for over a year. The sight of the beautiful Norton bike in Noël Coward's barn had rekindled his excitement. An idea came into his head.

He was about to venture farther when he heard Bill shout

his name from the house. He poked his head out into the rain.

"Bill?" he called. "Is that you? I'm in the barn."

There was no reply. The rain was much heavier and Simon quickly pulled his head back under cover. He heard the squelch of feet on the mud of the driveway and a moment later Bill appeared, running towards him. She was drenched by the sudden downpour and Simon stood aside to let her into the shelter of the barn. To his astonishment, she wrapped her arms around him and hugged him tight. She was shaking, and not just from the cold. Her shoulders heaved and she let out a cry of anguish.

"Anna's dead."

The brandy was very good and tasted expensive. Nevertheless Simon had no qualms about pouring a generous measure for both Bill and himself. This was an emergency and the brandy was medicinal. Bill cupped her hands around the bowl of the glass. Her face was ashen and she suddenly looked twenty years older. She had pulled her armchair next to the cast iron radiator in the corner of the living room and sat huddled in a strange, upright foetal position. Simon had never seen her so defeated before. He moved a footstool to sit at her side.

"Who was it you spoke to?" he asked.

Bill took a sip of brandy. "It was her landlady in the boarding house. They went looking for Anna when your friend Robbie and his cohort arrived to collect the documents. She was—"

Her voice broke and she shuddered. "She was on the bed. She'd been strangled. Her room's in the basement. They must have got in through the window."

"Were the police still there when you called?"

"They'd just left." Bill wiped her eyes and took another drink. "I feel so responsible."

Simon clumsily put his arm around her shoulder. "Come on old thing. You mustn't think that."

"But I am." Bill's response was swift and vehement. "Once Admiral Freddie Newman murdered your Miss Stockwell and attacked you, it was only a matter of time before he tracked down Anna. I should have thought of that. Why didn't I take the documents away from her? It's my fault."

"It can't have been him," Simon replied. "He's at Sandringham today."

"Whoever." Even when she was upset, Bill was not in the mood for being corrected. "Someone must have broken in, taken the documents and killed Anna."

"I don't see how they knew she had the documents," Simon replied.

"It's because I know Anna." Bill's voice was a monotone.

"Yes, but you know lots of people."

Bill looked up at him. Her eyes were red and puffy. "Don't be so dense, Simon. I mean I *know* her. Surely you realised that?"

"Oh, God."

Of course Bill knew Anna. She knew her in the Sapphic sense. He thought back to the day when Anna had arrived in Bill's office to talk about the coded document. Bill had been like an excitable child.

"Why didn't you tell me? How long have you—"

"Over a year." Bill sighed. "I was going to tell you. But somehow, I didn't. It's an odd thing."

"What is?"

Bill straightened up and turned to him. The colour had returned to her face and she was more composed.

"When you're *other*, you have to be so secretive. No one must know. And in the end, that becomes part of the thrill of the relationship. Don't you find? It's like you're back at school and it's a delicious secret. And you can't quite believe it's real. That you can be so fortunate. And you don't want to tell anyone, because you're terrified it will end. And that by telling someone you might somehow make it end. And so you keep it a secret. A wonderful, magical, secret. How humdrum it must be for normal people who have to announce their engagements in *The Times*."

Simon knew exactly what she meant. Ever since his innocent friendship with Robbie at school had gone so wrong, secrecy had become second nature to him, even with close friends. On reflection, it was no surprise Bill had kept her relationship with Anna a secret. It was easier that way.

"Do you want a top-up?" Simon reached for Bill's half empty glass, but she held onto it.

"No thank you, my darling. I need a clear head." She patted his arm and stood. "Thanks for listening. I'm sorry to make such an awful fuss."

"Bill." Simon struggled to his feet with difficulty from the footstool. "Anna's just been murdered. You've got every right to make a fuss."

"Do you think so?" Bill drained the remaining brandy from her glass. "Anna and I had something special. Very special. But as far as almost everyone else in this benighted country is concerned, it doesn't exist. It's impossible for two women to—"

She stopped. It was as though she was unable to complete her sentence.

"Be in love?" Simon finished it for her. "I know. But you were. And that's why you've got every reason to make a fuss. At least with me."

“Thank you.” Bill kissed him on the cheek. “You’re a dear. Infuriatingly dense sometimes, but a dear all the same.”

She crossed the room to a large oak bookcase and scanned the shelves.

“What are you doing?” Simon asked.

Bill pulled a large red-bound book from the shelves and held it out for him to see.

“I’m working. We need to look up that admiral in *Who’s Who*.”

24

There was a surprising chirpiness to Bill's manner as she carried the book over to a table and began to flick through its pages. Despite the devastating news she had received about Anna, it had taken her little more than half an hour to recover from the shock. Simon was full of admiration for her steeliness. A lesser woman, correction, a lesser *person* might have chosen to prolong their period of mourning. But not Bill.

Simon had never thought much about women and their affairs of the heart. He presumed they were like men's, only softer in some way. It was clear Bill was very fond of Anna. Perhaps in the same way he felt about Cameron. His desire for Cameron was not something to be talked about in public. It was illegal. Even if he wrote a love letter to Cameron and it was discovered they could both end up in prison.

Whether or not Bill and Anna had actually been *in love* was a whole other question. Of course, people in general considered it impossible for a woman to love another woman. Not in the conventional sense at least. Sapphic love was not a topic of conversation for polite society. In the previous decade the government had considered introducing new laws as draconian as the ones that outlawed people like Simon. But some law makers feared that such a move might encourage otherwise normal women to follow the Sapphic path and the idea was dropped.

Simon was curious about Bill's feelings for women and wanted to ask her more. If only she was the kind of person with whom he could have a decent conversation about these things. She could enlighten him, and perhaps help him understand his own feelings better. But he was certain if he was to broach the subject, she would dismiss him with a brusque "don't be absurd" or some such pithy phrase.

Bill thumbed through the copy of *Who's Who* with the enthusiasm of a child flicking through their first picture book. She was simply getting on with things. *What pluck, what courage* Simon thought. She had pulled herself together and was tackling the job in hand. She was just the person to accompany him on the journey he was planning.

"Nothing." Bill slammed the book shut as a punctuation to her statement. "You're sure Cameron said this chap was called Freddie Newman?"

"Certain," Simon replied. "Admiral Frederick Newman."

Bill stood and scanned the shelves of the bookcase once more.

"What are you looking for now?" Simon asked.

"It's highly unlikely," Bill muttered, almost to herself. "But I wonder if Noël has the German equivalent of *Who's Who* on his shelves. It's called *Wer Ist's?*"

"Why do you want that?"

Bill had got onto her hands and knees to check the lowest shelf of the bookcase. "Bugger." She looked up at Simon. "It's just a wild guess. This admiral chap arrived at Sandringham with Charles Edward, Duke of Saxe-Coburg and Gotha. He's from Germany—"

"Of course." Simon helped Bill back to her feet. "Which would mean Admiral Frederick Newman might in fact be Admiral Friedrich Neumann, and he's anglicised his name. Or Cameron misheard Neumann for Newman."

"Full marks." Bill dusted down the knees of her trousers. "But Noël doesn't have a copy of *Wer Ist's?*, so we're no further forward."

She tapped her fingers on the cover of the book. It was an irritating sound. Simon walked over to the window and stared out at the garden.

"I don't think I'm going to get anywhere while I'm stuck here in darkest Kent," Simon said.

"And where do you propose to go next?" Bill took out her cigarette case and picked up a lurid green onyx lighter from a shelf in the bookcase. "We can't go back to London. You'll get arrested straight away." She lit a cigarette and exhaled the smoke. "Dammit. If I went back, I'd probably get arrested as well for aiding and abetting a wanted man."

It was time to tell her.

"I'm going to Sandringham."

Bill narrowed her eyes. She slowly brought the cigarette up to her mouth and stared at him as she first inhaled and then blew out the smoke through her nose.

"I know you think I'm mad," Simon continued.

Why was he justifying himself to her? There was no earthly reason. He was his own man after all, free to make his own decisions.

"You are mad," Bill said. "But after what's just happened to Anna, I'm also mad. Not just mad, I'm damned furious. If you go, I'll cover for you here."

"That's very kind of you." Simon looked down at his feet. "But I think it would be better if you came with me."

"Oh, no." Bill waved the cigarette from side to side. "I might be mad, but I'm not foolhardy. What's the point of me coming with you?"

"Two heads are always better than one," Simon replied brightly.

"They may be. But they don't have to be in the same place."

"I thought you might map-read."

Bill sniffed. "What's wrong with your sense of direction? Only last night when we were in Patsy's car you were demanding a map to tell me how to get here. Even though I knew perfectly well where I was going."

"It's trickier on a motorcycle."

The cigarette fell from Bill's fingers and she dropped to the floor to prevent it from scorching the rug. When she stood up her face was flushed with fury.

"You can't seriously expect me to get on that infernal device?"

"Well, I can't take Patsy's car," Simon replied. "It would more than likely get stopped by the police—"

"And I wouldn't allow you to drive it," Bill cut in crisply.

"Which means the Bentley's out of the question as well, I suppose," Simon continued. "And that only leaves the motorcycle. I can't ride and read the map at the same time. I thought you could sit in the sidecar and tell me where to go."

Bill snorted. "That's a set-up line any comedian would give their eye teeth for. But I'm not going to demean myself by saying the obvious." She stubbed out her cigarette in an ashtray on the bookcase. "Do you know how far it is to Norfolk from here?"

Simon nodded. "If we leave now, we can be there by early evening."

"And what do we do when we get there?" Bill asked. "Knock on the door and say, I'm sorry to bother you Your Majesty, but your son, and a duke, and some bogus admiral are all plotting to assassinate you?"

"Not quite." Simon smiled. "But I do have a plan. Of sorts. And once we're on the road, we can stop by a phone box and I'll give Robbie a call. After what happened to Anna, perhaps he's more inclined to believe me. He might even get us some back-up."

"Ever the optimist." Bill strode across the room and went into the hallway.

"Where are you going?" Simon followed, and found her rummaging in a large cupboard under the stairs. "What are you doing?"

There was a loud crash from inside the cupboard and Bill swore several times. She emerged holding what looked like a brown leather football.

"Here. Take this." She handed it to Simon. On closer inspection he realised it was a very smart leather motorcycle helmet, complete with goggles.

"Noël brought it back from London once. He's never worn it. It's a perfect disguise. No one will recognise you in that."

Simon put it on and pulled the goggles down over his eyes. "What fun. I feel like a modern-day Don Quixote." He reached out for Bill's hand. "Will you be my Sancho Panza?"

"In a motorcycle and sidecar?" Bill snatched her hand away. "I think we're going to be more like Laurel and Hardy."

The gun was still under the bed in Noël Coward's room. He retrieved it and opened his satchel. There was not much in it. At least, not much that actually belonged to him. There was the black leather clutch bag with the initials S C inscribed on it. Then there was the small parcel wrapped in brown paper Miss Stockwell had given him. He removed it and pushed the gun into the bottom of the bag. He slung it over his shoulder, picked up the package, and went back downstairs to find Bill sat at the kitchen table studying several maps.

"Worked out where we're going?" Simon asked.

Bill ignored his question. "What have you got there?" she asked. "An early Christmas present for me?"

Simon handed Bill the parcel. She read out the name and address written on its packaging.

"Agatha Stockwell? Who's that?" Bill asked.

Simon put the package on the table. "She's the mother of the late Jenny Stockwell. This is the reason Miss Stockwell came to see me yesterday morning. It's a present for her mother. Jenny had run away from home six months ago. I think this was some kind of peace offering."

He left the kitchen and headed for the writing desk in the sitting room. In the top drawer there were some envelopes and a sheaf of plain paper. There was a pen and inkwell in a wooden stand on the edge of the desk. He sat and composed a short note for Mrs Stockwell.

"You're surely not going to deliver this parcel to her mother now?" Bill appeared at the doorway of the sitting room. "Isn't it going to be rather macabre for her to receive a Christmas present from her dead daughter?"

There was a wooden-handled blotter next to the inkwell. Simon rolled it gently over the text on the page, folded the paper, and sealed it in the envelope.

"I'm certainly not going to hold on to it," he replied. "And

I think it's better this way. In my little note I've told Mrs Stockwell that her daughter was remorseful for leaving home and wanted to see her again." He turned and smiled at Bill. "I think it would be a crumb of comfort to a mother in mourning."

Bill shook her head. "She'll see it as a letter from her daughter's murderer."

"I've not signed it, of course," Simon replied. "I simply wrote 'from a respectful friend'."

"You're a rank sentimentalist, Simon Sampson." Bill went back to the kitchen. "Now go and get that motorised contraption ready," she called. "There's not a lot of daylight left. Although that won't matter to me. I'll have my eyes tight shut most of the time."

The fuel tank was full. Even better, Simon found two more full cans of petrol stacked on a workbench nearby. Whoever rode the motorcycle had made sure that any local fuel shortages would not hamper their enjoyment of the open road. Simon loaded the cans into the sidecar and pushed the bike out of the barn onto the drive. He was hindered by the multiple layers of clothing he was wearing.

Bill had ransacked the house to make sure they were both warmly dressed for the long journey. Noël had an astonishing collection of clothing suitable for almost any climate. Simon wore two sets of cotton long johns, a thick pair of leather flying trousers, several naval pullovers, a leather flying jacket, two pairs of woollen socks and a stout pair of army boots.

He checked the motorcycle thoroughly, primed the fuel and gave the starter a kick. It roared into action on the fifth attempt. Simon put on the helmet and goggles Bill had given him, a thick pair of gauntlets, and swung his leg over the saddle.

It was good to be riding again, and he felt a thrill of excitement for the journey ahead. He had never ridden a motorcycle with a sidecar before, but he was sure there was very little difference in the technique. He put the bike into gear and rode it slowly to the front of the house where Bill was waiting for him at the front door. She held a large basket.

"What's that for?" Simon asked.

Bill handed him the basket and then held out her hand, waiting to be helped into the sidecar.

"Part of what was going to be our Christmas dinner," she replied. Simon jumped off the bike, helped her into the sidecar, and handed her the basket. "It's going to be a long journey and I'm quite certain we're going to get hungry."

"Excellent," Simon replied. "What have we got?"

"Honey roasted ham, a rather splendid foie gras Patsy got us from Fortnum's, some smoked salmon, and a decent burgundy."

"Do you think it's a good idea for me to drink when I'm riding this thing?" Simon climbed back onto the motorcycle and patted the petrol tank.

"Certainly not," Bill replied. "But there's no reason why I shouldn't. In fact, I think it's essential."

She pointed to the two petrol cans at her feet.

"What are those?"

"Spare petrol," Simon replied. "It's a long way and this bike's tank won't hold enough for the whole journey."

Bill stared at him. "Are you telling me I'm going to be charging along at fifty miles an hour inside this sardine tin, accompanied by two cans of highly flammable liquid?" She took the cover off the basket and took out a pewter hip flask. "I very much doubt I'll see 1933, so I'll wish you a happy new year now." She removed the top from the hip flask and took a swig. "Cheers."

Simon put the motorcycle into gear and they rolled at slow speed down the drive to the main gate. He turned out into the lane, accelerated and slipped into second gear. The sensation of riding was different to his previous experience with a motorcycle. The weight of the sidecar dragged the bike to the left and Simon had to concentrate to keep them in a straight line. Several times they nearly tipped into the ditch. Bill was quick to alert him of the impending danger, her voice loudly audible above the roar of the engine.

He moved into third gear and accelerated beyond thirty miles an hour. There was a right-hand bend ahead and Simon leaned into it as he would do on a solo motorcycle. To his horror the wheels of the sidecar left the ground as the shift in his body weight threatened to tip them over. He released the throttle and straightened. The sidecar crashed back onto the road. Simon fought with the handlebars to keep the bike following the curve of the corner and avoid crashing into the hedge.

"What in thunder are you doing?" Bill shouted. "We haven't even got out of the lane and you're already trying to launch me into space."

Simon shouted his apology. Clearly he was wrong in his earlier assumption that the riding technique for a motorcycle was no different when it had a sidecar attached. Bill tugged hard on his jacket.

"Do that again and I'm getting out," she shouted. "You can do your own bloody map-reading."

25

There appeared to be no one at home when Simon pulled up outside the little terraced cottage at the end of the high street in Aldington. Bill climbed out of the sidecar, picked up the parcel for Jenny Stockwell's mother, and left it outside the front door. She trudged back to the bike and pointed to a telephone box on the other side of the road.

"Aren't you going to call your little chum Robbie?" she asked.

Simon shook his head.

"Let's go a bit further. I don't want to risk being recognised around here."

"Don't be absurd," Bill replied. "You're wearing a helmet and goggles and there's hardly any daylight left. You could be Lobby Ludd and no one would recognise you." She held out her hand. "Come and help me get back into this tin coffin, and go and make your call. I'll sit with the petrol cans and shiver to keep warm."

Simon helped her into the sidecar and crossed the road to the phone box. Bill was right. It was getting colder. Even with all the layers of clothing he was wearing, it was going to be a chilly journey. It took several minutes before his call to Scotland Yard was answered.

"Could you put me through to Detective Inspector Mountjoy, please?" he asked.

"I don't think he's here at the moment," said a voice at the other end. "Can I take a message for him?"

Simon thought for a moment.

"Yes," he replied. "Tell him the same school friend called for him he spoke to earlier. I'll try again later."

"Who shall I say called?"

Simon thought for a moment. "Tell him that Norfolk's a damn fine place to spend Christmas. He'll understand." Simon hung up the phone.

"That was quick," Bill said when Simon climbed back on the motorcycle.

"He wasn't there. I'll try again in a while."

This time it took him eight attempts with the kick starter before the bike finally roared into action. Simon hoped it was not a bad omen. There was no fuel gauge on the bike, so he decided it would be sensible to top up the tank every fifty miles or so. He asked Bill to let him know when they reached the first fifty-mile point.

"How on earth am I supposed to do that, darling?" she asked. "You didn't provide me with a protractor and compasses. I'm afraid I'm not equipped to offer you the full navigation service."

She placed her thumb on the map and used it as a makeshift ruler.

"We'll head back to London on the A20 until we get to Dartford," she said. "That's pretty much fifty miles." She pulled on a pair of thick woollen mittens, wrapped her arms around her torso and hugged herself tight. "If we run out of petrol before then don't blame me."

The main road was very quiet as they headed back to London. What little traffic there was came from the other direction. It was fortunate the road had so few bends in it. The motorcycle and sidecar were far harder to steer than Simon had imagined, and it took a constant physical effort to stop them from veering off to the left. His enthusiasm for motorcycling had dissipated the farther they travelled. The refuelling stop at Dartford would be a welcome opportunity to rest his arms.

He thought about the task ahead of them when they got to Sandringham. Back at Goldenhurst he had tried to reassure Bill that he had a plan. In truth it was sketchy. He hoped that when they stopped, he would be able to get in touch with Robbie and persuade him to get the police involved. Simon shivered at the prospect of another encounter with Admiral Freddie Newman.

At least Simon had a gun with him, although he had not fired one for years. In 1918 he had missed being conscripted by a few days. His eighteenth birthday fell on the fifteenth of November, four days after the Armistice. Nevertheless, his father had insisted on teaching him how to handle a gun. Simon had learned how to use rifles and shotguns and he became a pretty good shot. But it was not a hobby that interested him much. Now his skill might be put to the test.

Despite the anticipated security, Simon was confident he could get them into the Sandringham Estate. Cameron had given him the phone number for the lodge house, and he knew the gatekeeper was called Dougal. He would ring ahead and convince Dougal they were messengers from the BBC delivering important technical materials for the Christmas Day broadcast. Once on the estate, he hoped to be able to enlist Cameron's help in finding either the duke or the admiral. Preferably both.

It was from this point on that Simon's plan became hazy. He had no idea what form the assassination attempt on the king would take. Nor did he know if it would be carried out by the admiral, or some other co-conspirator. A further disadvantage was that the admiral and the duke had the complete confidence of the Prince of Wales. Simon's intervention with a claim of skulduggery against the pair of them would doubtless be treated with suspicion, if not downright hostility.

By the time they got to Dartford, Simon was no closer to a plan of any detail. He would need to enlist the help of Bill and her brilliant mind. But first they had to find a telephone box.

Dartford was an industrial town, close to the mouth of the River Thames on the south side. It was home to an ugly sprawl of factories including a paper mill and a chemical works that made medicines for Britain and its empire. The streets were full of vehicles, from trams to horse-drawn carts, and Simon cautiously steered the motorcycle through the traffic. Up ahead he saw a pretty garden in front of a red brick municipal building with four telephone boxes close by. He turned off the main street and parked in front of them. The relative silence when he cut the engine was blissful.

"How appropriate." Bill pointed up at the building. "The town library. It's as though you chose this place for us to stop especially for me."

She climbed out of the sidecar and stretched her limbs. "You know, that thing's not so bad after a while. It's almost like being gently rocked in a rather noisy cradle. How are you finding the driving?"

"Ghastly." Simon dismounted the motorcycle and exercised his aching fingers. "The damn thing won't go in a straight line. The weight of you and that sidecar are pulling it over to the left."

"Well thank you very much for the insult." Bill walked unsteadily towards the phone boxes. She looked like a passenger on a ship trying to find her land legs after months at sea.

"What are you doing?" Simon called.

Bill stopped and turned. "I'm going to ring Noël's parents and tell them we're no longer staying at Goldenhurst. They might want to go back there for Christmas if Erik is well enough."

She resumed her haphazard walk towards the telephone boxes. Simon lifted the goggles from his eyes and took off the leather helmet. He reached into the footwell, retrieved one of the petrol cans and used about half of it to replenish the petrol tank. He replaced the cap on the can and slung it back into the sidecar.

He turned to walk towards the phone boxes and almost collided with a policeman. Too late he realised his face was no longer hidden by the helmet and goggles. He turned away and bent down to the motorcycle, pretending to examine the brakes.

"Is this your motorcycle, sir?" asked the constable.

"Yes, officer." Simon rubbed his hand around the front wheel.

"Very nice." The police officer bent down on the other side of the bike and peered at Simon over the top of the wheel. "1929, isn't it?"

"1931," Simon corrected him. He turned his face to one side and half-shielded it from the policeman, while he reached up to the saddle and felt for the helmet and goggles. "It's got the new camshaft arrangement. It's cut down the oil consumption quite a bit." He had no idea if this was true, but he made sure he sounded confident as he said it.

"I see." The officer lovingly slid his gloved hand over the petrol tank. "I'm waiting to be accepted into motorcycle division myself. Only way I'll get to ride a beauty like this."

Simon's shaking fingers made contact with the helmet and goggles. He tried to grab them but only succeeded in knocking them off the saddle onto the ground beside the policeman.

"Allow me, sir." The officer picked them up and handed them to him across the top of the bike. Simon took the helmet and shoved it on his head. It took him a moment to realise it was on backwards. He removed it, turned it round, and put it back on again. He pulled down the goggles, stood up and turned to the policeman.

"Thank you so much, officer." He held out his hand. "I mustn't keep you on this cold night."

The policeman stood and shook his hand. "Where are you heading, sir?"

"Oh, you know," Simon replied. "Back home. Eventually."

"Where would that be, sir?"

The policeman was being annoyingly curious.

"North London, officer," Simon replied.

"Long way ahead of you, sir."

You really do not know the half of it, Simon thought. He released his hand from the policeman's grip and was about to salute when he realised how ridiculous it might appear. Instead, he clapped his gloved hands together.

"Absolutely. I'm just going to make a quick phone call and then I'll be off."

The policeman showed no sign of leaving. Simon turned, gave him one final wave, and strode towards the telephone boxes. Bill was in the first one with her back to the door.

Simon reached for the door handle of the phone box next to hers. He was about to pull it open when he overheard a fragment of her conversation.

"It's the best test I know. Active duty in the field. Doing bloody well, in my humble opinion. I think you should take him on."

Bill leaned back against the door and it creaked open. She turned to exhale her cigarette smoke through the open doorway and saw Simon. Her eyes opened wide and she coughed noisily. The door slammed shut again and she turned away from Simon to continue speaking into the phone.

"Arthur, you can't possibly let Violet do all the nursing herself. She'll be exhausted." Bill turned to glance at Simon. "If he's doing so well then you should take him on. He'll make your life so much easier."

Simon picked up the receiver and dialled the number for Scotland Yard.

"I'll go now and let you get on with things," Bill's voice was fainter but still clearly audible through the small glass windows of the adjacent phone box. "We'll speak again. Soon."

Simon was about to ask Bill about her call when a voice sounded in the earpiece.

"Scotland Yard."

"I'd like to speak to Detective Inspector Mountjoy."

"One minute, please."

Simon held his breath. This seemed more promising. He turned when he heard the door creak in the phone box next to him. Bill was leaving. He pushed open the door of his phone box to speak to her and saw the policeman still standing by the motorcycle.

"Bill," he called quietly, but she carried on walking. There was a click in the earpiece.

"Hello," said a male voice. "Could you tell me who's calling, sir?"

It was not Robbie's voice. "I need to speak to D.I. Mountjoy," Simon said. "Is he there, please?"

"Is that the school friend who called earlier?" asked the voice.

Simon hesitated. Why was Robbie not available? Perhaps he had finished work for the evening. Nothing more suspicious than that. Simon looked at the clock on the front of the building opposite. It was not even five o'clock. Unlikely. Robbie would still be working, investigating Anna's killer. Perhaps he was out following a lead.

"Isn't he there?" Simon asked.

"Is that Mr Sampson?" the voice asked.

Simon hung up. Whether or not Bill was correct in her assertion that the police could track phone calls, he was taking no chances. He pushed the door open and walked back to the motorcycle. Bill was shaking hands with the constable. The officer turned to Simon, saluted him, and walked away. Simon nodded back.

"I thought he'd never go," he said to Bill. She was struggling to get back into the sidecar. "How did you get rid of him?"

Bill settled herself into the cramped cockpit of the sidecar and wrapped her coat around her.

"I told him we were on a top-secret mission to save the king from an assassination attempt."

Simon smiled. Perhaps it was better not to know how abrupt or direct Bill had been with the police officer. But the snippet of her telephone conversation he had overheard puzzled him.

"Why were you talking about 'active duty in the field'?" he asked. "It sounded like some kind of military operation you were talking about."

"Precisely." Bill pulled a map onto her lap and traced their route to Norfolk across it with her finger. "Noël's brother Erik wants to leave the hospital and live out the last few months of his life at Goldenhurst. Of course Violet, his mother, wants to nurse him herself night and day. Arthur and I are trying to persuade her to get this wonderful man who nursed one of Noël's neighbours. He's very good. I don't remember my exact words. If you say I said he'd shown excellent active duty in the field, then I suppose it must be true. It would make sense to Arthur. He was in the army in the Great War."

"A male nurse?" Simon queried.

"Don't be so old-fashioned." Bill pointed to the map. "Next stop, the Blackwall Tunnel under the Thames." She looked up at Simon. "I can't think of anything more terrifying. Riding in this tin perambulator full of explosive fuel cans inside a dark narrow tunnel underneath thousands of tons of water." She lit a cigarette. Simon watched aghast.

"You weren't smoking in there on the journey from Goldenhurst, were you?" he asked.

Bill exhaled a cloud of smoke. "Of course I was. I needed something to steady my nerves."

"There are two cans of petrol at your feet, for God's sake," Simon replied. "Didn't you think it might be just a little bit dangerous?"

"Nonsense, darling." She patted the saddle of the motorcycle. It's fine while we're going along. It's far too windy. Hop on and let's get going. You don't want us blowing up, do you?"

26

The journey through the Blackwall Tunnel was far less frightening than Bill had predicted. Simon found it an exhilarating experience as the roar of the motorcycle engine bounced off the walls of the tunnel. The journey across north London and on towards Norfolk was far less exhilarating. It was relentless and exhausting. Simon got used to the odd quirks of the motorcycle and the dead weight of the sidecar. He found he could push their speed up to a respectable fifty miles per hour. Any faster and the entire frame of the motorcycle began to shake and rattle so much Simon had difficulty holding onto the handlebars.

They passed phone box after phone box, but Simon had decided not to call Robbie anymore. It was apparent that Scotland Yard was now screening his calls.

He thought about the odd snatch of Bill's conversation he had overheard. She had claimed she was talking to Noël's father Arthur about finding extra nursing care for Erik, Noël's brother. But if that was the case, why had Bill used the phrase "*active duty in the field*"? Her explanation sounded doubtful. Had Simon heard her correctly? Perhaps he was mistaken.

His memory might be confused by the growing tiredness he felt.

They stopped outside a pub on the outskirts of Cambridge in the early evening to refuel. The pub was packed with people celebrating the end of the working week and the start of the Christmas holiday. The pub windows were partially steamed up but Simon could see a fireplace inside with a roaring log fire burning in the grate. It was warm and inviting.

A couple walked past them arm-in-arm, and stopped to admire the motorcycle.

"Nice bike, mate," said the young man. He turned to his companion, who had a bright red scarf wrapped around her neck. "What do you think, Doris? If I got a nice little motor like that, we could go off to the coast for day trips."

The young woman wrinkled her nose. She was not much older than twenty. "You won't catch me in one of those, Bert," she replied. "I wants you to get a proper motor. One with four wheels and doors." She pointed at the sidecar and laughed. "That's no more than a roller skate."

Bill's head emerged from under the canopy of the sidecar. She clambered out and stood in front of the couple. She was a good inch taller than either of them.

"That's quite enough of your damned impertinence, young lady." Bill turned to Bert. "If I were you, I'd find someone else to court who's got a better sense of adventure. This girl seems like a complete dullard."

"Well of all the nerve." Doris turned to her beau. "Are you going to let her get away with that?"

While she was talking, Bill had taken out her cigarette case, opened it, and proffered it to Bert. He looked from his companion to Bill, shrugged, and accepted the offer. He took out a box of matches and lit his own cigarette, and then Bill's.

"Merry Christmas, lady." He turned to Doris. "Come on you. Perhaps she's right. What's wrong with a motorcycle?"

He pulled Doris's arm and led her, still complaining, into the pub. Simon finished refuelling the bike and put the lid back on the petrol can.

"Sense of adventure, eh?" He chuckled. "I never thought I'd hear you say that."

Bill snorted. "Don't forget there's a world of difference between a sense of adventure and damned foolhardiness. Are you still planning to carry on with this ridiculous journey?"

"Of course I am."

Simon walked up and down and stamped his feet to restore the circulation to his legs. He was determined to continue. They had come so far. Sandringham was probably no more than two hours away. He took out his pocket watch. They could be there by nine o'clock.

"There's absolutely nothing wrong with me."

"Really?" Bill pointed at him with her cigarette. "Look at you, Simon. You can hardly stand after being astride that ruddy machine for hours. You're cold and you must be exhausted. I can't imagine how befuddled your brain is by now. What earthly use are you going to be when we finally get to Sandringham?"

"Oh, do be quiet." Bill was beginning to annoy him. He stifled a yawn and put the petrol can back in the sidecar. "The sooner we get going, the sooner we arrive."

There was a look of fury on Bill's face.

"What's the problem?" Simon asked. "Do you want me to leave you here instead?" He climbed back on the saddle and tried to kick-start the bike. The engine coughed but failed to turn over.

"I might as well," Bill replied. "It doesn't look like that thing's going anywhere tonight."

She shoved the cigarette into the corner of her mouth and narrowed her eyes. It was *that look.* A look that Simon knew very well. Lesser men had been reduced to quivering wrecks by *that look.* But not Simon. He sniffed and stamped down hard on the motorcycle's kick-start. The engine roared into life. He smiled at Bill in triumph.

"Well?"

The clock on Saint Margaret's Church chimed nine o'clock when the motorcycle and sidecar rolled into the market place in the centre of King's Lynn. Simon switched off the engine, dismounted, and stretched his arms. Finally, they were only a few miles away from Sandringham, where the king and his family were preparing for Christmas.

From Cambridge their route had taken them across The Fens, a low-lying, flat and featureless farming landscape. The long straight road from Cambridge was sometimes dwarfed by giant, man-made drainage channels, taking water pumped from the land back to the sea. Much of the area had been reclaimed from the sea in the eighteenth and nineteenth centuries and some of the land was below sea level. If it were not for the constant effort of pumping engines and the network of drainage ditches, the Fens would once again be submerged by the North Sea.

Bill rummaged in the basket of food. "Noël will find it killingly funny when I tell him we were in Norfolk. He hates the place. Never misses an opportunity to make a disparaging remark about it." She retrieved a mince pie and offered it to Simon.

"Happy Christmas, my dear," she said. "Pray tell, as we're almost there, what is this great plan of yours?"

"You can relax for a few minutes," Simon replied. "I'm off to make a phone call."

"Relax, says the man." Bill raised the bottle of burgundy to her lips and gulped down a mouthful. She wiped her mouth with the back of her hand and offered the bottle to Simon. "You're not going to call Detective Inspector Mountjoy again, are you? Surely it's a bit late to summon the cavalry now?"

Simon held up his hand to refuse the wine bottle. It was a shame. He could see it was a good vintage, but he needed to keep a clear head.

"Not this time," he replied. "I saw a phone box on the edge of the square. Back in a jiffy."

"Then who are you going to ring?" Bill called after him, but Simon chose not to answer. She would know the plan soon enough.

"Sandringham Lodge," said a man with a broad Scottish accent when Simon placed his call.

"Good evening. Is that Mr McAllister?" Simon asked in his best BBC English.

"Aye, it is," replied Dougal McAllister. "And who are ye?"

"This is the BBC in London, Mr McAllister." Simon was very pleased at how authoritative his voice sounded. "There's a dispatch rider with an urgent package to deliver to the BBC's wireless operations there. It's needed for tomorrow's rehearsal of the king's Christmas Day broadcast. We're calling to make sure he'll have no problem entering the estate when he arrives. I understand you're in control of the gates."

"It's ver' late," Dougal grumbled. "I wa' goin' tae bed in a wee while."

"You won't have to wait up very long," Simon replied. "The dispatch rider's already in King's Lynn. He should be with you in twenty minutes."

"Well, I suppose tha's all right," Dougal replied. "Wha's the fella's name?"

"Coward." Simon said the first name that came into his head. "Simon Coward," he added.

"Simon Coward," Dougal repeated. "An' he's comin' in twenty minutes ye say? I'll keep an eye out for 'im. But I'm warnin' ye, if he's much later, I'll be a bed. It's a busy day the morrow."

The line went dead.

Simon stepped out of the phone box and looked up at the sky. After the bad weather of the day, it was now a cloudless evening and the moon shone brightly. Not so helpful for a covert operation. But it would be useful to see where they were going, in what he imagined would be a wooded and unlit landscape at Sandringham.

"What next, my Don Quixote?" Bill asked when he arrived back at the motorcycle.

"I've got us past the lodge keeper," Simon replied. "Once we're on the estate, my plan is to find Cameron. That way he can give us the lie of the land. It will make it easier to find the duke and the admiral."

"And then what do you propose to do?"

Simon climbed back onto the motorcycle. "I'll tell you once we're past the gates. We need to get there before Mr McAllister takes his beauty sleep."

Dougal McAllister was exactly as Simon had imagined him. A stocky, red-haired man with a bushy beard. He was standing by the gates at the entrance to Sandringham estate when they arrived half an hour later.

"Two minutes later and ye'd be out of luck," he said to Simon. "Yon BBC man called and said ye'd be here in fifteen minutes."

Simon smiled at the distortion Dougal had made to the information he had told him.

"I'm sorry," he replied. "I got a bit lost on the way from King's Lynn. I've been told to find a Mr Cameron McCreadie. Could you tell me where he might be?"

"Cameron?" repeated Dougal. "He's the equerry appointed to the duke. They're stayin' at the Lodge Cottages over yonder. He's in the stables next to 'em. But right now they'll all be in the great house for the welcoming supper." He pointed down the long straight driveway that led away from the gates. "It's not yet ten, so they'll still be there. Do you want me to call ahead to the house for ye?"

"No. Please don't bother yourself," Simon said quickly. "It won't take us more than a couple of minutes to get there."

Dougal opened the gates and Simon rode through onto Sandringham Estate. The driveway was flanked by trees and rose in a gentle straight climb. After a quarter of a mile, they reached the summit of the incline. The lights from Sandringham House glowed in the distance. Simon pulled over to the side of the roadway, switched off the engine, and dismounted. There were copses of mature trees on either side. With the roar of the engine silenced, the sounds of the night came alive. An owl hooted and the wind rustled the branches of the winter-bare trees. Simon stood on the earthy ground at the side of the roadway and stretched out his aching arms.

"Now will you tell me what your brilliant plan is?" Bill asked.

“I’m off to find Cameron,” he replied. “Pass me my bag, will you?”

Bill reached behind her, pulled out the satchel, and handed it to Simon. He opened it and took out the gun he had retrieved from underneath Noël Coward’s bed.

“Where the hell did you get that?” Bill asked.

“Goldenhurst,” Simon replied. “Pretty handy, eh?” He held it up and turned to aim it at a distant tree. “I used to be a pretty mean shot. Still am probably.”

“Drop the gun, Simon.” Bill’s voice was strangely flat and characterless.

“Don’t worry, old girl.” Simon lowered the pistol and turned back to Bill.

She too held a gun. And it was pointing straight at him.

“I don’t like to repeat myself, Simon. Drop the gun on the ground.”

27

The pistol made a dull *thud* when it fell onto the woodland earth. Simon was not sure if he had let it drop, or if it had simply slipped from his fingers. Too late to pick it up now. Bill's gun was still aimed at his chest.

"What's going on, Bill?"

"Walk away from the gun, please."

Simon stared at her.

"Do it now, please," Bill's tone was calm, almost friendly. But the barrel of the gun pointing in his direction said otherwise.

Simon took a step backwards. Bill climbed out of the sidecar and placed her gun on the motorcycle saddle. She reached down and picked up his pistol. It was clear she was familiar with handling a gun. She flipped open the barrel, tipped the bullets into her hand, and flipped it closed again.

"That's better." She tossed the unarmed pistol back across the ground to him and pocketed the bullets. "We don't want any unpleasant accidents. I wasn't expecting you to bring that. Where on earth did you find that in Goldenhurst? I didn't think Noël cared for guns."

"You haven't answered my question." Simon bent down to pick up his gun and put it in his pocket. "What the hell's going on, Bill? I thought you were on my side."

She laughed.

"Of course I am, darling." She lit a cigarette and exhaled a plume of smoke. "In a manner of speaking, that is."

"And what's that supposed to mean?" Simon was infuriated. "Either you are or you aren't."

"Oh, Simon." She picked up her gun from the saddle and shoved it back into her pocket. "Surely by now you've come to understand that life is never that simple?"

Her patronising manner irritated Simon. He was also confused. Was Bill a part of the conspiracy to murder the king? He had known her for over three years. As far as he was aware, she was as patriotic as he was. He recalled how she had praised both the king and the queen for the compassionate leadership they had demonstrated during the crisis of the General Strike. She was full of admiration for Queen Mary in the way she had cared for King George when he showed signs of ill health. It had never crossed his mind that Bill might be a traitor. How much did Simon really know his friend Florence Miles, otherwise known as Bill?

"I have something to explain." Bill dropped her cigarette to the ground and stubbed it out. "And very little time in which to do it. I'll keep it brief. Before you ask me any more nonsensical questions like 'who's side am I on?', let me reassure you. I'm on the side of our country. Of our king. There's no question that I'm out to stop these fascist bastards just as much as you are."

"Then why point a gun at me?"

Bill chuckled. "Yes. That must have been rather alarming. The truth is, we didn't expect you to be quite as resourceful as that."

"'We'?"

Bill sighed.

"The intelligence services."

Simon was speechless. Bill was head of BBC Libraries. He had only ever known her as that. Two years before he moved from *The Chronicle* to the BBC's News Department, he had met her in the Fitzroy Tavern on his birthday. From the start, it had been a fiery relationship. But it was a friendship based on strong, mutually held beliefs. Bill was one of the few people in Simon's life that he could trust. Now she was telling him she was not who she claimed to be. He was shaken and angry.

"'The intelligence services'?"

"That's right," Bill continued. "The Secret Intelligence Service or MI6. They placed me in the BBC just under three years ago. Not long after we met, in fact."

"'Placed you'?" Simon repeated. "You mean you're not really Head of Libraries?"

"Don't be ridiculous, Simon." She lit another cigarette. "Of course I am. We women can do more than one job at a time. And we do them very well, as it happens. The SIS got wind of the BBC's plans to start up the Empire Service and they wanted someone to keep an eye on what it was doing. From a discreet distance, of course."

"Does Lord Reith know about this?" Simon asked.

"The Director General?" Bill laughed. "Absolutely not. He's such a simple man. He huffs and puffs with the politicians. Makes a good show of boasting about the BBC's impartiality. Surely you remember what he was like in the General Strike? Saying the BBC wasn't the mouthpiece of the government, and then slavishly broadcasting their public pronouncements without comment. The truth of the matter is the government foots the bill for the BBC. And they're not going to let it do what it likes. It's got to toe the line. We in MI6 simply keep an eye on it. If something's amiss, we put a word in the right places to get things sorted out."

Bill seemed to be enjoying telling Simon her revelations. It was as if she was unburdening herself.

"I'm not the only one, you know."

"Not the only what?" Simon asked.

"Monitor," Bill replied. "We make sure the BBC upholds British values. Especially now the Empire Service has started. We don't want them misrepresenting us when they transmit programmes to other countries. We keep a look out for Bolsheviks or Fascists who might be working behind the scenes to push their ideologies into programmes."

"'British values'?" Simon took a moment to digest Bill's words. "Don't you mean the government's values? It sounds like you're simply acting as the prime minister's lackey."

"Rubbish." Bill lit another cigarette. "Politicians come and go. What we're defending runs much deeper than the petty factionalism in Parliament. It's the stability of Britain and the Empire that's at stake. I thought you of all people would understand that. Goodness knows we've talked about it often enough."

It was true. The question of what constituted the values of Britain and the British people had been an occasional topic of discussion when he and Bill met. They were usually in broad agreement. For example, they both believed that the ancient public institutions established to run the country and the Empire were outdated and needed modernising. And that the revolution in Russia was a warning to all monarchies in Europe not to lose touch with the ordinary people. But most of all, they were united in the view that the king was doing a good job at keeping the country together and providing stability and leadership in a turbulent time.

To hear Bill tell him so casually that she was monitoring and potentially subverting the independence of the BBC was something Simon found difficult to stomach.

"Why have you never told me this before?" Simon asked.

"It's the SIS, my dear," she replied. "Where the S stands for secret. How could I?"

"Then why tell me now?"

Bill put the cigarette to her lips and inhaled deeply. It was a convenient prop to delay answering a question, Simon reflected. Perhaps he might consider taking up the vice for moments like this. Bill opened her mouth to release a cloud of smoke into the night air.

"We were always going to tell you," Bill replied. "But the buggers left it to me to pick the right moment. To be honest I kept bottling out. And anyway, I wanted to know what your great plan was once we got here. When you started waving that gun around, I decided it was time to call a halt before someone got hurt."

"You're forgetting something," Simon replied. "We're here to save the king. Stop the assassination. With brutes like Admiral Newman around, or whatever his real name is, there's a strong chance someone's going to get hurt anyway."

"Oh, don't worry about him." Bill waved her hand dismissively. "I'm sure by now he's already been dealt with. And Charles Edward, Duke of Saxe-Coburg and Gotha will have been sent packing with his tail between his legs."

Simon was astonished by what he was hearing. "How can you be sure?"

"Because a number of agents should have arrived here several hours ago. I'm sure they'll have mopped things up by now. We can go and meet them in a minute."

"I've been set up." Simon leaned heavily against a tree. Everything had been a lie. Bill had played him, while at the same time orchestrating events behind his back. The conversation he had overheard when she was in the telephone box in Dartford replayed in his head. She had used the phrase *"active duty in the field"*. She must have been talking to someone back at MI6. A surge of adrenalin coursed through his body and he calculated the possibilities of jumping Bill to tackle the gun from her.

"No darling," Bill said quietly. "You've not been set up. Evaluated, yes. And you've passed with flying colours."

She stepped forward and laid a hand on his arm. Simon pushed it away.

"Passed *what* with flying colours?" he asked. "What's my bloody prize for taking part in this charade?"

"To join us, my dear. In SIS. You're an ideal candidate. First class degree from Oxford. Fluent in French and German. With a smattering of Latin, I understand. But what's most impressive is how you perform in the field." She inhaled one last time on her cigarette before dropping it to the ground. "The section head's very impressed with you."

"So that's who you were talking to back in Dartford, when you said 'active duty in the field'. And you told me it was Noël's father you were talking to. About Erik's new nurse. And you'd said he was in the army. Which was why you used a military term."

"Did I? How clumsy of me." Bill chuckled. "Noël's father was in the navy, not the army. I'd be torn off a strip if my section head ever found out I'd made a silly mistake like that."

"What on earth makes you think I'd even want to join you?" Simon asked. Bill was still standing close to him. It was an ideal opportunity to grab the gun from her pocket. "You've lied to me, Bill. The secret services might suit you. But I'm not prepared to lie my way through life."

"Aren't you?" Bill stepped back and narrowed her eyes. It was *the look*. "Both of us spend most of our waking hours lying. I've just lost a woman for whom I cared very much. Do you think I can tell anyone about that? Of course I can't. I grieve alone. You seem to have feelings for young Cameron. If you told anyone about that you risk being thrown in jail. Even being given hard labour. The world isn't prepared to accept us as we really are. We're enemies in plain sight, Simon. Forced to lie in order to remain a part of Britain's genteel society."

She reached into her pocket, took out the bullets from Simon's pistol, and held them out for him.

"Here," she said. "Take them and do what you want. I know you're furious with me. I can see it in your eyes. But you can't deny you're the same as me."

Simon said nothing. He stared at the bullets in Bill's hand. Her reasoning had brought an uncomfortable truth to the surface. A truth they had seldom talked about, but silently acknowledged. They were both outsiders, forced to live a lie every day of their lives. What he found difficult to accept was that she had lied to him. Or rather, she had withheld information from him. And that one piece of information rewrote the story of their friendship. Was her friendship genuine? Or was she doing no more than using him in her role as an agent for the intelligence services?

"Simon? Is tha' you?" The voice came from farther along the roadway towards Sandringham House. As he came into view, the moonlight illuminated Cameron's face and the scarlet tunic of his uniform. He walked at a rapid pace, and glanced over his shoulder several times as he drew closer.

"And Bill. Ye both be here." Cameron stopped in front of them and panted, as though he had been running. "Thank God."

He took a step towards Simon and wrapped his arms around his waist. Simon put his hands on Cameron's shoulders and stared into the young man's eyes. Cameron smiled, and turned his head to glance behind him once more. He released his arms from Simon's waist and raised a finger to his lips.

"We've got tae hurry," he whispered. "I wa' goin' tae call ye from Dougal's telephone. Thank God you're here. I know how they wa' goin' tae assassinate the king."

28

Cameron beckoned them away from the driveway and into the copse of trees. Bill prodded Simon in the back and showed him the bullets from his gun. He took the bullets and reloaded his pistol before following Cameron to a large oak tree. The roofs of Sandringham House were just visible in the distance. A verdigrised copper cupola glinted dully in the moonlight.

"I see ye came prepared," Cameron whispered. "It's just a' well. Yon admiral's a vicious bastard."

"What happened to your cavalry of agents from MI6?" Simon asked Bill. "I thought you said it was all taken care of?"

"Never mind them," Bill replied. "I want to know what Cameron's got to say." She pulled out her gun. "Don't worry about the admiral, Cameron. We're both armed. Is he following you?"

Cameron shrugged. "Mebbe. I overheard him an' the Prince o' Wales talkin' earlier. I couldnae get away any sooner to call ye. I heard the admiral say the Prince o' Wales had nothin' tae worry about. The duke said he wa' only goin' tae drug the king for a wee while. Nothin' more. And it would last until after the broadcast."

"But you don't believe him." Bill said. "You think he's going to use poison. Why?"

"Because I saw it in the admiral's medicine chest when I unpacked his things," Cameron replied. "That wa' before he hit me wi' his cane an' told me to get awa' from them. I nigh on hit him back, but I didnae dare. I tell ye, he's a vicious bastard."

"What do you mean, you saw it?" Simon asked.

"It's a small bottle wi' a skull and crossbones on it and the word poison written across the label." Cameron shrugged. "Pretty clear tae me."

"Many medicines are labelled poison," Simon replied. "It could be perfectly innocent. His doctor might be treating him for a condition that requires it."

Cameron reached into his jacket pocket, pulled out a small brown bottle and handed it to Simon.

"Ye can decide for yeself," he said. "What do you treat wi' strychnine these days?"

"Very little," Bill replied. "It might still be used in lunatic asylums. But for the most part it's a rat killer. The days when it was used to treat palsy are long gone."

"You took this from the admiral's things?" Simon held the bottle up to read the label. "That's a hell of a risk. Let's hope he doesn't have any more."

A gunshot shattered the quiet of the evening.

"Get down!" Simon called out, and dropped to his haunches.

But Cameron was already down. He lay with his face in the earth, his body contorted. A part of the back of his head was no longer there. The shoulders of his scarlet tunic glistened with blood and brain matter. Simon placed two fingers against Cameron's carotid artery and felt his pulse fade to nothing as the life ebbed from him.

Simon rolled him onto his back and ripped his tunic open. He had read somewhere about how a man's heart could be restarted by putting pressure on it. But he had no idea how to begin. He lay his hands on Cameron's chest and pushed down. How much pressure should he apply? He pushed again, harder. And then again, and again.

The pool of blood beside Cameron's head grew larger. Simon lifted his hands and stared at them. He was making matters worse. His hands were doing nothing to restore Cameron's life. Instead, they were pushing the life from his body.

There was nothing more he could do.

He pulled the edges of the tunic together and smoothed down its creases, brushing away traces of mud from the scarlet fabric. He lowered his head and kissed Cameron on the lips one last time. Memories of the brief moments they had enjoyed together overwhelmed him. He felt angry and cheated. Cameron was a very special soul, older and wiser than his years. A man Simon wanted to get to know. To spend time with, even share his life with. Now that could never happen.

Another shot rang out and ricocheted off the trunk of the tree that shielded them. Bill fired two shots in rapid succession. A man cried out in pain.

"Got the brute," whispered Bill. But her triumph was short-lived. Another gunshot demonstrated that whoever was firing at them was still alive.

"Are you all right?" Simon whispered.

"Never better, old thing," Bill replied. "Caught a glimpse of him in between those two silver birches over there. I think

I winged him in the leg. Difficult to get a good shot from this position."

The clouds parted and moonlight lit the copse of trees opposite. Their branches waved in the breeze, causing confusing shadows to dance across their trunks. Every movement was a potential threat. Simon levelled his gun at a spot close to the ground in the clearing between the two silver birches. He exhaled slowly and waited to put his father's tuition to the test.

There was a commotion in a clump of bushes off to Simon's left. In his peripheral vision he saw the large shadow of a bird attempt to take flight. He kept his gaze focused on the clearing between the silver birches in front of him and saw what looked like the barrel of a shotgun. Simon aimed his revolver at a spot he judged to be near the shoulder of whoever was holding the gun and fired twice. The shotgun's barrel jerked into the air and there was a flash, followed by a loud report as the gun fired into the branches above Simon's head. The shotgun now lay abandoned on the ground.

"Bullseye," whispered Bill. "I think you've immobilised the blighter."

"Don't be too sure," Simon whispered back. "He might have another weapon."

But there was no further movement from the clearing in front of them. Simon kept his gun trained on the space between the two trees. With his free hand he reached into the undergrowth close by, found a decent-sized stone, and threw it at the butt of the shotgun lying on the ground. There was no reaction from whoever had been holding it a moment before.

"You there," Simon called. "Can you stand?"

There was no response. Simon got to his feet.

"Don't move. Put your hands on your head."

The voice came from a few hundred yards away. Two men walked up the driveway towards them from Sandringham House. They both carried rifles. Simon raised his hands and placed them on his head as instructed. One of the men spoke again.

"Who are you? What the hell are you doing here?"

"My God," Bill whispered. "It's the Prince of Wales." She grabbed onto a branch to pull herself to her feet.

"Drop that weapon or I'll shoot!" commanded the Prince of Wales.

Bill threw her gun to the ground and, still in a kneeling position, raised her hands.

The other man stepped towards Simon and prodded him with his rifle.

"Get on your knees next to her."

Simon did as he was told. He felt a boot in his back and he fell forward, his face hitting the forest floor. The man knelt on him, pulled his hands together behind his back, and tied rope around his wrists. Simon spat out a mouthful of soil and raised his head. He could see Cameron's body lying a few feet away.

"There's an injured man over there," Simon shouted. "You've got to attend to him."

"Shut up."

Simon saw the Prince of Wales walk over to Cameron and prod him with his rifle.

"He doesn't look like he's going anywhere. Unlike you two. You're coming back to the house to answer some questions."

Dogs had been locked up in the room. Recently. It was evident by the smell and the stains on the floor and walls. Now it was Simon's prison. His hands were still tied behind his back and the bindings were secured by a thick rope to an iron ring on the wall. He had no idea how long he had been there. Possibly an hour. Maybe more.

He wondered where they had taken Bill. Simon remembered his final glimpse of Cameron's body as they had walked away. He had looked so vulnerable on the ground in the cold of the night. No one had even had the decency to cover him before they had left.

The only light in the room came from a gas lamp on the stone terrace outside. It shone through a single, barred window and cast a flickering shadow of the bars onto the grubby back wall of the room. The side of Simon's abdomen throbbed from where he had been kicked by one of the men who had captured them. His whole body ached from the hours of riding on that damn motorcycle.

He closed his eyes, but the image of Cameron's lifeless body kept returning to him. He tried to picture him at a different time. The moment when Bill had left them to say their goodbyes in the mews in Bloomsbury. Simon had felt invincible then, without a care for what might happen next. He and Cameron had been connected by the adventure and the blind certainty that they would find each other once more. The memory was rapidly replaced by the sound of the gunshot and the feeling of Cameron's pulse dying beneath his fingertips. Simon shook his head and reopened his eyes.

There had been one, small victory. When he and Bill had been taken prisoner, Simon caught a glimpse of the body of the man who had shot at them. It was Admiral Frederick Newman. Simon's torturer and Cameron's murderer was dead.

Keys rattled in the door and it swung open. Simon was momentarily blinded by a bright light shone in his face.

"Sampson?" said a voice.

Simon squinted in the light. He thought he recognised one of the men who had captured them earlier.

"Come with me," the voice continued. "You're wanted upstairs."

Simon gestured to his bindings.

"I'm not going anywhere unless you untie me."

The man grunted and stepped forward. He pushed Simon aside and struggled to untie the rope that secured him to the iron ring. The man was several inches taller than him and far broader. With his hands tied behind his back, Simon knew he had a slim chance of overpowering the man.

He was prodded out of the room, along a corridor and into a hallway. At the far end of the hallway was a grand staircase. He looked up to see Bill at the top of the stairs.

"What the hell are you doing with him?" she called out. "Untie him at once. He can't be presented to the king in that state."

She walked down the stairs, and Simon stood and waited while the man grumbled and tugged on the bindings until Simon's hands were free. He rubbed his wrists where the ropes had chafed, and massaged his forearms to restore the circulation. Bill leaned forward and kissed him on the cheek. She sniffed at his clothes and wrinkled her nose. "You smell disgusting."

"I was thrown in the dog house," Simon replied. "Literally. How come you got off so lightly?"

"Hardly 'lightly'." Bill snorted. "I was locked in a room for nearly an hour until my section head arrived and explained what's been going on. Your chum Robbie's here as well, and what looks like half of Scotland Yard. It's quite a party."

"Did you say something about me being presented to the king?" Simon asked. "Is this a dressing down before I get sent to the Tower?"

"Not at all, my dear. The king's been put in the picture about everything. He now knows you're the hero of the hour."

"Really?"

"Absolutely. Now come on. He's waiting for you."

Bill led them up the stairs and stopped at the top.

"Try not to say too much, darling," she spoke in a low voice. "The king's been told what he needs to know, and that's all. You mustn't be alarmed by what you might hear."

"What do you mean, 'told what he needs to know'?" Simon whispered back. "Is this more manipulation of the truth by your intelligence services lot? And why didn't they turn up when you said they would?"

"Small territory battle between SIS and Scotland Yard," Bill replied. "They both turned up at the same time, thanks to your chum Robbie jumping in with both feet. Presumably the admiral picked his moment to skedaddle while they were arguing." She brushed down the shoulders of Simon's flying jacket with her hand. "Try to smarten yourself up, my dear. You're about to meet your king."

29

Footmen dressed in the same red tunics that Cameron had worn opened a pair of doors in front of them to reveal a modest-sized reception room. There was no trumpet fanfare, no formal announcement. It was not how Simon had scripted it in his head. The king and queen sat in armchairs on either side of a white marble fireplace. The fire in the grate was fading, flames occasionally licked around the charred embers of smoking logs.

When the doors opened the king raised his arm and beckoned them in.

"Please. Come forward," he said. "I understand I should be grateful to you for saving my life."

Bill and Simon entered the room and the doors slammed shut behind them. The queen looked up from a book she was reading and gave them a forced smile, as if they were intruding on her privacy. There was one other person present. A tall man stood a short distance away from the king and queen with his back to the door. He turned his head and nodded to Bill, as if it was not the first time they had met. Perhaps he was from the intelligence services.

"Stand there." The king pointed to where the man stood. "Next to Johnson where we can see you."

They walked forward obediently, and stood alongside the man called Johnson. The king approached and offered his hand to Simon, who was uncertain what he should do. What was the protocol? Should he kneel, take the royal hand, and kiss the ring on its third finger? He decided to shake the hand in the usual way. Before he did, he attempted to remove the leather gauntlet from his right hand. But it was difficult when his left was also encased in a gauntlet. He had to clench the obstinate glove between his knees to remove it.

"Your majesty." They shook hands and Simon bowed his head.

"Mr Sampson," the king replied. "I understand you're a veteran of the microphone. You may have heard I am to embark on a small broadcasting career myself." He glanced behind him at the carriage clock on the mantelpiece. "In a little over thirty-six hours. Do you have any advice?"

The king's voice was deep and resonant. His articulation of each word was measured and precise.

"Be yourself," Simon replied. "Whatever they might tell you. The microphone exposes anyone who tries to be something they aren't. It's brutal."

"Thank you, young man." The king seemed genuinely grateful for Simon's words. "No one bothered to tell me that." He turned to Queen Mary. "Or maybe that BBC wallah hadn't the balls, eh?"

They both laughed at what must have been a private joke. The king turned back to Simon.

"The wireless is becoming a new force in the world. It seems some wanted my voice silenced even before it was released onto the airwaves. I am grateful to everyone who came to my aid."

"It's not the first time that new inventions have posed a threat," Simon replied. "I'm sure that our future will lay upon us more than one stern test. But our past will have taught us how to meet it unshakable."

The king nodded thoughtfully.

"Very eloquently put." A playful smile lit up his face. "I may just steal that for my broadcast. If you permit me."

Simon smiled. "It would be an honour, Your Majesty."

The king laughed.

"Well done on bagging those two traitors. Sounds like you're a damn fine shot. You should come shooting with us one day."

"Two?" Simon turned to Bill. "Does that mean they've got the duke as well?"

Bill shook her head at Simon vigorously, and raised a finger to her lips. But the king had already heard Simon's question.

"The duke? What on earth do you mean? I meant those two traitors out in the grounds. That admiral imposter and the Scottish footman."

"But Cameron's not a traitor—" Simon began, but Johnson interrupted.

"I'm sorry Your Majesty. I understand Mr Sampson's not been feeling well since it all happened. He needs some rest."

"I see," the king said. "We're arranging transport to take them both back to their homes, aren't we?" He smiled at Bill. "You don't want to miss out on Christmas with the family."

Simon was determined to correct the king's mistaken impression about Cameron.

"Your Majesty," he began. "I *will* be heard. Cameron McCreadie is—was—an honest and patriotic man. He served the Royal Household to the best of his ability, and was instrumental in preventing the attempt on your life. He's not a traitor."

Johnson turned to stare at Simon. There was fury in his eyes. Simon refused to be intimidated. "When we met Cameron in the grounds earlier, he was on his way to the lodge to get help. He was the one who discovered the admiral intended to poison you with strychnine."

Simon pulled the small brown bottle from his coat pocket. "This was the murder weapon, and Cameron took it from the admiral's possessions to save your life. He's the hero, not me."

Simon swallowed hard to stem any unnecessary display of emotion in the presence of the king.

"And the admiral shot him dead."

The king looked from Simon to Johnson. He sighed deeply.

"Is this true?" he asked.

"Yes, Your Majesty." Johnson's voice was quiet, almost a whisper.

"Then why was I led to believe differently?" The king walked over and stood behind Queen Mary's armchair. He rested a hand on her shoulder. She patted his hand and smiled up at him.

"The queen and I are very aware of the constant threat to monarchies across Europe. We know we must be vigilant, and we take great comfort in the hard work of many people, like yourselves, who strive to preserve one's safety and the integrity of the British monarchy."

He returned to stand in front of them.

"For the country to be protected, for the Empire to be safe, we must be told the truth at all times." He turned to Johnson. "Is that clear?"

Johnson nodded. The king turned to Simon.

"You said something about the duke a moment ago. Do you mean Charles?"

"I do, sir," Simon replied.

"You think he's a traitor?"

Simon considered his reply. It was clear that neither Bill nor this man Johnson had told the king anything about their suspicions of the duke. He presumed there was a good reason for the deceit. While he refused to allow Cameron to be wrongly accused, he cared less about the duke.

"I couldn't say, sir," he replied. "The duke was accompanied by the admiral. It's a possible conclusion to draw. That they were both involved in the plot."

"No other reason?"

Simon could feel Johnson staring at him. But he was not prepared to lie any further. If the intelligence services had a reason to keep the king in the dark about the conversations between the Prince of Wales and the duke, then they could do their own dirty work.

"I'm sure Your Majesty is aware of our concerns," Johnson began. "The Duke of Saxe-Coburg and Gotha is an uncomfortable guest in our country. He has questionable allegiances in Germany and it would be prudent to keep him at arm's length. If Your Majesty agrees, we can arrange for him to return to Germany today. We'll find a plane and have it available at an airfield in Cambridgeshire." He bowed his head. "He can be back with his family for Christmas."

"But David will be very upset." Queen Mary used the royal family's private name for the Prince of Wales. "It was he who invited him."

"And I was opposed to the idea," the king replied. "All this nonsense about having them stay at the lodge house instead of here. I'll talk to the Prince of Wales." He nodded to Johnson. "Make arrangements for the duke to be flown back to Germany tomorrow afternoon. Is there anything else you failed to tell me?"

Johnson avoided the king's gaze. "We have everything under control, Your Majesty."

"That's not what I asked." The king turned to Simon. "You seem to be a man who might talk in a more... straightforward way. Thank you for putting me right about the footman. We'll have his body returned to his family. They're in Scotland, aren't they?"

"Yes, Your Majesty," Simon replied. "From Crathie."

"Oh, my Lord." The king shook his head. "I remember him now. And his father. He was a local lad brought in to carry the haggis, wasn't he? I recall the look on the poor boy's face. Absolutely terrified. Such a waste."

He put a hand on Simon's shoulder. "Thank you for speaking up for him. Was he a friend of yours?"

"I knew him slightly."

When Simon and Bill returned to the main hall, Robbie was waiting for them at the bottom of the staircase.

"Robbie!" called Simon. "Are you a sight for sore eyes."

"I could say the same about you." Robbie embraced him. "What on earth were you thinking of? Coming out here on your own. When we heard the gunfire, I feared the worst."

"Oh, you know me," Simon replied. "Can't keep away from a good story."

Robbie leaned in to whisper. "What did the king say?"

Simon raised a finger to his lips. "That's confidential I'm afraid, old boy." He pulled out the little brown bottle from his pocket and handed it to Robbie. "But here's your evidence. This was found in Admiral Newman's possessions."

"Strychnine. Good God." Robbie took the bottle gingerly and held it by his side. "What on earth are you going to do now, Simon? I can't imagine the BBC's going to have you back. After your face was plastered all over the newspapers, wanted for murder."

"I don't much care," Simon replied. "You know how bored I was with the job. Perhaps it's time I returned to *The Chronicle*."

"Excuse me sir, madam." A footman approached them and bowed. "I apologise for interrupting, but when you're finished with the Detective Inspector, we have a room where you can rest until your car arrives to take you back to London."

"Has the room had dogs in it?" Simon asked.

The footman looked confused. "No, sir. It's the queen's private drawing room. The dogs aren't allowed in there. The queen suggested you use it to rest in. The car's coming from Norwich. It will be an hour at least."

"How very kind of her," Simon replied. "Please tell her we're most grateful for her hospitality. Might it stretch to a couple of gin martinis as well?"

The footman grinned. "They're my speciality, sir." He pointed down a corridor leading from the entrance hall. "The drawing room's the second door on the left. I'll set your drinks out there."

Much to Simon's amusement the footman bowed again and walked away. He could get used to being treated like royalty.

"Do you need us for anything, Robbie?" he asked. "I presume you want to take statements? Only I'm gasping for a drink and a decent sit-down. And I've got a few questions I need to ask Bill here first."

"I'm around for a while longer," Robbie replied. "By the

way. That fake detective you told me about in Fortescue Place? He wasn't one of ours. And he doesn't belong to Special Branch either. Complete mystery."

He waved to get the attention of a footman. "I'm desperate for a cup of tea. Come and find me when you're ready."

Simon turned to Bill and gestured towards the corridor leading to the drawing room. "Shall we?"

The drawing room door clicked shut behind Simon. He leaned back against it and took a deep breath. It was as though he had been an actor on stage and was now back in the wings, out of sight of the prurient audience.

Bill lowered herself into a large, wing-backed armchair and lit a cigarette. "I know what you want to ask me," she said.

"Do you?" Simon walked over to a similar armchair opposite and sat. "Because I don't know where to begin. You've hidden so much from me, I've no idea what's real and what's not. First I find out you and your cronies at the intelligence services set me up—"

"We didn't," Bill interrupted, but Simon cut her short.

"Be quiet. I haven't even started. After I discover you've set me up, I then find out, from the king himself that you were prepared to implicate Cameron in the assassination plan. Cameron. The sweetest and most patriotic of young men. Who was actually on his way to raise the alarm when he was shot."

Simon shook his head. "What kind of a woman are you, Bill? I've always thought of you as a cool-headed kind of person. But I didn't realise until this evening that you've actually got a heart of ice."

"It's complicated." Bill put the cigarette to her lips. Her hand shook. "Johnson advised it was a better story diplomatically. It wasn't plausible that Admiral Neumann—"

"So he is German?"

Bill nodded. "A senior member of Der Sturmabteilung. But he went to school in Gloucestershire. That's why he had such an impeccable English accent. Johnson wanted to avoid implicating the Prince of Wales, and even the duke in the assassination plot. If it ever got out that they had been involved, there'd be a national scandal. But he decided it wasn't plausible to claim Admiral Neumann had been working alone. He needed an insider. Johnson simply told the king that Neumann and Cameron were collaborators."

"Hanging Cameron out to dry," Simon wanted Bill to feel the force of his bitterness. "And you went along with it. Knowing him to be an innocent man. And also knowing how much he meant to me."

"Johnson's my senior officer." Bill looked away and mumbled her explanation. "I had no choice."

The door opened and the footman arrived with their drinks. It was clear he sensed the atmosphere in the room. He said nothing, but placed the drinks on a small table between Bill and Simon, bowed and left them.

It was Simon who broke the silence. "But it wasn't the intention of the Prince of Wales to murder his father. Remember? Cameron told us he overheard him talking with the duke. They were only going to drug the king, not kill him."

Bill picked up her cocktail glass. "It amounts to the same thing. An attack on the sovereign monarch. Treason. The intelligence services couldn't let it be known that *Hamlet* was playing out in the House of Windsor."

She took a sip from her glass and set it down. "I'm sorry,

Simon. About Cameron. If it's any consolation, I did make Johnson aware of my objection to his little rewrite of history. Very forcibly."

Despite his anger, Simon smiled. He could imagine Bill in such a confrontation. Dammit. He had been on the receiving end of her forked tongue often enough. But there were still a lot of questions for her to answer.

"That day I met the fake detective by the alleyway, loading bags into an unmarked van. That was your lot, wasn't it?"

"No, he wasn't." Bill snapped. "And now that Mountjoy says he wasn't from Scotland Yard, we can only assume he was one of Neumann's lot, clearing up their dirty work."

She reached for her cocktail glass again. "You can't blame us for everything, you know."

Simon got up and crossed to the door.

"Where are you going?" Bill asked.

"I want to tell them I intend to go to Cameron's funeral," he said. "I need to find someone who'll put me in touch with the family. If I leave it until after we've left here, it might not be possible to organise."

"Simon." Bill stood and walked over to him. "We still need to talk about you and SIS. As I said before, there's an opportunity for you to do something more for your country."

Simon opened the door. "Go to hell, Bill."

30

They were the last two mourners standing at the graveside. It was a cold January morning and frost lay heavy on the grass in the churchyard. Bill threw a wilting carnation into the open grave and bowed her head.

"Thank you for coming," she said. "I don't think I could have faced it on my own."

Simon slipped his arm through hers. "I wouldn't let you suffer this alone, old girl."

They stood side by side in silence. A crow squawked high in a leafless tree. In the distance they could hear the low rumble of London. The peace of the churchyard was but a temporary refuge from the harsh reality of life in the first few days of 1933.

"Didn't her family want her buried in Poland?" Simon asked.

"Anna had no family to speak of," Bill replied. She took a handkerchief from her coat pocket. "This cold makes your eyes water, doesn't it?"

Simon hugged her to him and let her release her pent-up

grief. It was only a few days since he had returned from Cameron's funeral in Scotland. Two graveyards in as many days. A depressing scorecard. He envied Cameron his parents. They had welcomed Simon as though he was a member of the family. By the time of the funeral, Simon's face had returned to the newspapers, this time as *Britain's Hero: The Ordinary Man Who Saved the King.* There was no mention of Cameron's efforts. He felt a fraud. But Robbie had told him to keep to the official line that an unnamed, armed intruder had been apprehended by Simon, and Cameron had got caught in the crossfire.

Simon was uncomfortable with his complicity in the deceit. But at least it had restored his good name. The head of News Department had called several times to talk about *"an exciting new role for him in news reporting".* Simon was unwilling to discuss it with him. He had no idea what he might do next. It was too early to decide.

Bill wiped her eyes with the handkerchief and shoved it back into her pocket. She looked up at him and blinked several times.

"Sorry about that." She smiled. "Alarmingly unnecessary display of emotion. Won't happen again."

She turned away from him and walked towards a bench close to the church.

"Come and sit with me." She called over her shoulder.

They sat together, wrapped in their dark woollen coats and scarves, like the elderly couples Simon had seen sitting watching the sea at Budleigh Salterton when he used to visit his grandparents as a child. He was not ready to listen to any proposals from Bill. He was still angry with her about Cameron. Only their grief for the people they had lost united them in a temporary truce.

"Have you spoken to Robbie recently?" Bill asked.

Simon shook his head. "Not for over a week. You heard he solved the mystery of the keys?"

"I don't know what you mean, my dear," Bill replied.

"My spare keys," Simon said. "They'd gone missing. I blamed Cameron for taking them at the time."

"Something else to make you feel guilty." Bill lit up a cigarette. "Well don't. The dead die despite us, not because of us."

"I say old girl, that's a bit harsh."

"I said *despite* us. Not *to spite* us." Bill exhaled smoke into the frosty air. "Despite our best endeavours, our loved ones still desert us for the hereafter." She rubbed his arm affectionately. "It's not your fault. It's the way of the world. What happened to the keys?"

"The police found them among the admiral's possessions," Simon replied.

"That explains why you didn't see any evidence of a break-in that night," Bill said. "But how did he get the keys?"

"Mrs Nowell."

"Your cleaner? Why would she give them to him?"

Simon smiled. "She's too nice, that's why. Robbie met her when he was checking over my apartment. Apparently she told him that this nice man with a monocle bumped into her. It must have been the morning after Cameron first came over. The admiral claimed to be my brother and that he'd just arrived from Scotland. He told Mrs Nowell I'd promised to leave my spare key out for him and that I'd forgotten."

"Neat trick," Bill replied. "So much tidier than breaking into a place."

They sat in silence for a few more minutes. This time it was Bill who spoke first.

"I have a proposal for you."

Simon turned but Bill avoided his gaze. "I know you're not ready to hear this," she continued. "But there's still an opening for you with SIS. They want you in Berlin. It looks like things are really hotting up there. Herr Hitler is about to take supreme power. We're predicting a bumpy ride ahead."

Simon was curious. He missed the thrill of Berlin. His life since he had joined the BBC had been straitjacketed by conformity. In Berlin he had been able to be more like his true self. It was a gayer world. People there cared not who you might be attracted to.

"You'll still be with the BBC," Bill continued. "That's your cover story. You'll be their first foreign correspondent. Reporting on what's happening in the heart of Europe."

It was an attractive proposition. But he was not thrilled at the prospect of working with that man Johnson. A man who could twist the truth and besmirch the good name of an honourable man. He shook his head.

"It's an interesting offer," he said. "But I've seen the way the intelligence services work. And I don't much like it."

"You mean Johnson?" Bill took out her cigarette case and lit up. "Don't worry about him. He's gone."

"Really?"

"Yes. The king requested it personally. He was furious to discover he'd been misled."

"So you've got a new boss in SIS?"

"In a manner of speaking." Bill smiled. "And I'm going to be leaving the BBC."

This was a shock to Simon. Bill seemed to be so much a part of the fabric of the BBC. As though she had always worked there. "Where are you going?"

Bill knocked the ash off the end of her cigarette. "I'm the new section head in SIS."

It took Simon a moment to realise the corollary of her statement.

"You mean, if I accepted your offer, you'd be my section head?"

"Yes." Bill turned and raised her eyebrows. "Interested?"

ALSO BY DAVID C. DAWSON

The Necessary Deaths

The Deadly Lies

The Foreign Affair

For the Love of Luke

Heroes in Love

THE NECESSARY DEATHS

The Delingpole Mysteries: Book One

A young man. Unconscious in a hospital bed. His life is in the balance from a drugs overdose.

Attempted suicide or attempted murder?

British lawyer Dominic Delingpole investigates, with the help of his larger than life partner Jonathan McFadden.

Dominic and Jonathan uncover a conspiracy reaches into the highest levels of government and powerful corporations.

Three people are murdered, and Dominic and Jonathan struggle for their very survival in this gripping thriller.

Award winner in the 2017 FAPA President's Awards for Adult Suspense and Thrillers.

Available on Amazon

THE DEADLY LIES

The Delingpole Mysteries: Book Two

A man is murdered, and takes a deadly secret to his grave.

Is it true the murdered man is Dominic Delingpole's former lover? And were they still seeing each other just before his recent wedding to husband Jonathan?

Or are these simply lies?

This is more than a story of deceit between husbands. A man's death plunges Dominic and Jonathan into a world of international espionage, which puts their lives at risk.

What is the ruthless Charter Ninety-Nine group? Why is it chasing them across Europe and the US?

Dominic and Jonathan are forced to test their relationship to its limit. What deadly lies must they both confront? And if they stay alive, will their relationship remain intact?

THE FOREIGN AFFAIR

The Delingpole Mysteries: Book Three

There's a murderer stalking the gay bars of Berlin.

It's September. The time of Folsom Europe. Berlin's annual festival for gay men in leather.

And the city's become a dangerous place for them.

British lawyer, and part-time sleuth Dominic Delingpole is in town.

He discovers the attacks are linked to a sinister, Russian-backed experiment.

Dominic teams up with German lawyer Johann Hartmann, a man with the seductive charm and good looks of Dominic's late husband.

But whose side is Hartmann really on?

Available on Amazon

FOR THE LOVE OF LUKE

A handsome naked man. Unconscious on a bathroom floor.

He's lost his memory, and someone's out to kill him. Who is the mysterious Luke?

British TV anchor and journalist Rupert Pendley -Evans doesn't do long-term relationships. Nor does he do waifs and strays. But Luke is different. Luke is a talented American artist with a dark secret in his life.

When Rupert discovers Luke, he's intrigued, and before he can stop himself, he's in love. The aristocratic Rupert is an ambitious TV reporter with a nose for a story and a talent for uncovering the truth. As he falls deeper in love with Luke, he discovers the reason for Luke's amnesia. And the explanation puts them both in mortal danger.

Available on Amazon

HEROES IN LOVE

NOT EVERY HERO WEARS A UNIFORM

Can love last a lifetime?

Billy and Daniel never intended to be matchmakers.

After all, they're only at the start of their own love story.

But Billy uncovers a failed love affair that lasted over fifty years until it fell apart.

He and Daniel see their own fledgling relationship through the lens of the now estranged couple.

They vow to reunite the elderly lovers.

But as they set about their task, the pressures of modern life threaten to tear them apart.

ABOUT THE AUTHOR

David C. Dawson is an award-winning author, journalist and documentary maker, and lives in London and Oxford.

His debut novel *The Necessary Deaths* won Bronze for Best Mystery & Suspense in the FAPA awards.

As a journalist he travelled extensively, filming in nearly every continent of the world. He's lived in London, Geneva and San Francisco, but he now prefers the tranquillity of the Oxfordshire countryside.

In his spare time, David tours Europe with his boyfriend, and sings with the London Gay Men's Chorus.

Printed in Great Britain
by Amazon

83939974R00164